BY V. CASTRO

Immortal Pleasures

The Haunting of Alejandra

Mestiza Blood

Queen of the Cicadas

Goddess of Filth

Hairspray and Switchblades

IMMORTAL PLEASURES

IMMORTAL PLEASURES

V. CASTRO

New York

Published in the United States by Del Rey, an imprint of Random House, a division of Penguin Random House LLC, New York.

DEL REY and the CIRCLE colophon are registered trademarks of Penguin Random House LLC.

Hardback ISBN 978-0-593-49972-6
Ebook ISBN 978-0-593-49973-3

Printed in the United States of America on acid-free paper

randomhousebooks.com

1 2 3 4 5 6 7 8 9

ScoutAutomatedPrintCode

First Edition

Book design by Debbie Glasserman

Dedicated to A.J.D.M.

Thank you for being my support and pleasure.

And to my ancestors.

Thank you for the wellspring of inspiration.

Your stories are my stories.

IMMORTAL PLEASURES

Is it really our life? Perhaps we are gathered to dance to a shaman's chant we cannot hear until we find ourselves moving to the beat.

1

t's my last night in Dublin before I head to the south coast. Ireland was the first stop on my way to London because of its landscape, particularly its grass—that dreamy electric green, surrounded by dark cold waters and even colder winds.

That landscape had called to me while I was flipping through an airline magazine during one of my business-class flights across South America. The advertisement showed a green pasture that ended with a cliff dropping to leaping waves in the shape of giant conch shells. I had to see that grass with my own eyes, feel it beneath my feet.

You see, my name is Malinalli, which means grass in my native Nahuatl language. The glossy photo ignited my soul with wonder, and I knew I had to overcome my irrational fear of exploring this part of the world, Europe. It was a European who changed my given name Malinalli to La Malinche and Doña Marina. Neither did I choose, nor could I refuse as a human. At least as a vampire I could take back my name. Small steps.

But you may wonder why a Nahua vampire from the sixteenth century like me would harbor a fear of anything after being an apex predator for so very long. After all, my blood is powerful and intoxicating—it comes from a vampire made by one of the very first vampires. However, like the demolished temple Tenochtitlán, my heart still bears the scars of history.

Before this trip was even an idea, my concentration on work had been waning. I kept finding myself slipping into daydreams of distant places. My heart would sink to depths of emotion I could not allow myself to wade in. In train stations and airports, I used to walk with a smug swagger past couples if I saw an obviously out-of-sync partnership, and past families if I saw screaming children throwing themselves at the feet of exhausted parents. *Ain't no one holding me down or holding me back,* I'd think. But recently I'd also think soon after: *Ain't no one waiting for me either.* Walk enough crowded terminals alone, your hand swinging aimlessly by your side, and it starts to feel dead. And mine had hung empty for centuries. I couldn't care less about the offspring. As a vampire, my bearing a child was not an option. But lately I'd wanted to feel an arm around my waist. A companionship that lasted longer than a night would be nice.

Two days after the idea of traveling to Ireland first struck me, I received an out-of-the-blue opportunity to purchase rare Mexican artifacts from a dealer in London. I am a collector, buyer, and seller of antiquities from all over the world; however, my specialty is Mexico and South and Central America. As a blood huntress it was a natural fit.

Since 1972, I had made my living tracking rare objects, although I began my search for these objects long before I'd ever earned a cent. My career had begun not as a career, but as a sort of spiteful secret mission to reclaim our culture's lost treasures one object at a time from the colonizers. The more I learned about my new vampire life and all its strengths, the more I thought about my purpose in life. My work has given me purpose beyond servitude or mere survival. I could create some good for myself and others.

The artifacts are two skulls I first encountered when I was still human. When I read the email and saw the photos of the skulls, the excitement in my work that I'd lost came back, and I nearly jumped out of my skin. My instinct told me these were the very same treasures I had been hunting for since I began my journey in acquiring antiquities. One skull is carved from pure clear quartz. The other is an embellished mosaic of turquoise and obsidian set in a human skull with most of the teeth still intact. Judging from the photo, the gold that once plated the human skull had been scraped from the bone.

The skulls had once belonged to someone I loved dearly. Her name was Chantico. She was like a mother to me when I first became a vampire. She helped me find the will to live for myself.

I had been searching for centuries for these skulls with no luck, and I'd been on the brink of giving up on ever finding them. It wasn't until the birth of the internet that my journey began to gain a little momentum, though every path had led to a dead end until now. However, life can be as unpredictable as the height of waves crashing on a shore; now, at long last, the skulls were within my reach. The universe presented me the perfect opportunity to act on my desire to reclaim these treasures.

So I simply had to fly across the Atlantic to purchase those skulls and keep them safe. The catch was the skulls were now in London with a private collector. But this purchase was too important to leave to chance, to buy on the evidence of digital photographs alone, even if the photos I'd been emailed appeared legitimate. My usual London-based antiquities broker, Horatio Hutchings, a trustworthy man in the business, assured me it was not a scam. However, he did not possess the same skill that I did in detecting forged objects—and I had seen my fair share in my many centuries of existence. To reclaim the skulls—and with them, a part of my soul—I had to take the trip. And that trip would be first class all the way, including the best hotels. Everything paid for by the business I had built from scratch and the antiquities I'd acquired over time. I deserved to have everything I wanted in this life. Divine timing can be a stubborn bitch, but when she comes through, she delivers divine rewards.

And so, eager to finally possess the skulls, and with a nagging desire to travel, I created a four-week itinerary to explore Ireland and England at the same time. Spain would be the next place I'd visit—where perhaps I could finally lay my anger at its colonizers to rest—and finally Vienna, Austria, to see the Penacho, a rare surviving Aztec headdress, bright green and feathered, that didn't belong halfway around the world from its country of origin, in a museum for people who could not fully appreciate its true importance. Indeed, part of my mission has been to reach out to museums around the world and broker deals to give back stolen items to their original cultures. The treasures can then go on tour or on loan to museums in other lands; however, sole ownership belongs to the people who created them. That particular headdress had long been on my radar. I figured my kind emails to the museum were not doing enough, and that my power of persuasion in the flesh could serve me better. After years of practice, vampires can use their energy to influence the emotions of humans. We can't force them to do something, just steer them toward what we want from them. I was not opposed to using my vampire magnetism to get what I wanted, and I wanted this headdress back in Mexico City.

In my human life, as a translator, I'd watched villages and temples be sacked by the conquistadors. The terror and sorrow at one's powerlessness to stop the destruction of one's home is something no one should experience or witness. And with the treasures of our past stolen, our children would grow up without anything to remind them of their history or story. The children of Europe had no tie to this object and could, at best, see it only as a unique piece of history of a people they could not fully understand, but more than likely, as just a nice artifact with pretty feathers from a bird they had never seen before. But the headdress had the potential to instill pride and awe in my people if returned to its rightful place in Mexico. And that is exactly what I was going to do. The Hapsburg Archduke Ferdinand II was long dead—what would he care if an item he acquired out of imperialist greed was taken back?

And as soon as I landed on the distant cool shores of Ireland, I knew I had made the right choice. Even the sight of the drizzle on the small window as we landed excited me. An undercurrent of expectation made my body alert to every sensation and sight. The climate in Ireland differs greatly from my home. Although it is summer in Ireland, there is always a damp chill in the evening air. What a change from the heat I'm accustomed to! This is exactly why I'd made the decision to cross the pond to explore the Old World. My trip would be a gust of change to rid myself of my inner demons—and perhaps introduce me to a few new ones along the way, just for laughs.

All of this to reclaim the freedom once stolen from me back when I was a mortal. Imagine going from "Will this be the day I die as a slave?" to becoming the very embodiment of death.

And now I wanted to appease the restlessness that had settled over me the last few years. I am worth millions, but as life has shown me, cash only goes so far in creating a fulfilling life.

And so on this trip I felt open to the unexpected. Perhaps destiny had even brought me across the pond for a reason beyond the skulls. Part of me wanted to believe Chantico watched me from wherever her spirit hovered and sent me a blessing of joy.

2

Later that night, I am on my final stop on a pub crawl and my third glass of sparkling water with a wedge of lime. What a great way to end the evening: "Big Love" by Fleetwood Mac playing on speakers mounted on the front of the bar. The paunchy bartender wearing a rugby jersey bellowing "Last call" over the din of the bar. People guzzling whatever they're drinking and shuffling toward the door. Through the thinning herd, I can now see the corner booth.

And there he is, sitting with his mates at a table covered in Stella Artois bottles and pint glasses. His blue eyes flash with the same allure as his smile surrounded by a light stubble. The sleeves of his T-shirt creep over defined biceps. Candy for the eyes and body. A box of new books rests at his feet. The covers are all dark with red titles. One has a skeleton key and skull with what look like fangs. I chuckle to myself. He has a thing for vampires. I wonder if he is selling the books. Or did he write them? Doesn't matter. I want the pleasure of his company, or at the very least the comfort of his body.

During my human life, romance and sex for pleasure had not been options for me. I had gone from being a teenage hand-maiden serving the Tabascan royalty to being owned by the Spanish colonizer known as Hernán Cortés. Not only did I translate for him, we Indigenous women could not say no to any "advances" made toward us. First, he'd given me to one of his captains, Alonso Puertocarerro, then to himself, and finally to my Spanish husband, Juan Jarmillo, before my human death.

When I was reborn, I relished my newfound freedom, but I had much healing to do after the trauma of witnessing the con-quest in all its horror—and the horrors inflicted on me. My his-tory had left me with deep scars, one of them the fear of being used. There was the lingering paranoia that once my use was over so would be my worth, my life.

But after some time, I began to allow myself the luxury of physical pleasure even though I still was not able to give my heart freely. My experience of not being accepted, respected, or loved as a Brown woman by colonizer men made me self-conscious, about myself and also my vampire nature. Not all vampires felt like this, as I found out centuries later, when I fi-nally befriended one.

"Mortals only want one thing," that vampire had once told me, shouting over pulsating disco at a nightclub in New York City in the 1970s. White light refracted across our faces from the spinning disco ball in the center of the dance floor. The vam-pire's name was Catherine, and she was older than me by a few hundred years. She wore the best clothing in the current fashion and the brightest red lipstick, with a shine as blinding as the nail polish on the talons she filed to sharp points. Her life was a con-stant party; she was never not planning another wild bash, and she was never alone for long. If not planning that next party, she hopped from shop to shop for the best her money could buy. So I was curious about her thoughts about life as a vampire.

"And what is that? A chance at immortal life?"

With her hot-blooded gaze, she flicked her feathered, bouncy honey-blond hair and scoffed, "No, no. Very few mortals have the courage for that. Most really can't stomach the idea of being a blood drinker day in and day out. They want to feel close enough to life after death to not feel afraid of death itself. Humans are so full of doubt and fear of the unknown. They can't see the divine unless the signs hit them like battle axes and draw blood. And vampires tell them that death is an illusion."

Her bright lips spread to a sinister smile. "But also vampires do not deny ourselves pleasure. And pleasure is everyone's drug of choice."

She raised a finger and motioned for someone behind me. A young woman slid next to her, exposing her bare shoulder blade as she continued to move to the music. Catherine laid a sticky lipstick kiss on the woman's shoulder before pulling out a small velvet pouch from her metal clutch. The young woman giggled and purred with delight. From inside Catherine plucked a small white pill and placed it into the woman's mouth. Catherine didn't take her eyes off me as she bit deep into the shoulder blade of the young woman. Blood and lipstick stuck to her skin. The woman moaned and writhed in Catherine's embrace. Catherine still had crimson beads clinging to her lipstick when she pulled away from the young woman.

"All the lords and masters are dead, Malinalli. It is our turn to celebrate in the streets. We are not dead. I hope they are all burning in hell while feeling the constraints of the tight corsets some of us were forced to wear. Let them choke on sulfur for a change."

Catherine became a vampire during the thirteenth century in France. She had seen the evolution of Europe. As an aristocrat, she was by no means deprived or underprivileged in material wealth; however, her only worth was to be wed to create more of it. Her words hit me in the center of my chest even harder than the bass from the music. My wounds opened for a moment as the faces of my many owners flashed before my eyes. I couldn't argue with that sentiment. I hoped in death they knew intimately the pain they had inflicted. Part of me wanted to embrace the carefree nature Catherine had adopted, but my resentment still glowed a little too brightly. More time, something I had plenty of, was still needed.

She let out a wicked giggle before shouting, "I fucking love the seventies!" Her hand slid beneath the low-cut collar of the young woman's thin pink polyester wraparound dress to massage her breast. The young woman tugged at the fabric to expose her nipple. Catherine used the tip of her nail to flick the erect pink flesh. One swift swipe drew a bloom of blood, causing the woman to groan. Catherine bit her lip before lapping up the red liquid jewel.

Catherine hadn't cared about being inconspicuous. That was her way of getting vengeance against her former masters. And now, so many years later, I was slowly reaching the same point. I had once kept my true vampire self in shadows, and now it was rising to the surface.

The longer I am far from home, the more open I feel to wanting my vampire half and human half to be equally free. I have left my past in Mexico and I have traveled across the waters that brought the many colonizers to my world. It is time to confront their world. My work requires me to seem human. And I have kept my sexual relationships superficial so as not to reveal I am a blood drinker by nature. There was a time in my life when the thirst and the hunt gave me immeasurable pleasure, the only pleasure, as I had retreated into hiding as the last of my people attempted to fight off the invaders. I orgasmed in the throes of draining a soldier dry and tossing his corpse where I knew the Spanish sent scouts. Every part of me let go in blinding surrender. The look of horror when they saw the new me, the vampire me, let me know this was a side of me humans would never understand.

Yet the lack of intimacy in my life had only become another wound. My heart feels tied in ropes of thorn. I had tried to place a vast distance between me and others, as vast as the depth and length of the ocean between the New World and the Old. All the while I ached for real connection, for a profound love to blow away the profound hurt I was still healing from. But now I was resolved: I did not come this far or live this long to become a captive again. I want a lover to love all of me, the woman *and* the vampire.

But I don't believe we find our true soul's desire, or purpose—it finds us. Perhaps, when you meet a soulmate, it is a sign that all those long-lost particles blown to bits at the beginning of time have found their way to one another again—stardust finding itself in another body. Until we reunite with those parts of ourselves, our thoughts and desires will burn like meteors scalding skin, brain, bone, and soul. And that's how we end up choosing the wrong people, feeling the kind of heartbreak that teaches us lessons. After centuries alone, I hoped to find my soulmate as I did the treasures that made me my fortune. My soul's aching desire was to discover real love, to feel true equilibrium with my match. To make up for when I had been passed hand to hand in my youth without choice. At that time, I was merely a treasure to be taken.

As I look at the stranger, I can't tell yet how deep an encounter might be with him, but fate is somehow telling me I'm not going back to my room anytime soon. The question is: Will he notice the only Brown woman in the place, the one with the leather jacket, dress too short to bend over, large hoop earrings, and lips tinted so red they'd leave a ring around his cock?

The bartender shouts "Last call" again with a grumpy look on his face for those of us who remain. I drink the dregs of my water, waiting for a glance from the stranger. He's wearing a tweed newsboy cap, jeans, and a black T-shirt that reveals one tightly sculpted arm with a sleeve of tattoos. Is he strong? It makes me want both of his arms holding me against a wall with him inside of me. I watch him take the beer bottle into his mouth, then lick his lips with a slight pout. Perfect for nibbling bare skin. His physical allure was apparent, but I also liked that he was giving his friends his full attention. He didn't talk over them nor was he too obnoxious from alcohol. He had a sense of self-control and intensity when he didn't speak. Now I'm even more convinced I want to take him home. Just one last souvenir from my time in Dublin. Stardust or dark matter, in the spirit of this trip, I'll take a chance. He's perfect.

Our gazes lock when his group begins to say their goodbyes. His eyes are the color of stormy coastal waters and mine are so dark they look nearly black, or so I'm told. Suddenly my thighs are slick—something I notice since I'm wearing nothing underneath my thin jersey dress. The wetness between my legs becomes harder to ignore the longer I stare. His look says, "I'm here," and my body answers, "I'm coming." In this moment I'm a piece of driftwood being pulled to shore by a sensual current I can't control, and my thirst is the same vivid color as my lips. My belly moans like a siren looking for shipwrecked sailors to devour.

I walk over to the table; his friends eye the brazen woman

with a hungry gleam in her eye, straight out of "Maneater" by Hall & Oates. They are certainly drunk, talking too loud with heavy-lidded eyes, but he's not. He knows, with my predatory movements, that I've come for him.

I don't get the sense he scares easily, which is good. "Hey, fellas." I only greet the others to be polite, then I turn my attention to the man I'm even more physically attracted to the closer I get. He looks up from his beer and meets my gaze like before. I can hear his heartbeat quicken and smell sweat and the blood increasing around his groin. He is aroused. A stubbly five o'clock shadow covers his face, but it's not so thick you can't see his cleft chin. I touch his shoulder to let him know my presence is a formal invitation. Any inkling of unease will be forgotten as soon as he feels my vampire caress. A spark ignites in my mind. My vampire senses are similar to human intuition, but clearer: He wants to fuck me too.

Vampires may be dead, but we still possess energy; in fact, that energy is stronger than that of humans. Depending on the vampire, it can be used to send different emotions to a human through touch. My ancestors believed in something called tonalli. Consider it a type of soul energy. This soul energy even protects me from the daylight. I was born a sun worshipper, after all.

The magnetism of my being, this silken tonalli, I bend with my will, and I use it to tell him to relax. With one touch I could also send him running away with nightmares for the rest of his life.

"So, can I help you carry those books home?"

His Cupid's bow mouth curls to a slight smile. He looks at his friends, who are too gobsmacked to say anything. They just stifle their boyish schoolyard giggles. I could give zero fucks what they're thinking, because all I have on my mind is pleasure.

"All right then. I'm not far. My bookstore is just around the corner. My flat is above it."

"If you have no one waiting for you at home, show me the way," I say without looking at anyone but him before I make my way to the bar. The bartender is wiping down the wood counter scratched to the varnish, displeased we are still hanging around past last call. I pull out a one-hundred-pound note from my cross-body handbag and slap it down. "Their drinks are on me."

I can feel my beautiful prey standing behind me. His pulse pumps quickly, a tempo I hope he can match with his body. "I'm ready when you are," he says.

My tongue feels the sharp point of one of my fangs. I am ready.

We walk into the cool summer night. His arms shiver at the evening air. I don't feel the cold. I only see and feel the sights of this foreign, intriguing city. This is what keeps me moving forward year to year through my immortal life: beautiful objects, new people with unique stories, and discovering the secrets of the world.

It was my curious nature that kept me alive in those early days of the conquest in the sixteenth century, when my world was one of perpetual death and upheaval. The Spanish and the Tabascan traitors are the ones who taught me how to be a trader. I watched how they exchanged worthless beads for my people's riches and favors. In docility I facilitated these transactions. I was the object of a transaction myself, traded for a string of beads as long as the list of men I was expected to service, as numerous as the tears I cried. When I began my own antiquities business, I didn't consider it stealing if it wasn't the current owner's right to take the treasures in the first place. Cortés had conquered my people with treachery, double-crossing anyone when he could to get what he wanted. I learned from the best of the worst.

But that is history. My revenge is living my impossible life beyond mortal death.

And right now, I'm curious about this man with the books. "Tell me, why all the books in a box if you own a bookshop?"

He laughs, throwing me a playful glance. His eyes glitter beneath the streetlights. Hot damn, he is cute. "I had a book signing at a bookshop on the high street earlier this evening. A big chain. I'm a writer. My publisher says something about there being more traffic there, more visibility, blah fucking blah. Sell, sell. It's not easy, but I love it. When I'm old I want to look back and say I followed my passion." I like that he is an average guy doing his best to do something wonderful with his life. He has personality. We walk down a quiet road lined with the tiny cars people drive in Europe because the roads are so narrow. Bright streetlamps highlight the sheen of a recent rain shower on the sidewalk. It is not long before we stop in front of his bookstore.

"This is it." His voice is full of pride.

The shop is in one of those old lopsided buildings built in the seventeenth century. It's painted white, with exposed brown wooden beams on the outside. It's terraced, and the windows are dark. It's probably filled with ghosts. At one time in history this land was filled with people as pagan as my own. The crooked sign reads, *Horror, Occult, and Other Mischief*. Now I really like him. My soul calls out for the one who will not only complete me but *understand* me. I love myself too much for anything less.

Perhaps fate has set me on this cobbled road to a secondhand bookshop. And to his body.

He fumbles with the key before unlocking and opening a

door that creaks like a heavy coffin lid. The walls are filled with tightly packed frayed spines from top to bottom. It smells of coffee and musty paper. There's a large, tatty sofa facing the door, onto which I throw my leather jacket. He drops the books in front of it along with his hat. His hair is cut close to the scalp. It takes a certain type of man to pull off that kind of haircut, but with that face, he can do anything he wants. Only moonlight illuminates the room—just enough light to see each other, but dark enough to set the mood. I pull him to me by the waist of his jeans. "So, what do you write?" I ask.

"Horror. I write horror. Shall we go upstairs?"

My arousal is heightened when he says this. What I seek is some sort of intimacy through deep understanding. Could a horror novelist be the one to comprehend and accept my existence?

There is a room in the back with what looks like another sofa and desk. I don't want to wait and make small talk. I only allow in the things I want. Being this close to him makes my pussy feel like it's full of bees, their buzzing causing sticky sweet honey to leak from the honeycomb. I like watching men bathe in that honey as it coats their mouths and chins. "Take me back there."

He leads me to an office at the rear of the shop. A desk and plush red sofa face each other. A black varnished animal skull with large antlers hangs on the wall, its dark hollow eyes overlooking the entire room. I can't get distracted by details or get too personal, even though he piques my interest. I turn my attention back to him. Our mouths meet without any pillow talk or hesitation. His kisses are teasing nibbles, licks, and they tell me everything I need to know about him. I can already feel his cock hardening through his jeans, yet despite his arousal he continues to kiss me like we share a secret language using only our mouths. When did someone last try to seduce me? I never give anyone the chance. Too many emotional sword fights. Too many wounds from axes to the back I had to pull out myself with the blood left to dry on its own.

I push him onto the sofa while I sit in front of him on the desk. This dress is short enough that there is little work for him to do to hitch it up to expose my wet lips. My dress strap has fallen, unmasking one of my breasts, just enough to tease him.

A little fact about me: I've got a bit of a predilection for voyeurism. I like to see the excitement and anticipation on my lovers' faces. I take them to the edge of desire so once I allow them the pleasure of my body, they hold nothing back, giving me untamed, ravenous sex. Sexual gratification fertilizes the part of me where nothing grows, as hard as I might try. Since I'm a free woman now, I live my life without limitations. All the ones who ever told me no or held me back are dead in the ground from old age or disease, their empty armor hanging in museums. Moments like this, of pleasure and freedom, are the best revenge I could ever imagine.

"Stroke your cock," I mutter as I touch myself. Without protest he begins to remove his jeans, then masturbate as he watches me. I can tell he wants to reach out and feel me by the soft sigh that escapes his perfect mouth and by the pained look in his eyes. His hand glides up and down. Beads of pre-cum call for me to lick it off, wear it like lip gloss, but not yet. The anticipation of getting him alone has me feeling like I'm about to come, but I don't want to do it on my own. He will be rewarded for his patience.

"Get over here now. I want to come in your mouth," I breathlessly command.

He crawls on all fours toward me like a pilgrim at the steps of a church. He remains on his knees so I can rest my thighs on his shoulders. His tongue is soft, and it winds around my clit as if he's spelling my name without knowing what it is. Darting between my pussy and ass, his tongue draws sensations of pleasure from me like water trying to escape through a crack in a dam about to burst wide open. I push his head closer to my pussy. He sucks me to the edge of the universe and back with his blue eyes, tongue, and stubble that scratches my thighs. I have to steady myself against the desk as my back arches in ecstasy. It hasn't been long since I last had sex, but I can't remember when I last orgasmed like that.

Coming once is not enough, and his cock is still dripping with something delicious. I push him backward onto the floor with my stiletto, careful not to hurt him. I can't handle the sight of blood right now. It has been hours since I last fed. He smells wonderful, and I know his blood would stir my appetite for more than sex. My aim is not to harm him. I try to only bite to kill when threatened. A charmed snake will dance until you get too close to her mouth. Don't blame the creature for acting on its nature or curse the venom it cannot prevent itself from releasing.

I lower myself onto him slowly. I want to experience every thick ridge and vein of his cock inside of me. I'm about to ride him with bull rider precision.

He moans as I tighten my grip with my pussy. His hands find their way to my round, fleshy hips, holding on for dear life, like I'm about to throw him over the side of a ship without a life vest, his entire body tensing each time. I can tell he wants to come. But not before I get my seconds. The waves are cresting inside of me. My mind floats on a cloud with heaven in reach.

"God, woman, who are you?" he groans.

I lean forward, never stopping my grinding, slapping hips from increasing the friction against my clit. My lips are close enough to his ear to whisper, "I'm a horror story."

He grips my ass with a firm hold; if I felt pain it might hurt a little. I start pounding hard against his body as I orgasm on his cock. As my toes curl, joints freeze, and fingers push against the floor, I think I can hear him grunt through my own calls of release. We both get what we came for. I fall onto his chest, which is thumping with a heartbeat. Feeling satisfied for a moment, I close my eyes. Sex reminds me I was once a flesh-and-blood woman with needs that didn't get met. I can have what I want now, and I love that. Soft petals can still line my soul even after centuries of the most superficial watering. The thumping of his chest reminds me of the rhythm of life.

He's the first to speak, his fingertips rubbing my back lightly. "That was unexpected. I thought I was just meeting my mates for a few beers, then going home to write until I fell asleep at the keyboard."

His touch makes me feel nervous, a bit frightened at how good it feels. I raise myself from his body and sit next to him as I look for something to clean my wet legs. He takes off his T-shirt and hands it to me. This gesture stuns me. Sexy as hell, a great lover, and kind. Maybe pots of gold do exist.

"Thank you. You sure?"

He nods while staring at me with a faint smile on his face. The black skull with enormous antlers catches my eye again. It reminds me of a past life when we were all pagans without any scientific understanding of our world. We had blind faith the sun would rise, or enemies could be vanquished, if only we had the courage to offer our flesh and blood for divine use, like the papas I knew who consumed flesh and covered their entire bodies with sacrificial blood. Our lives were a ready offering for the gods and goddesses who watched our every move.

And then I think of the ones who arrived and used our faith in the gods to deceive us. Some of us thought the conquerors were gods themselves. Cortés manipulated many using our own religion, which he claimed was evil and false. They maligned our religion and faith as superstition yet told us the host was Christ's flesh once inside our mouths and the wine his blood once it caressed our tongue. We were not the only ones with wild tales to tell. But it did cross my mind after I became a vampire—what if it really was blood in the chalice Christ offered?

The skull on his wall is like a dark god who witnessed and blessed our unholy sexual matrimony. The entire room is dark and a bit macabre with spooky little trinkets meant as Halloween decorations but kept out year-round. He's my kind of guy—he's got an edge, but not so sharp you can cut yourself. Something tells me there are emotions, stories, and thoughts that drop off to dark trenches few see inside him. I'm always drawn to those places where not a ray of sunlight dares to shine—that is where you can sometimes find treasure. However, I can't forget he is still one hundred percent human. The few vampires I have encountered all roll their eyes at the very idea of any human-and-vampire romantic dalliance beyond consumption or pleasure.

His deep voice breaks my wandering thoughts. "By the way, I'm Colin."

"I'm Malinalli."

He's buttoning his jeans and picking himself up from the floor. "It was a pleasure meeting you tonight. Where are you from? I can't place your accent."

I lean against the desk. He moves closer, so close I want to kiss him again to show him where I am really from and what I am. His voice has an undeniable Irish accent that rolls off his tongue, another little thing that turns me on. "You've got those black eyes, that beautiful skin that is so intoxicating."

I know this to be true. Too much of me will give a normal man cirrhosis of the liver eventually.

He places a fallen strap from my dress onto my shoulder, and then his hands trace the lines of my neck, my breast. I'd be lying if I said it didn't feel good, to be touched like this. Most of my lovers never get beyond asking my name and not getting an answer.

It begins and ends the same every time, century after century. A change is long overdue. I want to begin a new cycle in this eternal life with a different ending to my story. The longer time goes on, the more I realize I am losing something precious— myself, my sense of place in this world, beyond my treasures, beyond blood, beyond sex. Something more than my original genius plan for revenge. Because revenge served cold is just that: cold.

And I would like to experience love for the first time in my life. The fear of heartbreak is a crown of rusty nails. I would like to take it off my head once and for all.

"You're right. I'm not from here. I'm from Mexico. It's my dream to explore all of Europe, one country at a time. I thought Ireland and England a good start. This excursion is business and . . . pleasure."

"Well, I am honored you chose me for the pleasure." His eyes are still large with excitement. There is an innocence in them I find very attractive. He's playful.

The rigors of sex must have worn off as his body shivers from the cold in this uninsulated old building that would probably cost a small fortune to repair because of its age. He rubs his forearms, then mine. "Aren't you cold?"

I smile to avoid the question and try to think what a human woman might say. "Got anything to drink?"

"Sorry! How rude of me. I didn't offer you anything." He walks to the other side of the desk, pulling out a bottle of whiskey and a T-shirt from a drawer. There are mismatched frames with pictures of people who somewhat resemble him. His family, I am assuming. There is a silver one with *Best Uncle* engraved on the bottom. A small boy hugs him tightly in the photo. I want to leave, but not be in such a rush as to appear rude. At least I tell myself I want to leave.

Because I like this man. He's into books—he's a writer, of all things—charming, and with looks as rugged as the landscape. The idea of us exploring each other more excites me.

But as he stretches his neck while pulling on the T-shirt, I find myself listening to his pulse. His heartbeat sounds louder now that my sexual need for him has been quelled. I realize I can't relax here much longer, because there's something else, a nagging need crawling beneath my skin. I'm hungry. The siren is awake, and she calls to be fed. If I wait too long, he will become my meal. "Thanks for everything tonight. Good luck with your book."

I start to walk toward the door to retrieve my jacket and go in search of fresh blood. His steps are quick against the hardwood floor as he follows me. Then I feel his hand gently touch the back of my right arm.

"Wait. I don't know anything about you. And what about a drink? What just happened was fantastic. How about dinner tomorrow? Meet at the pub around seven P.M.? The food there is surprisingly good."

His charm is irresistible, for a human. Maybe it's how sexy he looks in the moonlight or the way he asks, but my mouth says "Maybe" before my brain can tell it to say no because I am due to leave. I'd make an exception and stay.

I stop before I walk out the door. The rest of the night will be quiet for me, considering I don't sleep in the human sense. And I still want to know more about this man, even if I can't spend more time with him right then. My heart wants to open, feel a slice of sunlight. "Hey, can I have one of your books?"

"Hell yes. Writers are always eager to give out their books." He reaches into the box he carried previously. "Here you go. Hope you like it." One hand offers me the book while the other is a feather's touch against my thigh until my ass is in his palm. It takes every ounce of self-control not to devour him with my body and mouth. There is something about his touch that makes me feel alive. It amazes me that I didn't even know he existed two hours ago. He growls in my ear with his lips barely brushing against my cheek.

"I hope you like blood."

Once again, he reads my mind. He has no idea.

3

The moon is high in the sky. Its gray halo calms me because we are old friends—at one time one of my only friends. The softness of the light feels like rabbit fur, and it's just as gentle. So many things have come and gone in my life, but the moon and sun have always been steady companions that show up without fail. They look down on me without judgment for my past, or at what I am today. The heavens, and my faith in their unwavering power to shine, are my guides. I take no shelter in the opinions of others.

My name is Malinalli; however, I was also once known as La Malinche, or later Doña Marina, after I was forced into Christianity and, eventually, to act as its mouthpiece as I wandered through Mexico with Hernán Cortés. Some called me a traitor during the Spanish invasion, because so many of Cortés's translations were done by me.

But I was not a traitor. I was coerced to use my voice and words as a weapon. It was the world I lived in that traded me.

My own mother was the first. I didn't have much time to be a child. My father was a lord who died when I was just a girl. My mother remarried; it wasn't long before she found herself another man and bore him a child, thinking, like so many women in history, it might be a sure way to secure herself to him. But it is the weakest of chains, and they cost too much for both the child and the parent. As soon as I looked at her sweaty face and into weary black eyes after hours of labor with my new sibling, I knew my fate. She didn't smile at me when it was announced as a boy. We exchanged no words in that room saturated with the smell of blood and body odor. It smelled like a battlefield. A light scent of copal moved around with the presence of our unseen gods.

In my mind I could hear what her eyes wanted to say, *What will I do with you now?* That was it for me. My usefulness was gone in a single moment. There was a proper male heir to my father's position. So at twelve years old I was sold to another tribe, where I learned Mayan until I was bartered again at the age of sixteen to the people of Tabasco. To this day I can't sniff the stuff people put on tacos and eggs because for me Tabasco was just another betrayal, another place I had to go to without any say or control. I stayed there until the Tabascans gave me to Cortés. By that time, I had been a mistress to many.

But now I am far from Tabasco, living a completely different life in a different era. How could I have ever predicted wandering to a place called Dublin across a great body of water? The thought makes me chuckle, and I feel grateful that I can laugh at life; if I hadn't found a way to laugh again, I might be dead—or there would be far more corpses trailing behind me.

I walk through an area of Dublin known for its women of the night. I'll fit right in with the sex workers here, having spent centuries also living on the margins of society. Tonight, I want to find someone without a pimp who's working for herself. Whenever I can help a sister out, I do. Anyone can fall on hard times; no one is immune to life pulling the gravity from beneath your feet, leaving you at the mercy of powers beyond your control. I should know: I too was sold at a young age.

A young woman emerges from the shadows. "Hey, sexy, want to walk on the other side of the street for a change?" She looks me up and down. "Love your shoes."

She doesn't appear strung out or drunk. In any event, even if she had been, it is not my place to judge others' choices. Not with what I have witnessed or have done to survive. We are all made from equal measures of the stars. And so, while hard drugs are a no for me, I leave people alone to do whatever they want.

"Come closer. Let me see your arms, your eyes. Are you with anyone?"

She looks slightly put off and confused by my questions. "No. I'm on my own. My body, my cash. All of it. And I don't use. I smoke pot if it's offered. I drink occasionally."

"Honey, I've got cash, but I don't want your body; I want your blood. I'll pay you double and no sex involved. I promise there will be no lasting harm to you. I've even got a topical anesthetic to numb the pain of my bite."

She furrows her exaggerated drawn-on eyebrows. It's obvious she has no idea what I'm talking about. Her eyes scan me from head to toe again, probably using her extensive knowledge of people to suss me out. From my clothing and shoes she knows I have money.

"My blood? You want my blood, but you won't hurt me?"

I touch her arm to put her at ease. "Cross my heart. You can search me for anything sharp."

She looks me up and down again. "Triple for the kinky shit, and I want the money up front."

I give her a sincere smile of gratitude. God, I'm starving. "Deal. You don't need to tell me how much—this should cover it." I count out four hundred euros and hand it to her. Her grin tells me she is satisfied with the amount. We wander into a nearby park where we sit on a bench dark enough to hide us from a passerby. She must know this spot from her previous business dealings. The bench has one of those small metal plaques dedicated to someone who has passed: *She was a devoted sister, wife, and mother.* I can't help but snigger. Devotion is one of the most expensive things I know in existence. Especially when it is to the wrong people or things.

I wipe the numbing cream I carry in my bag on her outstretched wrist. She watches me with curiosity.

"Close your eyes and listen to music on your phone. I have earbuds if you need them," I tell her. She shrugs and obeys, pulling out her own AirPods. Her wrist is soft. It feels like thick cream in my hand. I bring it to my lips like a priest with a chalice filled with wine, then bite with just enough pressure to puncture the flesh and release her bloody gift to me. Her muscles tense for a moment before relaxing again. I glance at her face. Her eyes are shut tight, her fake eyelashes loose at the corners. I can feel her confusion. Her blood fills my mouth with the freshness of a bouquet of roses. I place one hand on her shoulder to reassure her again that I mean no harm. I allow her to feel, in this instance, that I am harmless and grateful for her blood. I know she receives this message, because a small smile appears on her lips. Feeding on her blood takes ten minutes. Before she has a chance to open her eyes, I rest her hand on her lap and rush into the darkness of the park.

When I reach the end of the leafy grounds according to the GPS on my phone, I stop to wait for my Uber on a desolate sidewalk. A fog has slowly descended, filling the atmosphere with a haze that glows slightly yellow from the streetlamps. I can tell the fog will soon blanket everything. It makes me want to shiver despite not feeling cold.

But there is something else in the atmosphere. My ears pick up movement nearby.

I look back to see if it is another sex worker. Couldn't be, because I would have detected a human scent, maybe perfume, or shampoo. This is different. It's as if whoever it is has deliberately masked their scent artificially. That is the only way I can explain it.

The sound draws near in the line of trees closest to me, where a public bus stops beneath a single streetlamp. Five people slowly file out of the bus. My Uber pulls to the curb behind it. I jog to my waiting ride. Before opening the door, I look back. Just as I hop into the back seat of the car, the bus screeches away.

I look around, swearing I can hear a scream.

4

For days in Ireland, he had stalked Malinalli.

As soon as he first glimpsed her in the flesh in Dublin, his memories of her came flooding back, and he couldn't look away. She moved like a big sleek cat. Those paws, so soft to the touch, but that hid lethal claws. She radiated confidence and raw sensuality—she was still stunning, a beautiful and rare creature he would love to stuff and keep on a mantle. But creatures like her were all beautiful, until they have their fangs and claws in you, bleeding your humanity dry.

Many times, back when they had both been human, he had had to hold himself back from smothering her in her sleep. In bed he often had to look away from her because of the burning hate in her eyes. She used this hate to cling to survival through the war. But he also had to keep her around to ensure his own survival and victory. She was nothing—and yet she was also everything when it came to his success. If there was one thing this woman had, it was the ability to make men do what she wanted even when she was technically their property.

And now, centuries later, he watched her from the shadows. He couldn't help his curiosity. Watching his victims aroused him. It felt like all the power he lost at the end of his human life was restored. Modern living in the twenty-first century was so complicated in some respects. And these days his true identity could not be discovered for any reason.

No one would believe he was *the* Hernán Cortés from the history books. The man who changed history and yet people hated today: In recent years he had sunk into a dark depression, as he saw the statues of his peers vandalized and their names given no respect. And so he went by Martin, his son's name . . . *her* son's name. As Martin Ruiz to the human world, he was adored as a savvy businessman who looked good for a man of sixty-two—the age when he had become a vampire and faked his human death.

When human, he had given Malinalli away to another man, along with a token grant of land, knowing she would die sooner rather than later in the hands of Juan Jarmillo. Juan promised him a constant supply of fresh slaves in exchange for Malinalli. Since she meant nothing to either of them, it was a fair deal.

And now Malinalli had to die . . . again.

Malinalli had been impeding his relic-trading business for years without his knowing who she was. John Hawkins, his business partner and fellow immortal, had his human lover, George, looking for the anonymous rival who worked so swiftly to undermine their business. When the email popped into his inbox, he felt overwhelming relief at the mystery finally being solved. But when he opened the email, his entire body shook: The black hair. The strong angles of her bronzed face. Those black cenotes for eyes that blazed with hate and strength. He had never loved her, nor valued her as a human, but he did respect her ability to survive. He could only stare at her photo, taken in New York City, where she stood alongside a broker named Horatio. That sixth sense possessed by vampires who cared to develop it swelled in his mind: He could tell she had strong blood. The word *Cuauhtémoc* whispered in his ears. John entered his office with a large smile. "Did you see the good news?"

Hernán couldn't tear his widened eyes from the screen. His hands hovered over the keyboard like claws about to attack. The longer he stared at her image, the longer his nails grew to sharper points.

"Hernán, I thought you would be pleased. Do you know who she is? Her name is Mali.

"Do you sense something about her? What is it? This isn't like you."

"Malinalli. Her full name is Malinalli, but she is called many things. She was with me during the conquest. And here we are again. What does fate want with us?"

John's smile dropped. "Nothing. We stick with the plan. It is a two-for-one deal. We get rid of her and then sell her piece by piece. Plus, I don't want to put George in any more unnecessary danger. He is still human, after all."

Hernán closed his laptop. "You are right about her. We still continue to disagree about your . . . *attachment* to a human. I have no business with her but for her to be gone."

Since that day he could not stop thinking about her. She was alive, she was his rival in business, and she was a vampire. It was a strange coincidence, because he didn't just trade in antique objects.

As a mortal, John Hawkins had been the Englishman who created a slave route from Africa to the islands off the coast of

America. Hernán knew of him from his exploits. They both changed history through torture and flesh during their human lifetimes. And now they sold the body parts of other vampires, from which they created Immortalis, their anti-aging beauty line for humans, along with other serums they were dabbling in for future product lines. Together Hernán and John had made a new fortune in stolen treasure and vampire bodies.

As a vampire in 1595, Hernán stumbled upon John Hawkins in San Juan. Hernán had been there looking for new business opportunities, and to create loyal vampires for his expeditions. The desperate ones made the most ferocious of servants. It was at an inn serving criminals and those down on their luck that he heard the name John Hawkins being discussed by a table of drunks looking for an easy means of making money. Hawkins was dying of dysentery in a cramped room on the top floor. Hernán had to see this fellow man of the sea for himself. When he walked through the doorless room, he covered his nose. The stench overwhelmed his acute senses. People were sleeping like rats on top of each other in filth.

"John Hawkins!" bellowed Hernán. A frail man lying on a stained straw mattress turned in slow, weak movements toward the voice. Hernán looked at him in disgust. This could not have been the same man who changed the way humans were bought and sold. Hernán walked to the dying man and leaned close, ignoring the stench of sweat, shit, and death.

John barely blinked. "I have nothing to steal or give you. Can't you see I am dying?"

Hernán flashed the sharp points of his teeth. "I do not come here to take anything but this miserable experience from you. I only ask one thing."

John's eyes rolled to the back of his head on the border of delirium. "What?" he asked in a shallow whisper.

Hernán slapped him hard across the face. "Your loyalty and your expertise. And your ruthlessness."

John nodded and licked his dry lips. "Anything to make the pain go away."

Hernán ripped into John's wrist and drank with greed. Just as the dying man was about to slip away, Hernán sliced his own wrist with a pointed thumbnail and poured his blood into John's gaping mouth. John sputtered and coughed the blood back onto his face. A loud gasp fled from his lips before his body convulsed. Hernán stepped back to wait for the old John Hawkins to be reborn as a vampire in service to him.

Since 1595 they had been partners in crime. But Hernán held no deep affection for John, nor for anyone at any time. Sometimes he wondered if he had always been meant to be a vampire because his blood had always run ice-cold. The slightest betrayal and Hernán would dispose of John. But John didn't know this. He thought they were blood brothers.

And he had no love for Malinalli either: Until he saw that photo, Hernán had never even thought about seeing her again.

However, here she was. His breathing quickened. The wetness of the night filled his nostrils. He stood behind the trees, imagining what her bare skin smelled like up close. Did the painful memories from her past still seep from her pores? Would he be able to inhale her pain? He imagined gazing at the reflection of himself in her eyes as life left her body. Then he would peel her skin delicately from her muscles, and remove her skeleton from her corpse. With every bone removed, he would then begin the painstaking process of extracting as much of her vampire essence as possible—it would linger in her blood, tissue, and fat. Once extracted from her corpse, that essence could be consumed by humans in small doses to slow down aging and improve their health without any vampire side effects. Because of her age, and who he suspected was her creator, she would have enough essence to set him and Immortalis up for at least one lifetime.

And so he had traveled to Ireland to watch her movements and find out more about her as a vampire to make the task of trapping her in London easier. His clinic was in North London, where the conditions would be right to perform the extraction of her essence. To preserve her essence, he needed to take her apart piece by piece in sterile conditions, and a park was not an operating room in North London.

The sound of the clicking of heels distracted him from his plans for Malinalli. *So close.* But he couldn't kill her now. A human woman, the one Malinalli just fed from, walked alone near him, counting her cash. By her pace she seemed to be leaving, probably because she now had more money than she could make in a week. His heart began to pound the longer he looked at her bare legs flexing as she walked. Every curve of her body was on show, her shoulder-length hair caught in the night breeze.

This tender piece of flesh would melt so easily into his arms and mouth. He wanted to taste the fleshy part of her thigh at the very top of her leg.

The woman was fading into the fog. It was now or never if he wanted to feed on a terrified human. To conquer. A willing feeder was not as satisfying to him. One taste, because who was she in this world anyway.

The heated desire to kill crept from his toes to his scalp. He felt less determined rage than when he had begun his journey of conquest when he landed in Cuba, but the desire to get what he wanted remained. He stretched his fingers and cracked his knuckles. He kept his long vampire nails meticulously filed short for his work. Keeping them filed also helped him to keep his darker urges of tearing flesh at bay. He would have to rely on his teeth tonight.

Another woman came into sight as the sex worker made her way toward a well-lit street. This other female with her backpack and sneakers looked like a college student. Between her fingers she held her keys—as if a scratch from them could stop him. There was no sound of another human nearby. Now was his chance to have a slice of the good girl.

Satiated and in my hotel room bed, I spend the night reading Colin's book, because I find it difficult to close my eyes and rest. First, though I heard some odd sounds in the park, I didn't pick up on any sensation of immediate danger. There was only the unease of being watched.

And I know that feeling, because in my human life I had been watched all the time—I could not under any circumstances escape my duty to Cortés or any of the other men I was meant to serve under the guise of marriage or ownership. In an entire country, there was no one to run to and no one to set me free except for myself. As a human it had seemed an impossible task—I had given up all hope of escape by the end of my mortal life. But centuries later, as a vampire, it has been a very, very long time since I have been in any sort of danger.

So my encounter with Colin is closer to the forefront of my mind. I have so many questions about him and what I am feeling after our possibly more-than-a-one-night-stand. I want to know what secrets lie behind his imagined other worlds. Will his writing reveal some truth of who he is as a man? The longer

I read, the more I long for his touch again. He has talent, wit, and tales I want to be told in front of a fireplace at some lodge in the middle of nowhere. I could spend days fucking him, feeding from him, finding out the things that have shaped him to create horror. Perhaps, my being a thing of horror and him being a creator of horror could be a sort of connection between us. I want to sneak up from behind him while he's writing, bite his neck, then swivel his chair around so I can hop onto his cock for a ride to ecstasy.

Even though I've spent so long avoiding anything meaningful at all costs, I am finding that I am ready for a taste of something more than a fleeting fuck. In fact, I am realizing that if I keep thinking about Colin, my mind might spiral into infatuation. I'm way too old for that shit. But I also sense a gateway opening to something great. I didn't think love would ever find me, or perhaps it was here and I just wasn't ready to see it. I still don't think I am worthy of opening myself wide open to love. I am still scared of the price tag that is the potential for heartbreak. We all have lessons to learn—no matter how long it takes for those lessons to sink their teeth inside of us until we *get it*.

I finish Colin's book—it is about zombies, but it isn't just about mad flesh eaters; it is about grief and hardship. He captured the raw emotions of the characters perfectly. And it is terrifying. It makes me wonder what a zombie vampire might be capable of. I stare at the business card I took from his office before leaving. I thought it was just a token at the time. But having been allowed into his mind after experiencing his luscious body, I am left feeling like a well that's nearly gone dry that begins to fill again upon heavy spring rains. If only he knew of the horror I have lived through in all my years. Could he, of all people, understand this weird existence of mine?

And so I text him that I'll meet him at his place the following night. It's easier to feign eating in someone's home than at a restaurant. I close my eyes to rejuvenate and think about my life. The life that has been so devoid of love because I've treated every interaction like a mere transaction.

That is who I have become. And what I seek to change.

5

Beads. My people were to be bartered like cheap beads as the spoils of conquest and war.

And then I had to incite lust and fascination in my owners if I was to escape with my life. Many women didn't survive those early days of conquest. They were simply discarded like sacrificed bodies to the gods. We were slowly eaten, by time and the invaders using us for their daily needs. Consumed limb by limb as the years wore away at our souls. My only duty at this point in my life was to serve and never receive. My flesh was weighed with the same scale as gold. And so I made sure all my mortal life I served my masters because things that are no longer of use are expendable.

I feared death, or worse, when I was presented for the first time to Cortés, like an exotic bird or large cat. There I was, dressed in finery so I could look like a prize deal from the Tabascans to the Spanish. My hair was in two braids falling just below my breasts. My cotton huipil was spotless. But with the way they seemed entertained by my appearance, I could have been a doll made from husk and clay.

The room felt heavy and hot from the heat emanating from the Spanish men waiting to take what they pleased, and the anxiety from the girls ranging from fifteen to twenty standing beside me. Not a sound escaped their lips except for the breath they no longer owned. Some of the daughters of the caciques were wearing gold earrings and gold collars when they were presented to their new owners. A collar is still a collar no matter what material it's made from. Many times, that collar became a pair of hands wrapped around your neck, a rope tying your wrists to a tree, rope burned onto your skin. But I could not dwell on the fear. I sharpened my ears and mind to parse the many conversations between the men.

I was pulled by the arm out of the line of other women by a short man with a patchy beard who was named Geronimo. He was a Spanish invader who had escaped being captured by one of the tribes during the earlier days of exploration. Eventually he learned our language and served as a translator; however, he didn't know all the local languages or all our various customs. He was still a foreigner. Geronimo spoke to one of the Tabascan men who brought us to the invaders before turning to Cortés and pointing to me. "This one, she will serve you well. Beautiful and also quick-witted, which can be good or bad. Since you are new to this land it might be in your interest to have her."

The man called Cortés could have been from another world for how different he looked from us. Some even whispered these new arrivals were gods. Sweat rolled down his pale skin until it was absorbed into his thick brown beard. He didn't appear too old, or too young. His hair receded slightly at the corners without any touches of gray. But from the way his eyes prodded my body and strained to see through the white cotton shift I wore, he was all too human.

The men's eyes inspected every inch of our faces and bodies. I continued to catch pieces of their language as the foreign men spoke with each other. My mind moved quickly; it always had, even as a child. From a young age I had a way with words, speaking earlier than most, or so I am told. Learning came easy for me, as did the talent for adaptation. The words these new people spoke would be stored and memorized. Knowledge when it came to dealing with powerful men was as valuable as maize to the starving. Beyond that, as a woman, I knew how to read the mind of a man.

Who would get which woman first? All I knew was I had to align myself with the highest-ranking one here. By the way he carried himself, beneath heavy armor in better condition than the others' covering his body, and how the others acted around him, I knew it was the one I was presented to first. Deceit and treachery would be my new mission the moment Cortés took one of my small brown hands into his large, sweaty palm. Did I really care who lived and died from that moment forward? Did it matter? My own mother had traded me away.

Although I left with Cortés that day, Cortés first gave me to one of his captains, Alonso. I knew he wouldn't do in the long term when I saw the grin on his pasty young face as he looked at me, his prize for sailing across an ocean and committing murders for his kingdom. Only Cortés, this man's leader, would give me the greatest chance of surviving. One way or another I would have his protection—and in my naivete, I hoped maybe one day freedom.

After all, even in the worst of circumstances, I always got what I wanted. I knew I had to make my own way to survive.

Cortés was not a god after all—just a man. There is always a way to nibble and lick at the hearts of men. Sometimes the tongue is mightier than the sword. Once you have swallowed every last morsel of their heart in front of their faces as you keep them hypnotized with your eyes, it's possible to make master into slave, even if it is only for an hour.

Alonso was young and filled with ambitions of power, yet he had no power of his own. It took me six months after learning enough Spanish to communicate, but I eventually convinced Alonso to return to Spain. We lay in bed, his belly full of hair rising and falling, filling me with disgust but at the same time giving me the courage to escape his clutches. Slowly I stroked the black hair sprouting from his sweaty body. This was my chance. "You know this will not last long."

"What do you mean? You are mine. Don't forget your place now just because you are beautiful and I'm fond of you. I see how the others envy that I got you."

"No, not me. How this will all go and end. The fighting has just begun. I know my place, but I also know my people. You might die before you experience recognition or even get to enjoy the riches you have found here. Do you want to re-enter your country a victor or a sacrifice on a slab, perhaps slit open with a macana? You are still so young, with much glory to achieve. Why risk cutting your life short in battle?" I planted that seed there as his eyes snapped open to stare into the darkness. I watched as the humidity of the night closed in on him. Feeling satisfied with instilling the fear of mortality within him, I turned to my side to try to sleep. The next step would be coaxing Cortés into accepting Alonso leaving—for good.

Cortés and I met every day to exchange stilted sentences, learning about each other's customs and different regions, and the various languages spoken. His face always appeared puzzled at how quickly I caught on to his language. I wasn't. His behavior told me he wanted to dismantle my thoughts and body. It didn't pass my attention how he watched my mouth or as I brushed my hair away from my shoulders. They are all dogs wanting to gnaw on a collarbone. I always gave them eye contact. Let them imagine me devouring their heart in all my Brown glory as I straddle their body in the dark. All the while my human blood had to run as cold as melted snow. It helped to numb my existence with them. This was a mere transaction of survival during an apocalypse.

I kissed Alonso goodbye, happy to never see him again after he fought in one too many battles and watched men die like he had never experienced before. It dawned on him he might not see Spain ever again or tell the tales of his exploits. Years later I learned in conversation with Cortés that Alonso died in Spain at the young age of twenty-eight. I felt nothing, because at that time what was one more death in a world built on a temple of blood and bodies?

Three days after Alonso left for Spain, Cortés arrived at my door after dark. His eyes met mine, then darted to the mat where I slept. Without words I knew what he wanted. I had expected that this night would come, and in those days none of us captives could say no. Without question or smile I stepped out of the doorway to allow him in. He was the one I had to stay close to. I knew in my bones I could become indispensable in those first precarious in-between days of first contact, but when they see you as "just an Indian" or "beautiful for an Indian," you must make yourself indispensable. And when my use was over would not be determined by me. With Cortés the bindings between us would always be loose. We could never marry because it was against his religion to have more than one wife. Cortés was a married man with his wife still in Spain, like many of them who came over. The only thing like a binding promise would be if we had a child—and if that child was a boy and survived. Not six months into our arrangement I realized I carried his offspring.

It was morning, and we were due to leave for another village. I crawled out of bed for a bit of privacy in the trees. My stomach cramped as my body folded in half. The scent of unwashed soldiers made me feel ill. My eyes could see his black boots before I reared my head upward. Hernán looked at me in anger. "Why are you here? Don't you know I need you?"

I clutched my belly from the nauseated sensation as I tried to remember the last time I had bled. There was no sense of time back then.

"I am with child. I know it."

He continued to stare at me. "You better survive. There is much work to do. I will see you get the care you need to keep you comfortable and by my side. Taking this village will give us fresh slaves. Choose one you want."

All I could do was nod while fighting back tears. This child would either end my life in childbirth or survive and protect me for a little longer. The smell of a burning fire in the distance made my stomach lurch again. But there was nothing left inside to expel. The pain of acid burned my throat, and it felt like payback for the lies I had been telling my people. The lies Cortés wanted me to pass on as truth. Be submissive, convert, accept their rule unchallenged. Through my peripheral vision I could see Hernán turn and walk away. He shouted at someone to bring the captured females to me. I would choose a young girl to help me during my pregnancy and be my servant; maybe I could keep her safe.

For the next nine months my body grew heavy, as did the burden of the work I had to do with Cortés. I could sense his growing resentment when my ankles were too swollen to move at a steady pace or riding on horseback proved too painful. In private I brought in a shaman to reassure Cortés it was a boy. At first he protested, "I can't condone witchcraft in my personal life when I condemn it out there."

In the firelight I kissed his hand, despite hating to do so. "It is not witchcraft to offer care or assurance."

His eyes moved to the shaman, who had his head bowed. The shaman dressed like a farmer because he could no longer be who he had been before the Spanish arrived. Everything about his faith had to be destroyed. He looked like everyone else now. To survive he converted to Cortés's religion. He didn't bow his head in reverence to Hernán; he bowed it out of shame—shame of no longer being his true self.

Hernán puffed out his chest. "Fine. I want to know more about the condition of my child . . . of my son."

I lay on a mat and motioned for the shaman to come closer. He gazed into my eyes, or at least I think he did. In the light I only saw black sockets. His hands touched my belly as whispered words escaped his lips. A wave of movement made him pull away. "It is a boy," he said to me.

Then he leaned closer and whispered so only I could hear. "But this is not your destiny. You are not destined to be a mother.

It happened with this man. It will be what it will be until you are born again too."

I grabbed his wrist. "What do you mean? Will I die in childbirth?"

He shook his head. "Other great things will happen in your life. Just wait."

My hormones were already sending me into bouts of despair and tears, then fits of anger that could explode like the volcano Popocatepetl at any moment. But Hernán was watching everything, and I could not speak to the shaman more without being detected. I thanked him and watched him leave.

"What did he say?" Hernán pressed.

"He said exactly what I felt. It is a boy, and everything is fine."

Hernán left probably not believing me, but I didn't care. I turned to my side and tried to sleep with the words of the shaman ringing in my mind. Was there a way out I didn't see?

During the later stages of the pregnancy Hernán's eyes and body wandered elsewhere, which suited me fine. That was the best part of carrying his child. I slept alone, untouched, only summoned when my translation skills were needed. There were also guards around me at all times. I would not come to harm, but I also could not escape. Toward the end of the pregnancy, I could only sit to do my tasks. Traveling was slow. In one instance I watched the villagers create a serpentine line to bring the priests and soldiers what few treasures they possessed. However, because of my pregnancy I could also take more liberties with the Spanish. One of them grabbed a village chief by the scruff of his shirt when he failed to produce enough in taxes.

"This is it? Lazy liars. All of you!"

He raised his hand, but I stood defiantly with my belly protruding tightly and shouted, "Stand back now. This is not your job. You are meant to be protecting me. Am I doing the talking or you?"

The soldier shot me a dirty look with his gaze shifting from my belly to face. "Whore," he mumbled. I looked to the soldiers behind him. "Take him from me. I cannot do what Hernán Cortés has given me to do with that around me. It makes me sicker than I already am."

Without hesitation they did as commanded. I motioned for the accosted chief to come forward with his tax. I didn't want to take it. In that moment when gold and a basket of maize touched my hands, I felt like a thief. The look in his eyes took my breath away when he handed me what he owed. He should not have been forced to do this, and I should not have been forced to make him. This was his land. I gave him a nod before watching him shuffle away.

Soon after, a son burst out of me like a bloody fish I didn't recognize, with the exception of his black eyes. Thank God it was a boy. I didn't choose to be his mother, but there he was, a new creation, both Indigenous and European, in a new world. I was so exhausted part of me wished I had died in childbirth. It would have been a dignified way to go, and I would have been given a warrior's welcome in the afterlife. Instead I had to find a way to live with men I didn't want and their offspring I had no real desire for beyond security and duty.

Hernán held him, inspecting every part. "I will name him Martin," he said before giving him to a maid and leaving me. Not by choice but by necessity I cared for Martin for a short period of time because he was of me, my sacred blood. And despite his pale skin, he still had my eyes.

The eyes say it all. They are the ink that creates the story of the vessel we call a body. His infant love for me and his soul knew nothing of what I endured. When Martin was born and I survived, our next expedition to Honduras was already being planned. Empire is a roaming, hungry beast, always on the edge of starvation, and always on the prowl. Even when its belly is distended from being overfull, it still covets more. I had to tell the midwives by my side on behalf of Cortés, "Make sure I am given all I need to recover. Hernán needs me soon."

Never had I seen eyes so cold, those of a bloodless monster, than that moment looking at Hernán.

It was a small miracle Martin and I survived.

Martin was taken from me, and I lay there feeling the warrior's exhaustion as two women wiped sweat and blood from my limp body. God, I was so tired of it all. There was relief Martin was born, yet I felt nothing at all. Who wrote this story in history, and where could I find the author to eat their heart in front of their eyes, then tear their hands from their wrists? It made me have no sympathy for the Christ they made me pray to. It was also at this time that my final master whom I was forced to call my husband in my human life was brokering to have me for his own. I knew it wouldn't be long before my use to Cortés had been exhausted.

As the son of a powerful man, I *hoped* Martin would not know what many others of mixed blood experienced. I *hoped* he would be protected and in turn protect the Indigenous part of him. That power was priceless if you were not a Spaniard at the time. But Martin was left behind when he was a mere toddler so Cortés and I could travel, conquer. I still remember his little eyes wet from tears and his chubby hand reaching out for me. Is it cold and heartless of me to confess that this still didn't incite much emotion from me? When he was not near me, I scarcely missed him. Yes, I did possess love for him, but his crying in the night made me remember why I would not find it hard to venture off again.

Martin was Cortés's only male heir at that time. He had to be protected and educated, and that meant he would be sent to Spain. And so Spain is where my son, Martin, lived for most of his life after I had to leave him when I was married off. The part of me living in him was to be forgotten forever when he died many years later in Spain.

6

The alarm rings on my phone, breaking my rest and awakening my memories. This morning I had planned to visit a museum, but the memories of my human life have left me feeling my long years. I take a deep breath and remind myself who I am. The business I built is testament that I am no longer the young girl relying on Cortés or the many other men to provide the smallest scraps of my existence, including the freedom to live. They had given me the title Doña as a sign of nobility after my years of forced service, but there was no true nobility in it. I created my own sense of nobility after my human death through my own resilience and the business I later created.

Instead, I decide to catch up on a few hours of work before heading out to the museum, followed by my date with Colin. Working cleans my internal slate every time by distracting my mind. Again I look at the email stating the skulls are mine. It dawns on me that once I have them in my possession, what will be next for me to chase from my past? There will be nothing as valuable to me to obsess over and sustain me. The headdress in Austria is a project close to my heart, but it is not as personal.

I guess that perhaps it could only be love that will set me free. And too many times I've found my eyes brimming with tears and my chest tight when I thought of someone putting their arms around my waist and kissing my neck tenderly. The ghost of this man who could truly love me was so vivid in my imagination that I swear I could feel this phantom lover's breath on my earlobe. I'd clutch my midsection with no one there. This usually only happened when I listened to a Sade song. But at last, the choice between fear and loneliness or hope and open-hearted faith had come to me, and I am ready to choose.

And then I remember: I can't believe I am actually going on a date like a modern human. I never saw anyone more than a few times, and what we did was not what you'd consider dating. The anticipation of seeing Colin again is so great, my belly feels like a cave filled with bats ready to take flight. I like this sensation of excitement.

7

olin buzzes me through the entrance to his building, and I walk up to his second-floor apartment. The door was left ajar, but I knock anyway.

"Come in," he shouts. "Sorry, I just need to finish this paragraph. After last night, I can't stop writing. By the way, I hope you didn't walk far. A body of a woman was found near here. It made the papers today. Terrible stuff."

My entire body tenses hearing this, even though I have seen thousands of dead women over the years. No amount of outrage or anger from us seems to match the hate directed at us, hate that we are supposed to readily accept as part of our existence. And so when anyone tried to attack me, or if I happened to see another woman being attacked, the terror I would inflict on the perpetrator knew no bounds. Over the years, I have piled up bodies of villains by the thousands. One more would be nothing if I found out who murdered the woman in the news article.

Colin sits in a black leather office chair with only the glow of the computer to light the room. The bookshelves that line the walls are filled with CDs, horror films, and more books. There are so many, his collection spills onto the floor in neat piles. It makes me laugh to myself—I tend to be in resting bitch face mode, but this man keeps making me smile. I want time to discuss our shared passions together. The office in my home in Mexico is filled with books, framed albums, and movie posters. Things I love. How have I been led to this individual so suited to my tastes? The room smells like laundry detergent and cleaning supplies. It's endearing that he took the time to make his place decent before my arrival.

"Where's the bed?" I say from behind him. He swivels around. Both of his hands reach for my legs and inch their way up the sides of my thighs. His caress is like having one of my appendages reattached after being torn away. I can't believe I'm being touched by the same person more than once and actually liking it. "You don't want dinner first? I bought a bunch of things, since I don't know what you might want."

I have to laugh at this. In the politest way, of course. "I have a pretty select diet. And you know that is not why I came here."

He looks into my eyes, then scans my body. I've got another minidress on. This one is leopard print, with lace at the hem and waist.

"Thanks for texting me." He pauses, looks at me. "Why don't you take that dress off? I like your sexy style, but I want to see you. All of you."

I have lived long enough to be mostly comfortable in my own skin. Who cares what someone you will never see again thinks? However, even that thought doesn't take all my insecurities away in this moment, and my memories of my old life from the morning have knocked my confidence a bit. Any damage to your body before becoming a vampire remains, and the depredations of my mortal life have left their mark.

His request makes me feel vulnerable, human. If I were capable of blushing, my cheeks would be a shade of scarlet. Sometimes being superwoman is exhausting; sometimes that guard needs to come down. Saying you have no fear can become as uncomfortable as a pair of heels worn too long.

"I have a scar, stretch marks. Let's turn off the light and keep this what it is: a fantasy. You're mine and I'm yours. For a little while, at least."

He stands to lead me to the bedroom and sits at the edge of the bed. There is a serious sincerity in his eyes now. This look has the same effect on me as flowers do for other women.

"I don't care what you look like. It's how you feel that matters. What your body did to me last night was mind-blowing. Don't hide from me. I'm sure as hell not perfect either. I still don't understand why you picked me out of the bar. You look like the kind of woman that could have any man you want."

I'd like to sit and tell him all the little things I adore about him, despite just meeting him. I want to discuss his book and take copies of all his books home to read tonight, but I've also been wet since he placed his hands on my thighs. And now this: The honeycomb inside is crushed and overflowing. My desire for him requires seeing to immediately.

Because he's right: I've never fucked a flawless human in all my hundreds of years of sex. Why should I trip about not being perfect myself? It has never bothered me before. This personal growth thing is not easy. I may have the power to kill a thousand men, but some human insecurities remain. Even the mightiest of beasts feel fear. And he's getting me to like the idea of experiencing vulnerability.

I pull off my silk chemise. He looks at my completely exposed body and then touches me. He kisses the rough scar that runs vertically on my belly of loose skin from two pregnancies. It is like crepe paper, folds of melted skin soft to the touch. His fingers trace my faded stretch marks, and his large hands grab my wide hips and pull me closer as he sneaks his tongue between my eager labia and moves it around like a finger saying, "Come hither."

He's teasing me, playing a game of sexual hide-and-seek with his tongue. My head rolls back, and I close my eyes. Tiny spiders of pleasure scuttle across my nervous system. Fucking him leaves me helpless to him. I want him to carry me away and drain me dry. He explores the rest of me with his hands. I push him backward, so I can now look at his lithe physique. He's not overly muscular, but his body has definition. I smile when I see that the small patch of hair on his chest turns into a furry trail that leads below his jeans. A tattoo that matches the skull in his office decorates the skin over his heart. What does it mean? I have to know, but I'll find out later. Now it's my turn to tease.

My tongue flicks along the shaft of his cock. I lick his balls, taking them gently in and out of my mouth as my hand continues to stroke his cock. He grips the sheets as he becomes harder in my hand. That always does the trick; he's ready for me now. His stiff cock and my engorged clit need to be reunited in perfect unwed bliss. As I move to face him, he grabs me by the waist, tossing me onto my back.

"I wish I knew what you are doing to me, woman. I haven't been able to stop thinking about you."

I want to tell him I feel the same. That I'd finished his book in one night. That I want more words, more touches that make me feel human again, but I keep quiet, allowing this to just be what it is in this moment.

He thrusts inside of me like a runaway train hitting the side of a mountain. His paw of a hand massages my ass. Volts of pleasure cause the hair on my arms and neck to stand up. His cock is an electric eel bringing me to Bride of Frankenstein life. His rhythm between my legs is incessant, going from a slow strum as smooth as Nile Rodgers's guitar to a vigorous beat like death metal. Our bodies intertwine as if we are in love even though in that moment I want it to be no more than lust. But with every squeeze I feel my heart open a little more to allow that love to come inside. His eyes, heavy in their intensity, pry my soul open like a crowbar at a rusty safe.

Our bodies fit together. His head is buried in my breasts, neck, and hair. Part of me wants to tether my heart to this man. Find the real version of true love. However, this thought, and his cock, begin to bring all my demons to the surface. My darkness, the blood angel inside of me, wants a playmate too. Her loneliness seeks refuge in another dark place within someone. I don't know if that kind of union is possible with a human.

He presses his body weight against me as I hold on to his ass with both hands so as not to miss an inch of the thing I crave so much. The harder he thrusts with my bucking hips, the hotter my skin grows.

And then all my sense of control slips through my fingers like severed rope. I can feel my fangs begin to grow. He's bringing out that other side, that shadow side, which I hid so well for centuries from humans. Now I have to look away, try not to let go so easily.

And then he does the unthinkable, finding my sexual Achilles' heel, as if the devil himself whispered my secret. Colin's perfect mouth, rimmed with just enough stubble to delight me, takes in my breast, scraping my erect nipple with the edges of his teeth. I come instantly, and he sucks harder, pushes his cock deeper, causing me to come again.

To hide the transformation that's going to happen whether I like it or not, I push him off my body, so he's on his back again. My lips want to find his cock. My long brown hair hides my changing eyes and growing fangs. His hand gently holds the back of my head with fingers caught in the spiderwebs of my hair. I want to suck him until he needs an IV to restore his fluids. The entirety of my mouth down to the back of my throat is filled with Colin. I would take his being inside me for an eternity if it was possible.

Colin's warm sea spray slides without effort down my throat. I continue to suck until his cock is so sensitive he can't stand the feeling of my lips stimulating the head any longer. I jump out of the bed and run to the bathroom. He follows, sensing something wrong.

"Hey, Mali, you okay?" I turn my back to the door and hide my face beneath my hair. He has done nothing to deserve me ripping his throat out in a frenzy. I keep my heart locked because when it is open, the heart of the vampire is unleashed as well. Predators in the wild are just what they are, their nature on show. It is only humans who have the capacity to hide and go against their nature. I need to calm myself.

"Just . . . later. I'm fine."

"Please. Did I do something wrong? I'm sorry I didn't warn you before . . ." There is panic in his voice.

"Go away," I roar.

"I'm coming in. You're scaring me."

There is no way to stop this. Whatever happens next is out of my control. He opens the door and steps inside. From the mirror I can see he's studying my body to see if I'm hurt in some way. His eyes stop and go wide. My nails appear bark-like, and my tensed outstretched fingers resemble the talons of an owl.

"Mali, your hands, your nails . . ."

"Please," I sob. I don't want to attack him or feel anything toward this man except sexual attraction. He was supposed to have been just a bit of fun before I continue my travels. Fuck personal growth, spiritual awakening, facing and chasing some silly meditative dream I had.

Now I'm the one scared of myself. But being a blood drinker is what I am down to my very atoms.

"Did I hurt you?"

I lift my head toward the mirror, so he can see the real me. "I told you I was a horror story."

He stumbles back, still naked.

"What the . . . what the fuck? This isn't real. Are you fucking with me because of my book? That's not cool."

"No, I'm not. This is me. I'm both alive and dead, a vampire. Calm down. I won't hurt you." My fangs are in full view and the red thread of veins in my eyes pronounced. I can smell the adrenaline in his veins. His heart beats with a sprinter's pace.

"No! Impossible."

I turn around and grab his wrist before he can move away, biting him hard enough to let him know I'm real. His eyes are filled with fear, traveling from my face to his wrist.

"Ouch! Fuck, that hurts! Am I going to be a vampire now? It's real? Those are real fucking teeth." He grabs a hand towel hanging off the radiator.

My heart rate is beginning to slow, my breathing stabilizing. It won't be long until I look like myself again. I've never allowed someone to transform me in this way. I've never felt so connected to myself or to another, so uninhibited emotionally. It's what I wanted, but all things come with a price. So now I am ready to accept this brief glimmer of companionship is over. "Do you want me to leave?"

The white towel wrapped around his wrist is now bright red,

like my lipstick that first night. He looks at me in my nakedness with only my waist-length hair to cover my breasts.

His blue eyes soften. "No. Don't leave. I've dated much scarier women."

I can't help but chuckle. The taste of his blood lingers on my lips. He tastes like nothing I can quite discern. I want more. As he moves to clean his wound at the sink, he sees me eyeing his wrist. The scents of sex on our bodies and his blood cause my mouth to water and belly to leap with the hunger of a thousand leeches dying to be fed.

"Come here," he says in a soft tone. I move close to him until I'm against his chest. Without thinking, I kiss the skull tattoo and rub my face against his chest hair. He sits on the closed toilet seat and pulls me onto his lap.

"Here." He lifts his wrist to my mouth. "I don't see why you can't have all of me. I knew I was yours from the moment you offered to carry my books."

My worst fear and greatest fantasy floats in his blue eyes that are no longer stormy seas but cool Caribbean waters that dare me to wade in. For years I have avoided visiting Europe, afraid of my lingering resentment from the days of Spanish conquest. Cortés. His name still sends me into a rage. I would travel to hell if I knew I could drain him dry of all his blood. It has taken this long for me to feel a sliver of peace to travel across the ocean.

In the spirit of giving myself to all that life has to offer, I take Colin's wrist into my mouth and drink deeply. I have to learn to accept the love presented in front of me instead of dashing for the door. Love has been a sort of Hollywood version of a vampire to me—something legendary, something not real. But I have reached a stage in my long life when neither garlic nor crosses can keep the yearning away. Up to now, I ran as fast and hard as I could, choosing to be my own husband. Not once did

I disappoint myself. That only lasts so long because I had to show up for myself every damn day. A hand to hold as the years grow longer would be nice.

Colin winces only once, then brushes my tangled hair from my face and neck. Lips with the soothing balm that only love can provide kiss my neck. The sticky juice that is Colin's blood invigorates my body. He's swimming through my veins, my heart, my brain. There's no going back the longer I drink. You don't find love when you're looking; it waits in the shadows, stalking you by night, then devouring you whole when your back is turned. In that moment, I love Colin for his desire to give me his blood for sustenance. I love his kindness. When his eyes are heavy, I know it's time to stop.

"Thank you. You didn't have to do that. Why don't we take this party to the other room? Want a beer?"

He kisses my bloodstained lips and pats my bottom. "Hell yes, I want a beer! And a shot of whiskey. And something sweet. My sister is fantastic at baking."

I roll my eyes. "Baked goods, really? Why?"

"Yeah, you know when you donate blood you need something sweet after for the blood sugar? You practically drained me! I'd like brownies. I think I still have a few my sister left me the other day."

Any concern I had is gone. "I barely scratched you. I'll be waiting with that beer when you decide to join me." I walk out knowing he's watching my bare ass shake.

We sit at his table that seats two, and he wolfs down a thick slice of brownie. He is looking at me as if he is trying to read my mind or figure out what this will lead to.

"I have to ask you a few questions. If that's okay?"

This moment was inevitable. I've decided to answer as much as possible, but a woman is allowed to keep some of her secrets.

"You can ask. Don't be hurt if I don't respond or you don't like the answer I give you."

"I'm guessing we can only see each other at night?"

"That's totally false. I love the sun. In fact, it's a source of peace and calm for me. Next question."

He's thinking hard as he finishes the last crumbs of his brownie. Then he jumps out of his seat. "Hold on. This is good." He walks to a drawer beneath the kitchen counter and pulls out a small pad and pencil. I don't know if I should be flattered by his interest or wary of it. My story has only ever been told by others.

"How do you live? Like, do you have a job? How old are you?"

I wouldn't accept this line of questioning from anyone else, but he's not anyone else. I also want to return the favor of giving me his beautiful blood. Perhaps being open about my life will prompt him to tell me his life story too.

"I deal in antiquities. When the Spanish came to the New World, their mind was on nothing but plunder and conquest. Their lust for riches was as great as their cruelty. I was given to a very powerful Spaniard and privy to all the Spanish secrets the longer I served. The internet is a fantastic invention and expanded my business across the world. As far as my age, I became a vampire at thirty, which would make me over five hundred years old."

He is scribbling on his notepad. "Only two more questions. Promise."

I remain silent.

"How much blood do you need? Is it like the movies where you drain a whole body? You didn't seem to need much from me."

"That is different for every vampire just like it is for humans. When I feel full and satisfied I stop. Because we are dead, we have to feed more than you would eat. However, drinking blood feels better than eating food. It's intimate and rejuvenates our bodies beyond what humans are capable of. The physical power can be intoxicating. That is why some kill—because we can."

He no longer writes and stares at me with a look of wonder. "Wow. That is so fascinating. I thought you were only a tale in books. But to hear how it really is . . . Okay, last question."

I nod for him to continue.

"Why are you here?"

I have to make a decision whether or not to tell him about the skulls. The tip of his pen rests on the paper. No one can write my story but me. "Because I am."

He opens his mouth to speak again. I lift my hand. My desire to open myself to others will have to be taken in steps. "Later. Tell me more about your sister. I recall a photo on your desk. Are you close?"

"We are a very close family. Guess I got lucky that way. Growing up, we had our fights, like any siblings, but we always worked it out. Her son, Luke, is one hell of a kid. I always thought if I became a father, I'd hope I could raise one like him."

This statement raises the hair on my arms slightly. As much as I like him, he is still human, and longs for an ordinary human life. Something I can never give him the way he might expect.

It's the evening. We order Indian food for him because he's hungry, then we curl beneath a duvet to watch *Fright Night*. For some reason he's in the mood. It also happens to be one of my all-time favorite films. Since I have no spare clothes at his apartment, he gives me an old Van Halen T-shirt to wear. Not only is his taste permanently in my mouth, his scent layers itself on my skin from the moment I slip it on.

Telling a few of my secrets to someone after so many years alone feels as soft as wearing a twenty-year-old T-shirt with nothing on underneath. There is no reason to leave his apartment. I have all that I need in this moment in time. I've somehow moved in without moving. This is our island within an island.

His idea of breakfast in bed is by far the best sex I've ever experienced and the only thing I want every morning. While I lie on my side, still drowsy, he greets me from behind with his erect cock, the wet tip sliding between my ass cheeks. As my pussy becomes wetter from his cock entering and exiting, he slides toward my anus. It's stimulated until it pulses like a little sea anemone trying to catch prey. His one arm casts around my own, so that his wrist rests on my mouth. His other hand, coated with lube, continues to tease my little puckered hole, sending shockwaves of titillation to my toes.

Once out of my pussy, he slides in and out of my ass, pumping to the cadence of a slow ballad like Foreigner's "Waiting for a Girl Like You." His breath on my neck and soft moans are a soothing lullaby. My fingers find my clit as he fucks my ass. I can't remember ever being this wet. His blood is in my mouth and his cock inside my body. There is no part of him that isn't part of me. I want to cry, to relinquish my soul to whatever demands the gods have of me, because I don't want this moment to ever end. Dreams must exist, because this feels like one in the space of the day that isn't night nor morning. We enter and exit each other's bodies from the dark morning light until noon. I've seen the cruelty of how short life can be, so I don't overthink what any of this means beyond this flat. The entire experience is some sort of emotional chrysalis. My heart and body speak to each other. Inside I am growing, sprouting new anatomy. I am connecting the parts of me that had once been severed by the sword of subjugation.

When I can tell I've weakened him too much from my feeds, I feel like cooking. Even though I don't eat food, the aroma of it has always been a comfort to me.

It reminds me of my time with Chantico. When I was helping her, the rhythm of preparing gave me the same sense of peace as weaving. I've missed that peace but pushed the memory of it far from my heart and mind. Now the opportunity to feel it has arisen again. If we were in my homeland, I'd be preparing our traditional food, full of chili, onion, and maize. Instead, I have pulled up a few easy dishes from Pinterest.

While I'm at the stove, Colin kisses my neck and strokes my ass, a glass of wine in his other hand. He's a creature of normality, making me feel desired so much more than the quick-fix fucks I've grown accustomed to. His allure is so potent, I've forgotten what other blood tastes like or that it even exists. This perhaps is what it feels like to be normal: You just live an average life day to day and hope for love to find you. I've been in hibernation far too long, and so I will give living at a slower pace another shot.

I read his books in bed while he writes. When he's working, I only sneak to his desk to bring him dishes I've never made before. It has been centuries since I have even considered doing anything of the sort. But I humor myself with this act of domesticity, even while he is *my* food source. When I am hungry, he nestles next to me in bed as I take a deep bite into his wrist and feed until I am satisfied.

He's writing something new, something with bite and blood and more gore than he ever had in a book before. I consume all his published books with fervor and then he allows me to read the stories no other eyes have seen. I feel privileged to be a part of something so deeply personal. The idea of doing something like that frightens me, but I am also intrigued to try. When my watch buzzes with an alert to a new email, I swipe it away. The thought of turning off notifications crosses my mind.

It's time to live for the moment, not the hunt.

Before I doze off Colin whispers, "Good night, Mali, my Nahua muse."

These words are wonderful to hear, yet I discover something I had not anticipated or experienced before: his human body heat next to mine for hours on end. That heat consumes the entire bed until the sheets take on the sensation of floating on a magma waterbed. As he lays draped over me night after night, it warms me to the point of needing to inch away from him. At first the heat makes me drowsy, almost like being drunk on love, but my body does not regulate at the same temperature as his. The cold doesn't bother me, nor does the sun. But this body heat does.

I kick off the covers for some relief from my rising temperature. I close my eyes to meditate and try to rest, as uncomfortable as it feels. As vampires age, the need for sleep in the human sense fades; however, restorative rest is still essential. My body still finds itself resisting the heat. I try to tell myself this is something that will pass, an adjustment. Or is it?

Then there is also the sound of his heart. The constant patter of it booming between my ears makes it impossible to completely relax. Again, I tell myself to press on with this experiment of love, even if the sound of his pulse repulses me slightly. His breathing in his chest also makes a rhythmic whistling sound out of his mouth before it hitches. Humans are noisy as hell at night. His blood and oxygen irritate me so much that it makes me wonder what lying next to another vampire might be like.

After two days I broach the subject of leaving the apartment. "You have either been in bed with me or at that desk. It can't be good for your health." He stands and stretches his back.

"I think you're right. And this can't be that exciting for you," he says.

Nearly naked, I shift my eyes across the room toward the door to remain cool and calm. I can't tell him this time with him is priceless. How I find myself growing in ways I had once feared would end my life if I even tried. Finding him, on this tiny little island in an unremarkable pub, is a one-in-a-billion chance. Yes, there are many people out there that would be fun to fuck, but how many of them can we truly feel a connection with? He is in my life, whether I like it or not, and the gravity between us is more than theory. It now rules our lives.

But my mind can't help overthinking, so I simply say, "Show me more of your town. Show me what I won't find in a travel guide."

His eyes sparkle when he looks at me. "You bet. Anything you want."

The gauzy gray sky makes the city feel as though it exists only in a sad memory. The dark gloom that settles in the morning remains until the night. Not a speck of sunlight pokes through even once.

I would be lying if I didn't admit to myself that I disliked the weather in Ireland from the day I arrived. The sun is too important for me. A creeping thought enters my mind. What if this is all he wants? This island and his bookshop? And a normal woman with normal needs on his arm to wear his T-shirt? Too enchanted by the last few days, I brush these questions off. The fragrance of what I hope is love is such a strong perfume it clouds my mind.

The skull in his bookshop also keeps popping back into my mind, reminding me of the skulls I had been searching for and that are now within my reach. Yet I continue to ignore Horatio's emails. I can't escape the uneasy idea that I cannot have both the dream lover and my career. *Don't forget your skulls!* I keep telling myself. This entire trip was supposed to be about retrieving the obsession of my long, immortal life.

But instead, I walk hand in hand with Colin down the narrow cobbled back streets that he finds most interesting, but also so he can show me the clubs where he'd watch punk bands perform, his childhood neighborhood, his old school. We sit on the park bench where he had his first kiss. How different we are in our beginnings, our current situations, yet we share deeper similarities. Before his parents were born, my soul secretly yearned for this kind of companionship. I suppose all our souls do on some level.

I rest my head on his shoulder as we sit on the bench, a light mist of rain falling over us. I close my eyes and wish I could actually become my vampire blood as it enters his veins, mutating his cells until we are truly one and the same being. I want a shoulder to rest my weary head upon for years to come. But will this stay good long enough for us even to get through the entire Netflix catalogue of horror films? I dare not fantasize about it lasting any longer.

Because if I am honest with myself, part of me wonders if only another vampire will do for my lifelong companion. It's hard for me to discern between my own voice and the voice of destiny. My worries about the complications of living alongside a human gather as thick as the clouds over my head.

"Tell me about the horned skull," I say to him.

He smiles as he stares into the trees. The few other people that are seated get up to find shelter from the rain. We are now alone.

"Well, I suppose it's what I might look like if you peel back my skin. All the things I feel, think, my regrets, the things that motivate me, look like that skull.

"A few years ago, I did a lot of hard drugs. I thought it helped me with my creativity, but one bad trip left me hospitalized. I felt like I was going insane. So I stopped. Stopped drinking for a spell too and took a road trip in America. This old guy was selling the skull in this little junkyard shop off the highway in New Mexico. I bought it straightaway and had it shipped to Ireland for an insane amount of money, but I couldn't let it go. When it arrived in Ireland, I had my mate varnish it. It somehow helps remind me to always be honest with myself and others."

Colin's ability to reveal himself to me makes me want to feel even closer to him. I kiss his lips, unbutton his jeans, slip my hand underneath his boxers, while his navy rain jacket hides my little misdeed. I watch his dirty blond eyelashes flutter as droplets of drizzle catch on the tips. His perfect lips quiver and smile with every stroke of my hand. He leans back, letting the rain splash his face. His body tenses and his jaw clenches as the pleasure coils in his groin, and he squeezes my thigh. The rain saturates everything, including us, but we could be on fire and we wouldn't notice. When he's about to come, I pull his cock out far enough that I can wring every drop of cum from it with my mouth.

Now this park bench has two special memories for him.

On our way back to his home, I hear a small basement bar playing funk and disco. It feels like a poor man's Studio 54 and reminds me of my time with Catherine. I turn to Colin. "We have to go in."

He smiles. "Lead the way."

The staircase down to the basement leads to a dangerously overcrowded club, the air humid with suffocating body heat. No one notices or cares about the overcrowding. We could all be celebrating in the afterlife in the middle of a field under the stars with an angel as our DJ. I drag Colin to the dance floor. At least I dance, while he watches me or shuffles his feet back and forth while sipping on a beer. He's happy to humor me and give me a little twirl here and there, as long as I reward him with a kiss.

If I could relive any decades, it would have to be the seventies. It was a never-ending party of pleasure and music. I had met Catherine, my only best friend, in New York City during the seventies. She was so wicked and sensual. She possessed the wild emotional and physical abandonment of the music created in those times. My affair with Colin would meet with her approval. She was a complicated woman helping women in ways that would have been denied to them in centuries past, especially those down on their luck or looking to free themselves from fathers, brothers, and lovers. She believed women who were previously told they were heretics and liars. Yet in other aspects of her life she was so utterly selfish it ultimately might have led to her demise. She had no conscience when it came to killing, even the innocent. But Catherine's life is another story for another time.

I dance Colin into a corner when I notice a roped-off room in purple velvet and low light. Glancing around to make sure no one is looking, I pull him inside, pushing him onto the velvet sofa before turning to close the curtains.

My hips sway to the beat of the music. I'm wearing heels and a red wraparound spaghetti strap dress that is very short, just how I like my dresses to always be. I keep my eyes on him as I slide a single strap off my shoulder. "I Want Your Love" by Chic is playing. I'm feeling nothing but complete abandon. He looks so good tonight in his loose jeans and T-shirt. His stubble is unusually thick today. I want to feel my nipples in his mouth. I want to be driven to hunger and back again since he knows how to do it so effortlessly.

I straddle his knee with one heel on the sofa, grinding my bare pussy above his leg, my dress lifted just enough for him to catch a glimpse of my wet lips. He reaches to touch me and I swat his hands away and turn around to grind against his cock, still dancing. Lost in the rhythm, I kick off my heels to dance the way I danced as a young girl, the way my ancestors danced, conjuring up the spirits and magic of my homeland. Perhaps that is the same magic that made me what I am today. I am so very close to finding out.

I whip my hair side to side then bend over to touch the floor, so he has full view of my ass and pussy. Before I make it to the floor, he grabs my thighs, and the stubble that drives me wild brushes against my ass. His tongue laps at my clit, then dances from my labia to my anus as I hold on to the table in front of the sofa. He moans as he eats me in gulps and slurps like he's gorging on sticky candy.

But this is all just an amuse-bouche. I turn around and see his jeans can barely contain his cock. He reads the look in my eye that says, *Pull those silly jeans down.* His fingers unzip his jeans. I love how I don't even have to speak for him to know what I want him to do. You don't need to speak when you want the same thing, when you need the other person inside of you like you need air.

My knees sink into the sofa as I straddle him. My ass and hips still move to the beat, letting the tip of his cock sneak inside of me before it's out again. I bob and plunge deeper onto his cock as the music becomes wilder, while he squeezes both of my nipples into his mouth. Either this man is telepathic, or the heavens decided to bless me with a seraph to fulfill my every wish. Or is it the devil leading me down the road of ruin, temptation that feels like a downy bed but is really a coffin? I continue to ride him harder and faster as the music commands and as his grip on my ass tells me to. He's moaning and biting his lips while sweat causes his T-shirt to cling to his chest.

As much as my body wants to extract every ounce of pleasure from him, I want to cry out, "What have you done to me?"

I remain quiet and direct his fingers to my clit, creating a hurricane of tension that results in orgasm. Knowing he's made me come, Colin places one hand on the back of my neck as he thrusts his cock as deep as he can manage then comes inside of me. I can't stop trembling as we just stare at each other, our foreheads touching, the sweat from his skin saturating mine. I don't hear music or people or know if there's anything beyond those heavy purple velvet curtains. He opens his mouth to say something, but before he can get it out, I kiss him.

We linger inside of each other, neither of us wanting to disconnect. I want to cling to him. We kiss for what seems like hours but is really minutes. I touch his face, kiss him once more until my kisses lead to his neck.

I bite, drink, take him into my beating heart so that I may live, because without his blood pulsing through my veins I would surely die. I can feel him harden again inside of me the longer I drink. His sweat rolls from the side of his face into my mouth. Blood and sweat makes a salty-sweet umami taste that tumbles around my mouth, causing my clit to become engorged again.

For the first time I understand what the term *making love* could mean and experience a capacity to feel something deeper than flesh level, to exchange something other than bodily fluids before getting off. I've never felt anything like this before—it is a vicious lie to think a slave could ever love a master. There have been so many lies surrounding who I was in history, but that I could have loved my captor is one of the most pernicious. I move my hips, grinding at a slow and deliberate pace. Small kisses find his mouth again until we both orgasm. His blood is life, his love salvation, and his body the cherry and whipped cream on top.

Before I can move from his lap, he puts his hand around my waist.

"Wait. One more question. Since a bite doesn't make someone a vampire, what does?"

Suddenly I'm trembling again. Does he want to share an immortal life with me? To be a vampire? The back of my mind says this connection we are having is just the flash of a warming flame, but not that I'm ultimately destined to share my life with Colin. It is hard to know: As well as I know myself from spending so much time alone on the hunt, I still have those lingering human feelings of doubt. I'm a broken thing, who had been brought back to life, but still carrying with her a fucked-up past and no knowledge of what the future might hold. I fear what will happen to Colin and me when the flush of excitement and newness wears off. I know the moment may come when the touch that feels so exhilarating to me now could become no more than a sure thing to get me off before I roll over for sleep. Because life is more than sex, dancing, and sharing stories.

And love is a story, and all stories must come to an end.

Against my better judgment I tell him how a vampire is made. "I ask you if you accept my gift of your own free will. Then I drain your entire body of your blood, but just before death, I give you my blood."

He's looking at the corner of the room, nodding, touching his puncture wounds on his neck. Only God knows what he's thinking.

"Thank you for telling me. Thank you for texting me and making these last few, I don't know how many days or weeks it's been, but whatever, it's been something special I didn't know existed. Like you." He kisses me tenderly and places my dress straps over my shoulders. I want to forget he's asked me that question because it just leads to more overthinking, more worries, more messy feelings that splash all over me like a wineglass filled to the very top.

As we walk home, the old dark streets, football matches blaring from pubs, and greasy chip shops make me forget I had planned to be in London. This is so different from the world I was born in and eventually created for myself. I've spent all my time in bed, cooking, reading, and feeding from him. I'd forgotten about my original plan, my desire to see the south of Ireland. The skulls. My lifelong pursuit. All my work has been completely neglected. It's been the one thing that has given me purpose, true joy, because it was all created by my own hand. I have succeeded—and not because I was on the arm of someone who believes they own me.

When I get back to the apartment, I look at my phone finally, and my inbox is a mess. Unlike my historical persona as "the traitorous La Malinche," my work reputation is spotless, until now. Love isn't just blind; it blinds you right back.

Suddenly, the apartment that felt like an ever-expanding universe is just an apartment. He is just a man, a mere fantasy I once had. I can already feel the little petals of my soul curling in on themselves. The vibrant roses have dry, brown edges. Their heads sag at the weight of their time being over. And then the petals drop one by one until nothing is left.

Everyone I ever loved in my life is gone. I never gave human lovers enough of a chance to know me, and I've never had many friends. It is the vampire way, it seems, to be rootless. The male vampires I have met are just as aloof as I am. The petals on their souls are long gone, with no chance of ever growing back because they refuse to add fresh water for the stems to drink. Before leaving Mexico for Ireland, I was very close to that point too.

Not everyone wants the gift of near immortality, and if I had been given a real choice in the matter, perhaps I would not have chosen this vampire life. At the time, it had seemed like the only way I could realize the dream of true freedom I'd mistakenly thought I could win through Cortés.

Will I take a chance on love even though the ones closest to us hold the sharpest stakes in their hands? I've got countless splinters inside of me that will never be plucked from my flesh. The overwhelming emotions I'm feeling are turning into ugly, fearful obsessive thoughts. Ugly like when I wake up without removing my makeup, with my black eyeliner and mascara running, my mouth smeared with red. I think of these things as I brush my teeth and place my toothbrush next to his when I am finished.

Not a damn thing makes sense anymore until he sits down to eat the poppy seed cake I made the day before. While he eats, I'm on my phone trying to catch up on work. There are so many transactions I have neglected. A few emails slipped through the cracks. When I finally send my last email for the day, he folds a newspaper and sets it on the table.

I glance at the newspaper, and the headline makes me feel uneasy. Another woman was found murdered. I can't read the rest of the headline because what he says throws me even more off-center.

"My sister just texted me. I'd love for you to meet my family. Is Sunday lunch okay? Do you like kids? You mentioned you were a mother once. Anyway, her kids are pretty adorable. I told you about my nephew." And there's the other stiletto dropping. My head hurts with hangover pain even though I wasn't drunk the night before.

"Colin, you know that's asking for trouble."

"Let's just go for dessert. Say you're gluten and lactose intolerant. I promise she'll be making her 'famous' trifle. She always does for special guests. They all keep asking when I'm going to fall in love. Now they'll know they can stop asking."

He's touching my hand from across the table, looking at me with those dreamy blue eyes that now look like a watery grave. I slowly withdraw my hand to my lap. I think of the hanging horned skull in his bookstore. Then my thoughts shift to my skulls. The two skulls I desperately want and that brought me here. Horatio had sent me a flurry of emails I've ignored over the others. I only read one, which possessed the tone of a man I didn't know. *Where are you? The seller is having second thoughts. Please get in touch. This isn't like you. Everything all right?*

I had already paid the deposit, and so I wasn't sure what the rush was about.

Then my eyes fix on a bottle of Cholula hot sauce on the kitchen counter among his menagerie of condiments. The image on the bottle is of a woman with a pleasant and placid smile on her face as she stands in front of a kitchen. I want to take the bottle and throw it hard against the wall until it shatters with all its red-orange contents splattering everywhere, even if it hits our eyes, causing them to burn. Cholula. It reminds me of the eventual massacre there.

At the same time the word *love* that has savaged my heart for years has escaped his lips. He loves me, just like I hope to love someone someday. The word *love* terrifies me like my existence terrifies humans. I can't breathe.

But isn't this what I wanted? My fantasy could become reality. I just need the balls to take it into my mouth and bite. Once again, messy thoughts of consequences, of the pain if it all goes bad, stab the front of my forehead until I feel dizzy. I go to the other room to find my things and toss his T-shirt into the dirty laundry, even though I want to keep it.

"Hey, you want to go out? Give me five minutes to . . ."

"I'm going. You're staying here. I had a plan for my life, and I'm sticking to it."

"I thought . . ."

"You thought what? There is an ocean between us, more than one, in fact. I'm not human! I can't give you children or a life or all those things people want before they expire. No more children for me. I don't do family or romance."

He grabs my hands. "I don't need kids . . . I don't think. I'm nearly forty. If it was going to happen, it would have happened by now. I'm sick of being in and out of relationships that are nothing but constant ups and downs, never knowing what drama is going to crop up next. There's no bullshit with you. There are no expectations with you. You can have my blood for as long as you want. You already have my heart." He wasn't going to let me go easy.

"Maybe I'm tired of drinking the same blood. Ever thought of that? And how can you be sure if you want children or not, knowing it's not a possibility with me?" I spit these words at him like venom.

Now I'm just being cruel. He looks wounded. I want to embrace him, kiss him, tell him I don't mean it. Making love to him this second would make me forget the silly notion that leaving was the right thing to do.

But I shake my head. No, this is better. This is a web I walked into. I allowed myself to get spun tighter into *his* world. Not a world created in mutual union.

I walk out of the door and don't look back. As I step onto the street, a gust of cold air blows against my body. It sobers my drugged senses. The chrysalis around my heart has cracked open, yet I don't see the change. I head back to my hotel to focus on work for a few hours before checking out, namely calming Horatio down. After, I will begin my original itinerary.

Four hours later, I call Horatio from the car. To my surprise he answers after only one ring. "Malinalli! It's so nice to hear from you. Please tell me you are on your way. I really need to conclude this business . . . I mean, for you. This has been a long time coming."

He doesn't sound like his usual cheerful self. There is a frantic urgency in his voice.

"Everything all right, Horatio? You don't exactly have money problems, and I've already sent a deposit. What's another day?"

He remains silent. He is searching for the right words through his heavy breathing. "The seller. They are eager to move forward and will go elsewhere."

Now I know he is lying. "You said it was all arranged and there were no other interested parties, considering I was willing to pay in crypto."

"You know the business. Things change. Please come as soon as you can. These skulls are magnificent. They are haunting. You must see them to believe their beauty."

My mind can't juggle Horatio and my emotions while also navigating a car on the opposite side of the road. "I'll be in touch." I hang up, too agitated to give Horatio's strange behavior another thought.

I want my fucking skulls. I want to close more fucking deals for more goddamn money before spending a crazy amount across Europe. If only Catherine were still around for me to call.

When I am finally on the open road, it takes me back to that journey to Cholula. Today, they call it the Massacre at Cholula.

During the five years of translating for Cortés, giving birth to his child, and the brutality of conquest, I didn't have the energy to appreciate anything, not even the breath in my lungs. All I could feel were the blisters on my feet as we traveled across the land in the name of God and crown. Cortés would say without mercy, "Come, Malinalli. You people were formed with the animals during Creation. Surely you don't tire that easily." I remained silent about my needs because I had to, and to conserve my energy.

My people's resistance to Cortés and the colonizers was met with yet more violence. My throat remained hoarse from speaking on behalf of Cortés. And after I was done with that, he wanted me to either entertain him or explain everything we had seen and heard on our journey in detail. Hours I spent recounting the history and differences between the tribes.

I've bled bodies of all their blood as a vampire but only after my victims were received by death. But Cortés bled me in a different way while I was still alive: He worked me until the exhaustion left me with nothing. Then it all had to be repeated the next day.

There were moments I could do nothing but squat alone with my arms wrapped around myself. My own embrace was the only thing that felt real. It was the only true tenderness extended to me. Only my determination to survive another day helped me get to my feet when it was time to move again. I had to constantly be on the move with Cortés on his exploits, stand by tyranny and terror. At night I would stare into the night sky as if waiting for some miracle to occur. Every cell in my body screamed a prayer. No such thing happened. My calls for miracles were only met with more bloodshed of my people.

I remember one such moment when Cortés and I were side by side. Two gold cuffs adorned my wrists. All that was missing was a chain connecting them. After another battle, we watched black smoke rise in the distance. I didn't know whether it was burning bodies, temples, or villages sending plumes of stinking clouds into the atmosphere. Probably all three, because the stench of burning flesh is one you never forget. I turned to my right to see Hernán's reaction. There was none.

From the beginning of our travels, I could already see Montezuma's demise was inevitable. I spoke multiple languages fluently by then and picked up Castilian with ease, as my fear of these new people was as great as my curiosity about them. If the Spaniards existed, what else was out there in the world? How many other people were arriving on other shores with boats to do the same to other unsuspecting people?

The road to Cholula and the eventual captivity of Montezuma were the destination I shared with the invaders. My people had experienced bloodshed and territorial fights before, but not by a completely different race of people, and not in this way.

The god they wanted to give us, and the emperor named Charles we had to serve, were as distant and foreign as a star in the sky.

Side by side with Cortés I walked through rain and blood-sodden dirt, felt the heat of the sun on my cheeks. Inside it felt as if Tlaloc, the god of rain, himself caused a rainstorm to blow into my soul. When fighting broke out as we encountered a hostile village, many Spanish were wounded. In one village they found a woman with a soft and round body. In obvious shock from the terror of the attack of people she had never seen before, she allowed them to pull her away by the arm from her dead husband, who was lying on the ground with a gash on the side of his skull. Without mercy or question they slit her throat as she looked me in the eyes. There was no fear or judgment in her gaze. Just surrender. Both of us had surrendered to our fate. I knew there was no way for me to intervene. We bonded in an instant before there was nothing behind her eyes. Her death would give them life as they used her body fat to treat their wounds. Her body was stripped of flesh like they were handling a dead animal. At least they had the decency to bury her after they took what they required.

I retreated to the back of the brutal scene and just watched from inside my chameleon's disguise. Terror and tears have no place on the battlefield or in conquest. When the Spanish men were rested, we moved on.

With a downcast gaze I entered villages where I knew I had to play the good Christian, a mother Mary of diplomacy. *Look at me! I have converted to the one true god to save you all from your dirty and depraved existence,* Cortés had me say. The words sounded like my voice but felt like burning copal. My throat had become a brazier of destruction and hypocrisy. The praise of beauty and cleverness always laid upon me felt untrue, just like the lies I had to spread like I was transmitting a disease. I had to look adoringly at *my lord* Cortés and say there was nowhere else I would rather be than by his side on this most *holy* mission. I couldn't appear to be traitorous; otherwise *my* body fat would be used as salve. To do what I could to help others, I spoke to some of my people individually, pleading with them to be compliant, stay out of our way, keep the ones you love and your treasure hidden. If I had beads to give, then I parted with them. I had Cortés to barter myself with. It was futile to try to stop the tide of our new *brothers and sisters in Christ*. All of this happened in the face of certain death either by my own people, who would gladly sacrifice me along with my consorts, disease, or one word from the mouth of Cortés. Death was my constant companion. It was as sure as the sun and moon. When even the Spanish men faltered in their conquest and betrayed their worry and their tears, I kept my face stoic and back straight. What other way could there be? But I felt like I was being torn apart.

Because there were also those moments when I had to strip others of their flesh. It happened on our pursuit of Montezuma as we headed toward the Aztec capital Tenochtitlán.

After meeting with the Tlaxcans, the enemies of Montezuma, we arrived at Cholula. We entered with one thousand Tlaxcan warriors standing guard outside the perimeter of the city. Within the lively and crowded city stands a mammoth pyramid dedicated to the feathered serpent, Quetzalcoatl. It rises high and dignified, inspiring awe as you have to crane your neck to take its magnitude all in. We were welcomed with food and shelter by the nobles of the city.

For me it was all the same as it had been on our journey, and with the same outcome. A few caciques already knew of our movements as we made the journey to Montezuma. There was a woman who continued to follow us upon our arrival. She stood at the front of the crowds to catch a glimpse of the strangers. Her eyes fixated on me. I noticed her because she was dressed better than the others. And her gaze was filled with a poison and pity that made me feel self-conscious. I often heard what was whispered about me in the villages we entered. "She saves her own skin by helping to skin others!" There was also, "Where is her shame? She wears stolen gold!"

But I was a slave when others were not. Sometimes the real fight is surviving to tell the tale so others can hear it.

I did not see the woman again until after dark, once we had an informal meeting with the leaders of the city to discuss their dislike of Montezuma. These fools really believed they could retain their power while bartering with the new devils. But I remained mute about my knowledge. Cortés used discord between my people to create a noose by which they all hanged themselves. It would enable him to capture Montezuma and take Tenochtitlán. The apocalypse came full circle after Cholula.

After a long night we were finally lodged. I never slept in the same quarters as Cortés in the event he wanted to bring other women to share his bed.

I lay there frustrated at the trap I found myself in. Every day we were in constant motion, but I was never moving and could not see any way forward toward freedom. There was noise outside my door. At first, I thought it was Cortés come to find comfort or ask questions as he usually did in private. But it was a woman's voice. I lit a candle next to my mat before opening the door. It was the woman from earlier in the day. Her eyes darted all around, but there was nothing there but the darkness of the night and homes full of slumbering villagers. She wore a huipil, so I knew she wasn't of the lower class.

"Can we speak? I won't take up much of your time because there is none left."

I nodded and invited her in. "What is it you need to say at this time of night?"

Her eyes welled with tears that slid through the thick creases at the corners. "You must believe every word I am about to tell you. Please leave these men and come with me. There will be fighting, and none of them are intended to survive, save a few who will be sent to Montezuma. I have a son. Marry him. Join us. I know you can't be happily bound to the leader who keeps you tied to him like a shadow."

My entire body quaked. I knew the precipice on the horizon where our world would fall into oblivion had arrived. A choice had to be made. But first I needed more information.

"How do you know of this attack? What are the details? I have much wealth with me. If I am to go with you, I should not want to lose it."

A wide smile appeared on her sun-baked skin. Deep wrinkles around her mouth and eyes folded like lightning bolts of flesh.

"My husband is part of the fight. For three days they have been plotting the attack as you move through Cholula. They've dug ditches to hide our warriors before the attack. You do not belong with them. Choose a side."

The intensity in her demeanor made me want to cry, because her intentions were pure, and there was real sincerity in her. In that moment I truly did not know what to do.

"Go now. Let me gather my things," I said.

She placed her hand on my arm, fully trusting me. "We will win this war. I don't want to worship their god or give them our land. The things I have seen . . . who knows where they come from and what problems they bring with them if we allow them to stay. What will the future look like for us?"

I watched her go into the dark and looked up into the clear night filled with stars. I wanted guidance, but deep inside I knew the answer. It floated to the top like a dead fish in a flooded river. There would be no turning back. After what I had experienced up to now I knew there was no hope of standing against Cortés and the others like him. Without waiting I made my way to see Cortés and tell him of the plot. The side I chose was my own. No one else would choose me in battle.

The following day, without a second of sleep, I walked into the large courtyard with Cortés and his entourage at the foot of the grand pyramid. All that work and ingenuity of my people's creations were now coming to an end. I knew the pyramids would soon be swept with blood, screams, and terror.

And so I watched those accused of treachery die without any show of emotion as Cortés commanded them to be executed before they even had a chance to attack us. The slaughter would be a message to others who might have been considering resistance before we continued toward Montezuma. I looked to the clear blue sky and just wanted to know: *What was all of this for?* There had to be some destiny being shaped, even if it was the worst imaginable reality. Why was I given this life and position? How would it end for me? I breathed in deeply to fill my lungs with what could be the last of my breaths depending on how this all played out.

Cortés placed his hand on my chin and moved my face toward the ensuing attack on the Cholulans. He leaned in close. His breath escaped through his nose and slapped against my cheek and ear. "Look at the power you wield. Look at what you accomplished with your quick thinking and diplomacy. You are a dangerous woman, La Malinche. It is a good thing I hold the leash. You have served me so very well."

My breath trembled inside my chest as I struggled to contain my rage and sorrow. Hernán loved nothing more than to display his power. Severed limbs and heads scattered across the earth is the lowest form of enforcing power. I did not see the woman who came to me that night, and I was glad. The sight of her being skewered or tortured would have driven one of her soldiers to grab his sword and pierce Cortés through the neck. But what would that do?

Cortés was but one of many. If I had my own power, I would have freedom. He removed his hand from my chin, but I knew I could not look away from the slaughter. Instead, I fixed my eyes on the apex of the pyramid and prayed to whatever gods might give a fuck about me.

I'm asking once more for a miracle. God or gods, whatever you are, if you truly exist, show me the meaning of life and death, because this life of mine is neither. Take me beyond my wildest imagination or give me eternal peace.

The Spaniards' firepower and horses soon overwhelmed the Cholulans. It was a massacre.

As we left the city, we encountered two paths: One had been deliberately strewn with boulders and cut-down trees. The other was as clear as a summer's morning. We followed the clear path with no one standing in our way. As Cortés bounced on his horse, I could detect a small smile on his lips. He only saw the unobstructed road ahead and the glory that awaited him.

I continued to walk without a sign from any god or gods and lived to speak for someone else another day.

9

I spend the next few days driving around the Irish countryside in torrential rain or fog as thick as sheep's wool with only short spells of sunshine crowning the beautiful hills. The peace I'm looking for is like the cloud-covered sky. It feels like what my restless soul wants to hold is waiting for me somewhere in its white, blank vastness.

The pubs are all the same, reeking of stale beer and salt-and-vinegar crisps. Humans I don't know talk among themselves like they have known each other their entire lives. There's no stardust chemistry to be found here. No boxes of books for me to offer to carry.

I'm as fucking miserable as the weather, not knowing if I did the right thing or fucked something up. I knew what I wanted. Yes, Colin was a start, but was he the one to truly stop me in my heart-hungry tracks?

My travel guide is open to my next destination in Ireland. But I wonder if I'd rather just skip it and head straight to London.

There are still so many sights, so many strange veins to drink from, so many bodies to explore. My instinct takes me back to my old wounded headspace that tells me to simply take solace in the pleasures of the flesh. But I don't go on to London, because I have already derailed my plans enough: I will follow through with seeing Ireland before retrieving the skulls.

Once that mission is accomplished, then what comes next if not love?

When I'm in my car, I drive faster to drive these thoughts out of my mind. The roads are narrow and lonely. There's more sheep than people in some places. I finally reach the edge of the island, the cliffs reminding me of home, my real home. The water below, like my emotions, would surely drown me if I allowed it to.

Colin is the kind of man that haunts you with one look and possesses your body after just a single touch. And he doesn't even realize he's doing it. Well, maybe he does a little. Part of me wants to know if he is a permanent tenant in my heart or just a poltergeist of my own imagining. Surely in a place as religious as Ireland I could find a priest to exorcise these obsessive thoughts of him from inside of me.

I feel trapped: I don't want to drown in my insatiable lust, nor can I just ignore it. Some doors, once opened, are impossible to shut. We all hold the keys to the gates of heaven or hell within ourselves.

But here in this neon-green landscape with breathtaking views, I find that there is no peace for me. Beautiful things are meant to be shared. And with the world changing so fast, who knows how much time any of us has left? When the seas rise and the climate spoils like rotten eggs, there will be nothing left of any of the islands in the world.

My treatment of Colin makes me realize I need to continue

my quest for healing. All I did was run away from my feelings. I've seen enough death to know none of us leave this rock unscathed, and there is always time for change.

I was now resolved: I would give Colin a chance and see where things between us led. Colin could be the love of my life or the lesson I had to learn before finding the true love of my life. Either way, my courage could not fail me now.

I'm supposed to drop my rental car back at the airport today, but I really don't give a fuck. I've caught up on all my emails, profusely apologizing for my unavailability, and that's pretty much the extent of what I care about. And at some point I will need to find blood. I wander into one last pub to see if I can score an easy meal, since Colin may not turn out to be available tonight or may be too hurt to see me again after I left. It's now four P.M., and there are only two other people in the pub. And it's a small village, consisting of a pub, a minimarket with a post office, and a few stone houses.

An elderly couple tend bar, their faces weathered in a way I will never experience, but here, in this remote place that could be on another planet, at least they have each other. I know they are together by the way they move around each other in a familiar dance. Small touches and glances of reassurance that make it clear that they will be there for each other until either is buried.

Watching them reminds me of the skulls I seek, because now I feel like one of those skulls, like a piece of quartz with a massive crack down the middle. "Islands in the Stream" by Dolly Parton and Kenny Loggins begins to play. The old couple both sing along off-key to the chorus, glancing at each other. My heart feels as withered as their skin.

The old woman touches my hand when I order water. My face must have betrayed my heartache. Her thin hand is warm. Her frail skin is so close to the bone and devoid of fat that it exposes the veins that crawl the length of her arm. If only our paths could be that easy to navigate and see. I want to walk upon a clear blue vein to my destiny.

"You look lost, dear. You won't find answers in here. I'm much older than you, so I should know." This stranger's kindness warms my heart, makes me chuckle to myself.

If only she knew my real age. Usually touching people allows me to understand what they are feeling in that moment, or I can relay an emotion that I want them to feel for me. This does not happen. Instead, I receive a message just for me. As clear as my own voice: "I am afraid of myself."

This message is not from her. She has no fear of where she stands in life even with the knowledge there is not much time left for her. With my fine-tuned senses I can feel her heart beats erratically, even though it is too subtle for her to notice. She had perhaps two years tops left of working in the pub. Maybe she didn't feel so well every day, but she showed up every day to the pub to be next to her love. It gave her pleasure to talk to her friends who came into the pub, so she enjoyed her work even on the days she didn't feel so hot.

Instead, the message was from me, for me.

All the hiding I'd done as a vampire was because I have been afraid of myself. Not because I'm haunted by the Spanish or Cortés or Juan. I have been afraid of all aspects of me coming together in my chrysalis to form something new, to be a complete version of me. If I allowed my power to consume me, what would I accomplish, or find? What if I allowed the power I felt when I ran next to a jaguar to be unleashed? The jaguar thought nothing of it. What would people think? Does a bird with beautiful feathers or a buck with magnificent horns hide them away? No, they are simply part of its being. The piranhas of the Amazon swim with mouths open.

I am a worthwhile being, a product of creation; otherwise I and others like me would not exist. Sure, some have done despicable things, but the things I have done are not who I am.

The old woman pats my hand. She's right, though. I don't touch my water, and I leave a fifty-pound note for her. Disregarding speed limits and rain that leaves no visibility on the road, I drive straight to Colin. With no stops, it doesn't take me more than the rest of the day.

Finding true companionship in this long life is what I want. But I want it with me never hiding any part of me. What power I possess is mine to wield.

I knock on the door of the bookshop that says, "Closed until further notice." Those words leave me feeling deflated. Did I just throw away something so very precious because I'm too chickenshit to face my fears? I've made a lot of mistakes in my life, but this might be the worst if he doesn't answer. If he doesn't open the door to the shop, I will break down the door that leads to his apartment. I'll give this a shot with as much gusto as I do my work. Then I see a silhouette approaching though the glass in the door. He answers, and I can't help but notice a carry-on suitcase sitting next to the entrance.

He doesn't say anything, only pulls me to his chest and kisses me. I'm on the verge of tears. "I'm sorry. For everything. I'm an asshole for leaving like that. What's with the bag? Are you leaving?" His arms envelop my small frame.

His blue eyes shine with lighthouse brightness. "I wasn't going to let you go that easily. I know there is a lot more to your life than you're telling me, and that's okay. We have time. I was about to try to catch you before you left Ireland. I didn't care how long it would take, as long as I found you." I don't speak, only kiss him with the softness of marshmallow melting over an open flame.

"Where are we going?" he asks me through kisses.

I grab his bag. "We're going to London. Got a bit of unfinished business so a little change of plans. The skulls I have been hunting for years are ready to be mine."

He takes a step back. "Skulls? You didn't tell me that story."

10

We decide to take the ferry to England as a romantic excursion. The entire journey would be more driving than floating on the body of water separating the two pieces of land. Part of me also wanted to experience what it was like to cross by boat the way the invaders did. The dark water in constant, tumultuous motion seemed like the perfect metaphor for my human life.

After Montezuma was overthrown, we set off for Honduras again. From the start I knew something was afoot as Hernán kept his distance from me until we made camp. Without ceremony he took both my hands into his. "Our journey together is over, La Malinche. But I appreciate what you have done. All this belongs to me because I could see your use. As a token of my gratitude, I give you a Spanish husband and a parcel of land."

I was happy to be rid of his company; however, I had to fight the urge to vomit knowing I would belong to someone else. I was traded again without any say in the matter. In some encampment in a village I cannot care to remember I had to marry this man Juan Jarmillo. Cortés gave me to Juan because he had other shores to conquer and needed other translators—not to mention because of the wife he scarcely mentioned. If the man were to drown in a lake of love, he still would not feel or see it. I never saw him again. He used me like cheap beads. Even though he'd left me with a little land, it was a mere token that would belong to my "husband."

And so it was that I stood there on my wedding day in front of a drunkard with bloodshot eyes, a bloated face, and stinking of eggs, who would soon be that husband. His missing teeth made him look like a walking sacrifice. But *I* was the sacrifice. And again, I could not say no. Our marriage resulted in a child straightaway, a daughter named Maria. There were no more expeditions, but I had to tolerate the life of playing wife to a man I detested. So much for the freedom I thought I could swindle from Cortés.

Marriage to a Spaniard was not something I aspired to, far from it; however, because of my hand in translating for Cortés, it was the only way for me to have any kind of life in the newly constructed world. We women were traded with the same ease as gold yet cared for so much less. The value of my existence was in what I could do for these men and their place in my home-land. It tasted like venom every time they kissed me.

But then, two years later, another wave of smallpox ran through the village with the ferocity of wild beasts. No one knew who it would strike or when, only that no one was im-mune. When my fever struck I knew I was sick. How bitter I felt after the path my short life had taken. It couldn't end like this at thirty years of age.

All my land, and now my life, was about to be taken from me. I had been dutifully hoping for some grand universal reward after all my suffering. Where was it? When the first symptoms began, I dropped to my knees so hard I thought my spine would snap and cried until my throat could no longer make any sound. I looked to the moon and screamed for another chance. A miracle.

For years I had asked for a miracle to unlock a different destiny, one of abundance and freedom, a chance to make right the guilt I felt for being an accomplice to the slaughter. What choice did I have, being viewed as a piece of property? For the first time since I was traded by my mother I experienced what it meant to be alone.

But this loneliness was like nothing I had ever felt before. I sobbed from the pain in my body that didn't compare to the pain of being alone when all I wanted was comfort. I wanted someone to tend to me in my time of need, yet there was no one but myself. In that darkness it saddened me that I had never been in love nor experienced someone loving me. My soul wanted that. Was it too late now?

Exhausted from crying, I fell asleep in a small hut away from the main hacienda to prevent the illness from spreading to the others in the household. My husband, Juan, could die for all I cared, but I did not want to infect Maria and the servants. I would never want any child of mine, even if it was from a miscreant like Juan, to endure what I endured. Like Martin, her skin was pale, but her eyes had the black sheen of blood on an obsidian blade at night. Just like mine.

Alone I lay at death's cenote, falling in and out of sleep. That is when she came to me: Malinalxochitl.

In my dream I saw the goddess mostly known because of her brother; however, she is a grand woman in her own right. She is a powerful sorceress with black flowers entangled in her long brown hair that falls to her waist. She has no need for any other adornment because her natural beauty changes the atmosphere around her. Her aura emits a faint green glow that is reflected in her brown eyes. Her name is similar to mine in translation.

When she appeared to me, she kneeled next to me, not saying a word, yet I could tell she meant no harm. There was an excitement in her eyes, like she had a gift for me she couldn't wait for me to open. She parted her full mouth, exposing pointed canine teeth. Blood dripped from her tongue in the shape of tears. As the viscous fluid fell onto her lap it morphed into a scorpion the size of my palm. Small beads of blood dripped from the point of its stinger, leaving a trail as it scuttled away from me. I could feel myself wanting to follow it.

Then Malinalxochitl raised her arm and pointed to the door. It was important for me to follow. I don't know how I knew this; my aching, desperate heart collapsing in on itself beat the knowledge through my chest so I might hear its call. I rose from my bed, my body feeling as if it waded through water. The sensation was dreamlike, but I wasn't dreaming. Instead I knew I was sleepwalking. The gravel stuck to the bottom of my bare feet. Sounds from the village tickled my ears. Who knows how long I was walking in the middle of the night?

My next memory is of lying on a mat in a hut with an old woman, a crone, next to me. The hut smelled like copal and roasted maize. The sun was nearing the time to rise; the sky was dark indigo with a pale illumination of yellow on the horizon. Since the Spanish arrived, we were not allowed to practice our own religion. I had played my part in this. No offerings or prayers *our* way. We still swept our houses according to tradition. But sunrise remained an important time for offerings.

The old woman was clad in clean but worn clothing and sisal sandals. She brought a gourd toward me when she heard me stirring. I felt myself returning to the real world with a groggy head. "Who are you? Where am I?"

She looked kind, and her old age hadn't diminished any of the beauty of her bronze skin and white hair with its thick black streaks. "Freedom, La Malinche."

"Don't call me that," I snapped. "You know why they call me that? Because Cortés was considered my captain and I was always by his side with no choice but to survive like a pet. Then he gave me away."

"I am sorry, Malinalli. I just wanted you to know I know who you are. My name is Chantico."

"What freedom can you possibly offer me? The Spanish aren't leaving. Have you not seen what has happened to us? There is no freedom but in death, and I am almost there without ever having had the opportunity to live any of my life my own way. I shouldn't be here. I'm sick and will die soon."

"Is it really *our* life? Or are we gathered to dance to a shaman's chant we cannot hear?"

A man stepped from the shadows. He appeared regal with his square jaw, ear plugs made from turquoise in each earlobe, and a septum ring made from jade. He wore the clothes of a king but they were tattered from wear. I recognized him. Cuauhtémoc, the last ruler of this land. How was he still alive? He had been killed by Cortés, or so we thought.

"I am offering you death and life. Everlasting life. You can do as you please without any human having the ability to stop you, us."

I scoffed, not caring if my face showed contempt. "That is what all the Spanish priests said about their god. Many times I said it myself to the masses of our people. I do not want your cross, and I am done preaching on behalf of men."

He stepped closer to me just as the sun was rising behind

him. A blood-orange halo radiated from the crown of his head of shiny black hair. The sun continued to rise with fluorescent pink highlighting serpent-like clouds stretched across the sky. He opened his mouth enough for me to see he had the fangs of a serpent.

"Do you accept my gift? It will rid your body of illness for eternity. You will be stronger than any man, any human in fact. And never die or feel the bitterness of illness. All you need to do is stop wallowing in self-pity and take my blood."

I scurried backward toward the wall, my fever breaking out across my entire body. My panic made it hard to breathe. I wondered if this was part of some delirium from the illness. The old woman picked up another gourd and poured it over my head as if she could read my mind. The cold water made me gasp, almost choking on my own breath from the shock of it.

Chantico had no expression when she said, "You are awake. This is real."

The water dripping from my hair onto my face made me forget my fever momentarily. "But what is the price? I have carried so many consequences. So much guilt and pain. I do not want to belong to anyone. My only master will be myself. I will not bow to you or worship you if you give this gift to me so freely."

His face turned dark. "You do not owe me anything. I want to create more of us. For revenge. You have many talents as an extraordinary woman despite how history has treated you. I harbor no ill thoughts of you. The only master you will have is the one inside of your heart who insists on surviving—*your hunger*. You will have to feed on human blood, or you will die. Go and kill Cortés and your husband in their sleep for all I care. Eat your child, considering what they did to countless of our children. Drain them all dry. Massacre every priest with stolen gold hanging above his head. Steal their treasures and take back our gods."

The fury in his eyes had the power of the sun.

Without any control, I began to cry. Many nights I had wanted to sob in the darkness, but my body refused to relinquish any more tears from the exhaustion of creating them. The anguish never ceased to torment me for the role I played and the way I was viewed. My words were important but not my story, not the truth of it. To the world my truth didn't matter. And as much as I wanted revenge on the men who made me theirs without permission or love, they were also fathers to my children, who needed their protection in status and wealth. *My* children.

Mestizos. I am the mother of the mestizos, they say, an entirely new people on the Earth.

In that moment I knew I had a choice to make, and without knowledge of the details. It would require complete surrender to one path or the other, that was certain. Yet I could not help but think how this option I never thought possible had occurred just before my death. I took it as a sign. My body relaxed, relinquished to the notion death would come to me one way or another, as it does to every living creature. I looked inside the other gourd next to Chantico. It didn't appear to be filled with water or pulque.

My heartbeat began to pump hard against my temples as my mind spoke to me in gibberish terms, trying to find logic or reason for all of this. More sweat leaked from my entire body in gourdfuls. I took a deep breath and listened to my heartbeat, allowing the fever from the illness to burn through my thoughts so I could hear the truth.

"I accept your gift."

Cuauhtémoc kneeled next to me. With one of his thick, crimson-stained fingernails sharpened to a spike, he sliced open his wrist. "Take this gift and live. You will transform over many days, but you will recover here." I took his rough brown flesh into my mouth and drank quickly so I would not have time to rethink my decision. The musk of his blood was a mixture of manzanilla and palo santo. I could taste those aromas on my tongue. The sun seemed to burst through the window of the hut, bathing me in heat. My skin allowed it to make love to me. Welcoming kisses of the sun's radiation filled me with ecstasy. It embraced me with heaven's gifts of eternal regenerative life.

He pulled his arm away, but I was still filled with an unquenchable thirst. The gourd filled with blood next to Chantico made me shake with hunger, my tongue a hardened piece of clay in my mouth. She held it up to me, and I took the gourd in my hands and drank every last drop. Ecstasy slithered down my throat.

The old woman laughed softly. "You have a great thirst. It means you will grow strong in your new truth. If you could do in your new life what you did in your human life, I can't imagine what the world can expect when you go through this change."

With her words and the gourd empty, I fell back onto the mat. My muscles went limp all at once. I couldn't move if I wanted to. The man's potent blood had rendered me helpless. I imagined myself as an infant just born. My vision focused on hanging dried herbs above my head. Their scent filled my lungs with thoughts of the soil. I could feel myself travel deep into the ground to the underworld, where I fell into a cenote of blood.

My body thrashed in the pool as my anatomy changed. Overhead, red thunderclouds rolled into my vision. They clapped and sent bolts of blue lightning across the patch of sky I could see through the hole in the earth. Blood rain fell onto my body. Without seeing what was behind me, I floated to the top of the cenote until my feet touched land. Something still lingered near my back. The caress of a ghost or warm breeze licked me with the sensual teasing of a lover.

I turned to see a column of blood shifting into different shapes of animals until it formed wings and flew into the air as a red vapor. "Blood angel," I whispered. The clouds gave way to more fat drops of crimson. I lifted my hands and opened my mouth. The taste baptized me into a new life. I drank my past fears, the nightmare existence of the conquest, the dreams I didn't know I had, the gift of never asking for permission to just exist. My second chance. I could feel myself laughing hysterically, my heart bursting with gratitude and joy as I stood sodden with the plasma of life.

What wonders existed that we could not see. Now I was fortunate enough to see it all. I remained in the same spot, completely nude, allowing the surrender to the unknown seep into my marrow. I stretched my hands to the sky before allowing myself to float away into my dream within a dream.

Three days later, as I was told, I opened my eyes to Chantico sitting by my side weaving. "You are back."

The sunlight streaming through the window hurt my eyes. My mouth was as dry as before. She put her weaving down before holding out her wrist. "Go on."

I lifted myself to a seated position, feeling light-headed and hungry. "Why are you offering me yourself? You are old."

"Because you are deserving. Women always pay the price for the ambitions of men who see themselves as great. If I was younger that would be me waking up on a mat to take back what was lost. My body would not survive a complete metamorphosis this late in life. Besides, I can be just as much of a helper on the other side after I die."

I licked my lips. With an inviting smile, she raised her wrist closer to my mouth. Still hesitant, I bit into her dark brown flesh. Blood flowed into my mouth. My body celebrated the taste, the gift it offered. The sun no longer burned my eyes. My limp muscles twitched. I drank until she placed a hand with crooked fingers on the back of my head. "That is enough, dear."

Cuauhtémoc stood in the doorway. "Rise, Brown Queen. Blood Goddess reborn."

I rose from the mat with blood still dribbling from my chin, falling to the dirty huipil I still wore from when I first arrived. With slow steps I walked to join him outside. The sun wrapped her arms around me again, welcomed me back to life. My heart quickened with the sounds of the world. My body wanted to move to relish this new existence.

Without warning I leaped into the air as a head start into a sprint. In my mind I could hear Chantico say, "Should we stop her?" He responded, "No, let her run. Let her feel it for herself. Only then will she know what she is truly capable of."

I didn't have any destination in mind, but my body demanded to experience its full potential. My mind lacked any control over this; it was something else inside of me that knew better. Before I noticed my surroundings, I was in the forest running through thick foliage that hit my face and legs. Birds flew into the air as I approached. From the corner of my eye, I spied a jaguar. She ran next to me at full speed, her silky black coat catching the rays of sunlight breaking through the trees. Her powerful legs ran with abandon. Everything moved in slow motion compared to us, including the other creatures of the natural world. I felt power in its purest form.

I ran, jumped, shouted, and laughed. No one could catch me ever again or take my screams for themselves. Everything about me was my own. In my mind I could hear the man who made me call me back. I stopped in a clearing, allowing the stillness of the forest to see me as I was. The jaguar stopped as well. We looked each other in the eyes in acknowledgment. Then she turned and pounced into the forest until she was gone. I picked up my feet again and began to run with the intention of returning to the hut.

Before reaching my destination, I could hear water not far away. I followed it, wanting to clean my muddy and bloody legs. A small stream cut through the forest. I did not sense anyone nearby. As I peered into the water, I gazed at my moving reflection.

The movement of the stream changed the shape of the image from one moment to the next. It made me think how all the men I met were so attached to the image of me in their mind, they could not really see how the image is not one set thing, or the real me. This was their greatest weakness. I promised to not allow it to be mine. I'd love the ephemeral moving reflection of myself and not the carefully constructed woman who could be burned, torn, slashed to pieces. Besides that, I loved the color of my skin. The warm hue resembled the beauty of leaves changing color. And like the trees, I had undergone a transformation in the best of ways. In this life cycle I was always destined to live and come into full view. A great mariposa born from shadow.

Memory is a funny thing, though: I saw the papas with their confused expressions as I tried to explain to them about the rapture and joy this new God offered. The words tasted like the scent of rotting corpses in the sun. But I had to do it. I knew I was a walking corpse.

"For an Indian you are a beauty. And smart."

I couldn't help thinking, *For a brute you are . . . still a brute smelling of pork and body odor.* That was all behind me now.

I took off my filthy clothing before squatting into the stream to bathe. The coolness made me feel like a fish swimming in a calm current. Peace. Bliss. It's hard to look after others when you need looking after yourself.

I sat with my legs spread and my torso propped up by my arms next to me. I found the running water jumping over stones between my legs arousing. It tickled the soles of my feet. I threw my head back, imagining a lover of my choice pleasuring me. No shame or guilt in my body experiencing what it was built to experience. There was no containing the smile on my face. My arousal dissipated, and contentment in the present moment took its place. I felt at peace for the first time since I was a child. A childlike sense of freedom prompted me to splash the water on my face and kick my feet. The illness in my body had been defeated through blood.

My miracle had arrived.

Then the flash of reality as I heard my own laughter that was the same as when I bathed my own children. *My daughter, Maria.* These clothes. I thought I should go back to my own home before returning to Chantico. The smell of my human life left me with sadness as I slipped on the clothes stained with the illness my body had purged.

I would return to Maria as something else. Her mother lived, but at a price. Being a mother was a complicated thing for me. I looked at my offspring knowing they were part of me, but no matter how hard I tried I couldn't close the chasm to get near enough to enjoy them. Not the way I was taught you should.

My daughter. I would watch over her like a guardian, a keeper. I didn't want to abandon her the way I had been. Only if I saw she was being led down a path that mirrored my own would I intervene in the light. Other than that, I would work through the Nahua woman, Patli, in charge of Maria to take her to safety, even if it meant sending her to the same place they sent Martin. I had secrets and information to trade like beads to get what I wanted from the right people.

How would I reconcile my new existence with the old? I surrendered everything with no alternate plan and a mind full of questions. This blood-drinking form I knew nothing about had to be the destiny I was meant to live. There was truly no turning back after my leap of faith. The questions were large clams snapping at the bottom of the ocean, wanting to make a pearl out of me. But that is what uncertainty and fighting fear can do. It can make you into a pearl. They are incredibly valuable and beautiful treasures of creation.

This idea was also the only thing I possessed when I returned home, then found myself forced to leave again with only the dirty clothing on my back.

I shuffled into the hacienda somewhat dazed. It appeared odd through these new senses. The scent of food wafting through the kitchen was a mix of spices and roasting meat, with the people who prepared it chattering away about their lives. The aroma made my stomach turn. The household help stepped away and stopped their chores upon seeing me, as if their senses knew it was me in another form. Stillness gripped the property.

I'm sure I appeared like I had crawled from the underworld with my hair braided, body clean, yet my clothing muddy with blood and sweat stains. This was a strange place that never felt like home, but I considered it home because my daughter was there and it had always been bound to a man who held my fate. All the land gifted to me by Cortés my husband, Juan, already considered his own despite me doing what he could never do in ten of his pathetic lifetimes. No rights, or even extra concern, extended to me like the ones the Spanish wives brought over from Europe were given. They were still at the mercy of their husbands but seen as less expendable. We didn't receive the same respect or dignity.

Patli had a sad look in her eyes upon seeing me. She knew something I did not. Her head shook, telling me, *No.* I was about to discover my absence had created a chain reaction. Someone alerted Juan, because he stomped out to the center of the hacienda.

"There you are. We have looked all over for you. Where were you? Do you know what I went through, the time wasted searching for you?" His eyes narrowed as they ran the length of my body. I could hear his pulse slowly rising the longer he looked at me. There was no love in his eyes, never was to begin with. Our union was a transaction. Most things in my life had been mere transactions at that point. Alonso, Cortés, and Juan were my menage à trois of pain, deceit, and survival. His reaction did not affect me.

"Was it a lover? Some *Indian* man you have been keeping in secret? And he had enough by the look of you. They *all* eventually get their use out of you."

Despite my newly acquired power, I stood there filled with shame in my filthy clothing, not knowing what to say or do. The patrol that had been searching for me stared at this spectacle that should have been a private matter. I wondered why they were still there. Not long before this moment I had run with a jaguar. And now I lost my nerve in front of a mere human. My fear of him still infected me.

"No . . . I was sick with the fever. I didn't want it to spread . . ."

He puffed his chest out and walked close enough that I could see the baggy skin beneath his left eye twitch erratically. "So you came back? Were you in the forest practicing your ungodly savage religion to try to cure yourself? Leave now. There is no longer any space for you."

"You mean you no longer need my services, and you are through with me now you have my land."

His eyes went wide, and his pulse picked up a few beats. I was taught not to speak too loudly or show any dissent to my husband. Then his pulse dipped, remained steady. Some inner knowing I did not possess before told me he had already planned my removal; however, he did not know how or when. I spoke the truth without knowing how I knew it was so. He wanted a way to rid himself of me now that he had everything he wanted after securing land for himself. At the very least even Cortés hadn't turned me completely out with nothing when he left for Honduras. Now this man wanted to give me nothing of what was my fair due. In all honesty, I didn't want his dirty blood money.

I had a power within my possession he would never know as a mortal man: time.

Without thought I blurted, "What will you do with our daughter?" I could feel my body trembling. The vampire in me wanted to tear him to pieces, but Maria was present. I could hear her voice in the distance as light as the beating wings of a dragonfly. My heart could hear her even if my eyes could not see. Fear gripped my muscles, creating a tension from holding back my new physical strength, yet weak from not knowing what to do. What if I ripped my husband to pieces then couldn't prevent myself from harming anyone else, including the house-hold help? The armed patrol created a circle around me. An urge to slice through flesh was building inside of me. My fangs protruded, cutting into the inside of my lip. Copper coated my tongue.

"She will be married to a proper man in Spain. I will get a good dowry for her. But that is no longer any of your business. If you have the fever, then you are a dead woman. My men will escort you out. Go back to the forest. I'm sure you will find someone else to take you somewhere if by the grace of God you survive. You always land on your back. But I can't have this household infected with the fever or your heathen religion."

In that moment I cared less whether every last colonizer in this land perished from a horde of whatever I was. I understood my maker Cuauhtémoc's mission of destruction. But my own flesh and blood was here. It was time to make a hard choice no parent should have to make. In my mind, I saw the difficult life we would be forced to live if I took my daughter with me. She was a vulnerable little creature. And I was vulnerable too, since I did not yet know who or what I was. How could I adequately nurture my daughter when I needed nurturing myself?

I allowed myself to be taken away from the property but vowed to myself to come back. No matter what I did in that moment, my daughter would pay the price. Either way she lost a mother.

My feet shuffled away at the same speed I shuffled toward Cortés when I brought to him whatever he required when he first arrived. I was marched away feeling like an ant in the presence of large boots. It would be nothing to squash me in a second. I can't tell you how that sense of vulnerability has the ability to incinerate every ounce of soul within you, then blow it away with a single puff of breath from someone's lips.

I had asked myself as I stood before Cortés all those years ago, *What do you have within you to make this easier? To find some means to escape?* When you have nothing, it pays to get creative. As I left the hacienda, I thought of this again.

In that moment I had only my strange existence. It would somehow have to be enough. *God, make it enough,* I always prayed.

I felt utterly lost as I stood outside the hacienda with the doors shut. I had asked for freedom since the first time I was sold as a young girl; however, I could not help wondering what kind of plan this was.

I walked away thinking how every lover and relationship reinforced the idea that pain was just part of the deal. Hurt is just what happens when you are with someone. You have to deal with it like you deal with anything in life. But the constant undercurrent of fear was not normal. It's not really living to be always looking over one's shoulder, expecting a bitter look or harsh words. It's not normal to live with an invisible plank on one's back to keep you on your knees.

I no longer had to accept any of it if I didn't want to. Despite not having any concept of what the future might hold or how I would survive, I held my head high and walked away from my old life. As I neared the forest, Patli caught up to me. This was unexpected. She was out of breath and with red cheeks, and her eyes darted toward the hacienda. "Hurry. Let us go into the trees." She carried a leather satchel. "I brought you clothing. Come at night and I will let you see Maria again. None of this is right. Not from the moment *they* arrived."

I burst into sobs, unable to control my body from erupting into violent hitching. Her hand rested on my shoulder. She touched my face, then pulled her hand away. She stared at the bright red blotting her fingertips before wiping it on her skirt. "I always knew you were different. Special, of the gods . . . our gods. I don't know what this is. I will not fear. Hear me now. No one can take away that you gave birth to her or survived what many did not. It was you who gave her that first kiss. It is yours and yours alone. We, us women from the Earth, are daughters of the sun. We have its power. Go in peace now. When I leave a bowl of moon water by their window you will know it is safe to watch her."

"Thank you. Don't worry about me, Patli."

Her brows remained furrowed with her eyes seeing right through me. For a moment I thought she might tell me to forget about her helping me, but she didn't. "Make sure you take care of yourself. Rest. Listen to your body."

I nodded and fled back to Chantico in the forest. Tears streamed down my face from knowing I would still see Maria, but it would have to be under the cover of darkness as a silent guardian angel in the shadows. The overcast sky made everything appear dull; perhaps it was also caused by my mood. It was the color of defeat by one who always seemed to have the upper hand despite me having so much new power in my rebirth. My fear made me walk away like a mouse.

"You are back." Chantico looked up from shucking maize.

I nodded, trying to hold back more tears. My muscles felt as if they hung from my bones. All my energy had been used trying to control myself at the hacienda. And by my despair of not being allowed to touch my daughter one last time.

"Come sit next to me. Help me weave a basket. Think about what you want it to look like only once, then begin the weaving. Focus on your hands, the movement. Sing a song if you like. But we will sit here until it is done. And I have two beautiful helpers to watch over us." She rose from her spot and brought over a basket with a lid. Her frail hands pulled out a quartz crystal skull the size of two of my fists. Even without sunlight it dazzled the eye. I could feel myself smiling and my spirit lifting. "May I?" I asked her.

The clear crystal skull looked to me like a single, solid tear composed of all the tears I had cried alone.

Chantico nodded and passed it to me. The sensation it radiated was far greater than the weight of it in my hand would imply. It was flawless, the craftsmanship so very perfect. It was as if it had always simply existed in this perfect form and had been plucked straight from rock. She handed me another skull from the basket. This one was human, but small, encrusted with square turquoise tiles. The eye sockets contained two large, smoothly polished obsidian stones, and both were surrounded by serpents. You could easily see your reflection in the obsidian. I balanced it with the crystal skull in my other hand. I felt an ethereal, cleansing lightness when I touched the crystal skull, but when I touched the human one, it was a grounding sensation. I closed my eyes as I held both, allowing my mind to ease out of the blinding storm of emotional pain.

"Both are necessary. The skull made from rock is tied to the world we cannot see, and the other is tied to the present moment. Both create our world we live in. Like two people who are meant to be together. When they are together and become one, magic happens, magic that can only be expressed by those two souls together. When this happens everywhere, the universe, consciousness may even shift so that the entire world changes. Great things happen when balance is achieved. But the balance must be struck inside of you first."

I opened my eyes, hearing the passion in Chantico's voice. It sounded as if she had herself once experienced this type of union. Her aged skin glowed in the sunlight, and her eyes glittered like water reflecting that very light. This sentiment was something I found hard to believe in since I'd never experienced it myself. But she had faith. I had no idea what I believed or even who I was. When she saw me staring at her in confusion, she took the skulls from my hands.

"That is enough. You have much to learn. They will sit next to us as we work."

"Where did you find them and who made them?"

Chantico pushed a pile of dry palm fronds and reeds in front of me, then paused before speaking and continuing her own weaving.

"They were given to me by Cuauhtémoc. After he became a vampire, he returned to take back some of our treasures. He gave them to me for safekeeping. The other items he hid. It was a small cache, so he has no idea what they were used for or who created them. They had to be saved. Any more questions? You are a curious one. Must be why you have such a quick mind."

Her lips and eyes told two different stories, but I didn't press for more. "Where is Cuauhtémoc?"

"He is off taking care of his big plans. I told him to take his time. Think. But he has always been more lava than rain. It is his nature to always *do*. He never could just sit still and weave."

My mind raced with more questions pertaining to the how and why of everything. Chantico remained calm with her lips curved in a permanent crescent moon. Her eyes never left her work. Her ability to be calm despite what she had lived through baffled me. She was old enough to see history change for our people, including the disappearance of her entire family.

"Can I ask you another question?"

She paused with more patience in her eyes than I had ever seen. "Of course."

"Chantico, where were you when they arrived?"

"Me? I was busy living my life in our village. Already an old woman, they left me alone. No one noticed or cared about me. But as soon as I saw the very first Spaniard, I knew that was it for us."

She paused and touched my knee. "I can see your thoughts are moving fast. Too fast. Start your basket. Remember, the idea first and only once. Let the basket create itself."

The image in my mind was strong. It was a basket I made for my firstborn. I made it for Martin in the event I died during his birth. We sat there in silence until she put her weaving down for me to drink from her wrist. I drank with the rhythm of her heartbeat, listening to when her body told me to stop. She also guided me with her calm words.

"This is how you will learn control. It comes easy for you because I think it was always meant to be. You know where your power comes from? The soil. It is in what creates everything we see and cannot see. The Earth nourishes everything. So no matter where you are or what you are doing, it is always there for you."

I wiped my mouth and bowed my head in thanks before picking up my weaving again. This would be my new routine as I transformed. The hut was a sanctuary for my maturing emotions. Chantico guided the part in me that felt lost and in need of healing. I also sensed she was showing me how to heal myself.

No one bothered us so deep in the forest. The Spanish were too busy raiding and attempting to keep villages and towns under their control. Time was kept only by her human need to eat, sleep, and relieve herself.

Then there were the nights when Chantico felt the desire to build a fire. Her frail body moved slowly, but when the flames jumped into the air she had renewed energy. She swayed and danced like a young woman possessed. Her thick gray-and-black hair was a tangle of vines. The once-lush curls she must have had in her youth were now a jungle of frizz. "Join me. My mind remembers what it was like to be young even if my body does not like it. I will ache in the morning. Come," she said with palms outstretched. At first this struck me as odd, but then she took both of my hands into hers.

"Why do you walk around with your body and shoulders balled so tightly? We are dancing and there is no one around.

Everyone believes you are dead! Rejoice in your death from death! This is your second chance. Open your palms and receive your new life. Second chances are gifts to be explored and celebrated."

Her body of a crone became that of a maiden in that moment. Her hair and eyes blazed with sunlight despite it being night. She still retained all that made her vibrant, beautiful, and worthy. We bonfire danced and laughed until she had to stop to catch her breath and drink water just as the sun began to rise above us. As she sank into a deep slumber, I would take out the two skulls and think about the life I had lived until that point. What were all those experiences preparing me for, or was this just another cruel turn of fate?

I weaved with Chantico until I had to leave the hut to find more palms and reeds. In those quiet days I created countless items for Chantico and other women in the nearby village to trade or sell. The swift dance of my fingers brought parts of my broken human soul back together, but with these came new aspects of myself, the instincts of a blood drinker. The motion allowed my mind to focus inward, listening to the vampire inside and getting used to the body of a vampire, her needs. I could just be with Chantico. No judgment or pretense. For the first time in my adult life, I could breathe without anyone looking over my shoulder. It felt as if a sun lived within me, its radiating heat warming from the inside. For the first time I possessed love for the present moment, for my new life.

Sometimes at night when Chantico was asleep, I would return to the hacienda. Patli helped me look in on my daughter. I would sing songs or watch her sleep. My hope for her was for her to know all the languages I knew to help her navigate this New World and possibly find her way back to herself if she was ever lost or in need. She was not conceived out of love, far from it, but she did not have to suffer the way I did. Everything she would need to survive she possessed within her, like me. I hoped she would never have to be as malleable as the edge of a lit candle.

Before dawn I would retreat into the forest. I cried all the way on my walk back to the hut despite the freedom I felt during the day. Two worlds. Two parts of me with one having to hide half the time. Sometimes when I could hear the soft, heavy breathing from Chantico upon my return, I would take the skulls into my hands. I cradled the smooth cold quartz and stared into its vacant sockets. What did it see from the other side? I twisted it around and tried to look through the other side.

Then I took the other one into my hands. This skull was once covered with muscle and housed a brain with thoughts. Now it was an ornament. Where was its previous inhabitant? In that moment I understood why the origin of the skulls didn't matter. Not really. It was simply how the skulls reflected the world in the moment I regarded them.

We pass through life like a ray of light through clear quartz. We are only temporary. And we walk around like an embellished skull, hiding the many things we hold inside.

Colin joins me on the outdoor deck of the ferry. "Sorry about that. My publisher loves my new work. This could be *the one,* the book that changes everything. You will have to keep feeding me your stories, inspiring me with your body. Come with me if there is a book tour."

He's still a beautiful creature. His charm is undeniable, and I'm happy for his stroke of good fortune. However, following him on his book tour is not exactly what I had in mind for myself. The breeze on the outer deck of the ferry is colder.

In my eagerness to find what I was searching for, did I rush to hold tight to what is only a damn good replica? Through my work I encounter forged artifacts all the time. My acute senses make it easy for me to spot them. That instinct is what made me millions. But I found that examining the heart and emotions for their authenticity is a whole other matter.

Clouds are breaking, and I can feel the sun hit me directly in the middle of my forehead. *Tonalli.* I send out a call to the clouds, the penetrating power of the sun, for me to find real love, a true counterpart, and not a replica. After all, I am a hunter in my heart. I want to know it as soon as I see it. I want it to hit me like the hottest and longest day of summer. I want a clear sign I can understand, because otherwise love is an easy place to slip into self-doubt. And are there not enough places to curl up and wither away in this world?

11

John Hawkins sat at a café beneath St. Paul's Cathedral, waiting for his phone to ring before George arrived. He looked around to see who could be watching before taking out his monogrammed silver flask filled with blood and pouring it into a teacup filled with what was now called "builder's tea." With a small spoon he swirled the milk and blood into a mixture he could stomach.

He looked at his watch again. Ten minutes late. "This is getting tiresome. I have a life," he mumbled. He looked around again, taking in how much the city and British Empire had changed since he was born. But it still felt like home and gave him a comfort not found anywhere else.

He had met George here. Since meeting George, all he wanted was to enjoy the fruits of his labor instead of running around for more. To take the time to enjoy the world and life properly. He wandered through London sometimes in awe of the changes to the narrow cobbled back streets. Graffiti on overflowing bins, bursts of laughter from groups of youths spilling out of bars, Primark workers standing outside having a smoke break. For hours he would walk around his city, simply observing its human inhabitants.

It was the city in which he'd built his business. After Hernán turned him, John promised Hernán new connections in England. They could create fresh opportunities built on blood and treasure. He barely remembered the events of the weeks before becoming immortal. His dysentery had taken him to the border between delusion and reality. At first he thought it was all a dream, or perhaps just punishment for his sins, when he saw a man with fangs draining him of his blood. But then he awoke in his own filth with a strength he remembered from his youth. He sat upright. The man with fangs sat in a chair, staring at him. "How is this possible?" asked John.

"My name is Hernán Cortés. And I need men to build new empires. And for that, we must drink blood for eternal life. A small price to pay."

John looked at his body, which felt full of vigor. "I am your loyal brother for restoring my health. What did you do to me?"

Hernán stood to leave. "Get up, because you look and smell awful. Soon you will need to be fed. Until then I will explain what I know. There is still much to find out about this existence that defies Christ."

As humans in the sixteenth century, both had been giants in commanding fleets and leading trade. John Hawkins and Hernán Cortés. Now they had to reinvent themselves as other people, with the world thinking them both dead. Today, they traded rare artifacts to private collectors but didn't care how they were procured. There were also the diamonds—again they had no conscience about the details of how they were obtained. And more recently they had built a business on unique biological products from vampires. Both men made a fortune in these worlds.

But there still remained those who were getting in their way.

His phone vibrated on the table, rattling his teacup. He scrambled to answer it.

"What is taking you so long?" he said without masking his agitation as he spoke to Hernán.

Hernán matched his irritation. "Malinalli is on her way. She got distracted by a warm body. Some guy. Are you ready? I want her dead."

"I know. I want her dead too. George and I have travel plans soon. You've never taken so much time to stalk a potential victim. But I suppose with your history with her . . ."

"I will be there soon. She won't stand a chance."

John hung up the phone before jerking his head to the left. A group of pigeons took flight as people left the cathedral. The bells rang out in loud gongs. As he began to rise, a hand pushed him down again. He could smell day-old blood. He looked up to see the face of the man who had been keeping tabs on him and tracking him for such a long time. It was Alexander J, the bounty hunter who was known for picking missions that would let him right the wrongs in history. His black eyes were framed by shaggy black hair, and he wore a long khaki-colored duster coat over dark brown cargo trousers and a matching T-shirt. His combat boots were muddy—fashion was not something Alexander cared about. Alexander's lips curled into a smug smile.

"Hello, John Hawkins. We are finally meeting. Not like you to hang around one place for long. And who do you want dead now?"

Originally from Judea with Aramaic his mother tongue, Alexander still had a bit of an accent. It was also well known that he spoke Arabic, French, and Hebrew fluently. John's face twisted into a sneer. If Malinalli hadn't taken her sweet time, Hernán would be here and she would be dead.

And Alexander wouldn't have found him.

"What do you want? I have a business to run. Since I can't sail the way I used to, I am usually running to catch a flight."

"I'm here to shut you down. This isn't the sixteenth century, and you have been responsible for thousands upon thousands of deaths. And that is what you did in your human life as a trader. You created the English slave trade triangle. Your time is up. No more dealing in bodies."

"And what are you going to do? You won't kill me. I know that for sure. You have a code. How much were you paid to catch me?"

Alexander stared at him, expressionless. "I won't be the one to kill you, but I will question you, and then you will be entombed until those who paid your bounty collect on it. And for the record, I took this job for free. The human and vampire world is safer without you in it."

"I'm not telling you anything, and you're not entombing me. You may be older than me, but I don't hold back on blood drinking like you. I'll kill you, then I'll drain you."

Alexander leaned toward John. "You *will* follow me. You *will* answer for your crimes. And you will answer all my questions truthfully. I know and my client knows you have a business partner who wants to keep their name under wraps and hands clean. Hope you like the concoction that's about to run through your veins. It's one of your own you use on your victims. I found it in the last lab of yours I burned down."

A voice called out from the distance. "John! Sorry I'm late."

Both John and Alexander looked at the human man who couldn't have been more than thirty. He dressed smartly in fitted jeans, a collared shirt, and Chelsea boots. An expensive watch dominated his left wrist. John flashed Alexander a sly, wicked smile. "Perhaps another day."

George looked at Alexander in curiosity as he placed a hand on John's shoulder. John touched it with care. "George, an old friend saw me here and stopped to say hello. Meet Alexander."

George gave him a quick smile. "Nice to meet you, but we are running late. Maybe the restaurant can accommodate another seat?"

Alexander rose from his chair. "Thank you, but I have other lunch plans."

John stood and matched Alexander's stare. "Another day."

He left hand in hand with George.

"Fuck," Alexander muttered under his breath as he walked to his double-parked car with the fake police badge in the front window, allowing him to park wherever he wanted. He would head to Max's clock shop for blood and to map out another plan. Vampire bounty hunting work wasn't easy.

And he couldn't stop thinking about who this woman was that John wanted dead.

Max's clock shop rarely had any patrons, and it kept the lights low to discourage humans from wandering in. The shop was an old front for a safe haven that supplied vampires in the know with fresh, packaged blood sourced from willing donors. Struggling NHS doctors who needed cash sold extra blood supply to pump money into flailing community clinics. The shop had been founded in the eighties by Max and had kept going since. Max Powell, a vicar of seventy, sat next to Alexander and handed him a pouch of blood and an iPad.

Alexander took long gulps. "You know, I prefer drinking cold blood instead of from an actual human lover. They always get in the way."

"John Hawkins has spent a lot of money keeping his trail clean thanks to his human lover, George Morland," said Max as he picked up an antique watch to take apart.

"Shame, because George seemed like a nice enough guy. Wonder how much he knows. He didn't seem to know who I was." Alexander scrolled through files on Max's tablet. "Send out an email to those who might be interested in giving us more info on George. We need to find out about the woman John is looking for and that business partner of his."

"So much for entombing him. But you must find this mystery woman," Max said with a large grin.

"On the hunt tonight for a female vampire from out of town? Great."

"It's good you are getting out to mingle with the opposite sex."

Alexander raised his eyebrows. "This isn't a date."

"Who knows, she might be nice. I will keep digging, then finish with this little beauty I found at a market stall."

"I don't know. Anyway, I will see you later. Need to sit and meditate on it and see what comes to me. I didn't spend enough time with John to get a full read; might get sparks of information. If she is old enough, I will hear and feel her presence."

12

We arrive in London with clouds and rain to greet us, but all I feel is Colin next to me with his arm around my waist or searching for my hand. His comments on the ferry are bothering me less, even if they remain super-glued to the back of my mind. Despite those worries, I've decided that I'm ready for another adventure with this man to pass the time until I am due to meet with Horatio. The skulls are as good as mine.

The first line of business is to find our Airbnb. I have a hotel booked, one of the best in London, but I want to share a proper, homelike space with Colin, like his home in Dublin. Might as well try on living with Colin for size to shoo away my misgivings until I am sure. I was still desperate to cling to the notion of a sacred union written in the stars, preferably one that felt romance novel–worthy. Despite my lingering doubts, I go along with the flat I booked on the ferry instead of the hotel room.

We are staying in the middle of Notting Hill. It's the perfect location to reach most places easily on the tube. There is a constant bustle of residents and tourists among the multicolored, brightly painted terraced homes. Restaurants serving every cuisine imaginable line the narrow streets. Cheap trinkets are sold on the sidewalk, including the umbrellas that are indispensable in rainy London. A large marketplace with food, clothing, and all sorts of crafts is the center of activity on Portobello Road.

Blood, sweat, and the aroma of food fill my imagination as we move from the street to the small shops. The collective energy from all the bodies gives it a wonderful buzz. Sparks of information about these people fill my mind. The images of their lives are like a kaleidoscope. The neighborhood is a melting pot of people speaking different languages but enjoying many of the same delights. When I walk among this crowd, I feel grateful for the many experiences of this extended life. And it is mine to experience if I so choose.

What a dream it would be to share my long life with someone. But wouldn't I prefer to share it with someone I would not have to watch die? Where does that leave Colin?

I settle into the flat while he goes out for groceries. The man must eat, and for me to feed from him, he has to keep his strength up. The Airbnb is a tidy flat furnished with simple IKEA furniture. It's comfortable without being inviting. And the rain is now hammering against the windows. Colin will return soaked. As I search for towels, I notice his backpack is unzipped next to the bed. The title page of a manuscript is visible. Part of me wants to read it, but I don't want to betray his trust. He hasn't told me anything about this story. We'd spent hours talking about his books, even the ones that were works in progress or hadn't seen the light of day. Why would he keep this from me unless he didn't want me to know what it was really about?

I want to read it because it's called *Demon in a Dress*. I don't know how I feel about this, seeing the title. Is he trying to re-imagine my existence? I'm not a demon. There is writing in pencil. *She is only out for blood. Can she be changed? Have to change the name. The hero makes her human again. No more demon at the end.*

I snap the bag shut because everything inside of me drops with the suddenness of a tropical rainstorm. I'll ask him later about the book. But if he really sees me as nothing more than a demon in a dress, then I should give him what he might be expecting. And if he thinks I can be anything *but* an immortal creature, he has to think again. Our plan is to go out after he's had dinner here. It will avoid the awkward situation of him ordering food while I stare down a glass of water. The only Bloody Marys I can enjoy are the ones I mix myself.

He returns from the supermarket dripping wet and with two large bags filled with food. "I hope you like this kind of weather because this is pretty normal. Get used to it."

This remark pulls me deeper behind my protective walls. Silence is all I have to offer him right now. I am helping him unpack everything when my phone buzzes. More emails that need attention. Reading that note on the manuscript has soured my desire to walk hand in hand in the rain with him.

"Do you mind if I stay in for a while? I have work to do. You can go explore if you like," I say to him.

"No way. I can hang back. You know, I'll bake some bread. It will give you enough time to do what you need to do."

Sarcastically I say, "Irish soda bread?"

He throws his head back to laugh. He is still cute even if the daylight has dimmed his shine. "Yes, that is exactly what I will make. Let me see if they have what I need in the cupboards; if not I'll head back out."

I give him a smile and allow him to get on with his project while I begin mine.

He stands at the counter kneading dough in nothing but baggy jeans and a T-shirt. I watch his arms tense then relax as his flour-covered hands and forearms work their magic with the dough. My mind mulls over the title of his book that he didn't tell me he was writing.

There is a swell of heat inside of me. A little desire for revenge mixed with excitement. I want to drink from him. Fuck him immediately. I walk across the room with the grace of a jaguar ready to pounce. He sees me from the corner of his eye and knows what I want. He continues making his Irish soda bread. I drop to my knees.

Once between his legs I unzip his jeans, allowing them to fall to his ankles. I can hear his pulse from his femoral artery. It whispers my name, and there is no ignoring that call. As I dig my teeth into his thigh he groans because my right hand is stroking his cock. Both my hand and bite become a little rougher. Demon rough. My hand moves with slick ease along the length of his shaft. His artery is open to me, filling my mouth with luscious stickiness that's causing my pussy to become increasingly wet.

The deeper I gulp, the faster I move my hand. I feel rabid, voracious, greedy, sensing his pulse is beginning to weaken. I must stop even though I don't want to. Then he will see the real demon in me. "Mali, please. I'm feeling a little light-headed."

Now it was time to quench his thirst since he was such a good sport about mine. I spit on the open wound to close it tightly. His eyes are heavy. "Baby, why'd you stop stroking me?" I look up to him with my hand teasing my clit. "Because demons want to get theirs too." He is so eager for my body these words don't register in his brain. Without any other words spoken between us, he joins me on the floor.

"Taste me," I purr, bordering on a growl. I push him back and climb over his body until I'm seated over his face. His hands squeeze my ass, covering us both now with flour. His mouth seeks out every drop of moisture from my pussy. His tongue is like a trident puncturing me with torturous pleasure. I fall onto my hands and allow him to take control of my hips and ass as he takes each labia into his mouth. He sucks them in turn, making sure they each get the special treatment. I'm desperate to come. I push my pussy into his mouth so he knows I'm ready to be carried over the threshold. One of his fingers finds my anus as he takes my clit between his lips.

I lift from the floor with wobbly legs; my muscles don't want to work but I'm not finished with him yet. I step to the counter and grab a handful of butter. Knowing he's watching, I bend over and proceed to lubricate my ass.

His eyes go wide with wonder and arousal. "Oh my God. Get over here now."

I shake my head as I make him watch me play with myself.

"Please," he begs. I lower myself to the ground and slather the rest of the butter on his cock, which is so hard I feel it might split in two. I turn around again and squat over his cock. I plunge his erection straight into my ass.

As he enters me, he cries out. On all fours I ride him backward. The butter leaves little resistance as I move my hips so that my ass is like a monstrous squid pulling its prey deeper into its mouth. Unfortunately, I'm not thinking about love; my heart is tied up in my hurt, confusion over the little crumbs leading me to the conclusion this will not end well. He wrote an entire book calling me a demon, all the while feeding me other stories instead.

When was he going to tell me? I pound harder, the anger building up inside. And then he comes hard. I can't help but feel less warm. Just like all the times before, I am left feeling hollow despite him being the gourd of blood I drink from.

I rise from the floor without a word to shower for our planned day out. He shouts, "Hey, I'll finish the bread, then we can make a move."

In my mind I'm thinking, *Fuck the bread, because I can't eat it.* And I know that this Airbnb is where I will leave Colin when I'm done with him. This truth makes me feel lonelier than before. But I can afford to be fickle now and do whatever the fuck I want.

I walk into the bathroom to clean myself off. My mind goes hazy, and I can feel a pull, a voice in the distance. It must be another vampire in the vicinity. But the connection is strong. I feel it rising from my pelvis to the crown of my head. I look into the mirror, hoping to receive some vision or spark of information. There is only my reflection.

"What are you doing, Malinalli?" I whisper this to myself, hoping that finally I can change my life.

The weather outside is downcast like my mood. The sex satisfied my base physical need, no different from all the other detached sexual encounters I'd had over the centuries. So much for true love. But I'm glad that as long as we are out, I don't have to make small talk with him. For now, I just want to experience London.

We begin at the Clink Prison Museum located near Borough Market in Southwark. The museum is a tiny place once you descend. It shows you all the vicious ways the ones on this side of the pond tortured their own back when they were calling us "savages." I read every explanation and try to inspect as best I can all items behind the glass. The most interesting is a cap made of human teeth. I'm an educated woman and I know history, yet the irony of these torture devices does not escape me. I have read that in Spain there is a large metal bull they would force people to crawl into before lighting a fire beneath it. This was to compel them to confess to their misdeeds. Eventually, I want to see that metal bull with my own eyes.

On our way back to the flat from the Clink Prison Museum, we stumble across a tequila festival on the South Bank. The path is lined with large black streetlamps adorned with large grumpy-looking fish with their hungry mouths open. Gabriel's Wharf is a small area on the Thames where the water laps a filthy beach. It's odd to hear the water hitting the shore with the OXO Tower behind and black cabs zooming past on the other side.

This area of London on the Thames River is teeming with art, food, and music. From here the Houses of Parliament, the London Eye, and Big Ben are visible. Their lights cast bright colors across the placid river. The festival is a riotous celebration that resembles Día de los Muertos if it were in summer. There's salsa playing loudly with people dancing where they stand. Colin's hand clasps mine tightly as he drags me to join the crowd.

"I still don't know much about your past. I want you to tell me everything. But first we drink! Or at least, I'll have a drink. I want to celebrate!"

Colin lets go of my hand, and for a moment he is absorbed into the crowd of humans. He smells like them, and I can't discern his location; then again, I'm not trying. He calls my name from the crowd. He is at the bar, waving me over.

I go along, still imprisoned in my own mind, but excited to

see all these new sights. How wrong I was to read this so-called love affair as my ultimate great love affair. Bright papel picado blows in the night breeze with fairy lights strung above our heads like multicolored fireflies. Within the space of two minutes, he pounds two shots of cheap tequila. There is a large grin on his face as he attempts to take my hand. To avoid his touch I move to the music and dance away. "Let's see what else is going on here," I say.

I can tell he is feeling the alcohol and the buzz from his good news: I know from my own experience nothing beats the high of big breakthroughs in life that take you to the next level. Despite my misgivings about the relationship and not feeling fully satisfied about where it could lead, I want him to be happy. Thankfully, the music is so loud there's no need to speak, and we walk through the crowds in silence. He stops and pulls his phone from his pocket. "Hey! You won't believe this, but my friend Nolan saw my Twitter post about coming to London. He wants to meet up. You up for it? He can be here in twenty minutes."

I look around, not wanting to meet this Nolan at all, but I feel responsible since I brought Colin to London. "Sure."

"You are the best. I also need to call my agent back."

"Go on then. I'll sit at that pop-up bar."

He kisses me on the cheek and walks to a quieter spot. It is nice to have the space from him, now that I know he is writing a book about a demon based on me. And that I will never change.

As my thoughts drift I can feel someone close. Someone not human.

I turn abruptly. And there he is. I see a man with wavy black hair and eyes as black as mine that reflect the moon. His skin is the color of desert sand. Not sure why that image has floated into my mind. He is an eclipse and all its dark power. There is a wild look to him. I wouldn't be surprised if, like me, he is an ancient one, a vampire.

"Hello."

His voice is an unexpected wave toppling me over. I feel like a metal pole being struck by lightning. From that moment, Colin could have been just another memory from another century.

"Is this your territory?" I say to him, not wanting a fight.

"No. I'm Alexander J . . . I sensed your presence in the crowd and had to meet you."

"I'm Malinalli."

With an intensity that doesn't wane, he maintains eye contact with me. "Malinalli. A goddess. Malinalxochitl. Her name is grass and flower combined. But she also has the venom of scorpions and snakes. Beauty and power. She's someone to be revered."

"What?" I can't believe he knows this. Not even the men in my own country ever brought this up. That he knows it touches something deep inside me, like his presence has. My sudden softness catches him off guard, and for a moment, his rough-cut exterior grows smoother. He stammers, "The mythology from Mexico. You make me think . . . Never mind. I study beliefs and religion from different cultures . . . among other work."

"And what is that other work?"

He pauses as if to find the right words. "I'm a sort of detective. Some would call me a bounty hunter. Others say I do the good work of finding the bad guys. It's not always easy. I've also been called a traitor."

I smile. Now, this is intriguing to me.

"Am I in trouble with someone?" I playfully tease with a grin.

His face turns slightly serious. "I don't know. But there are others here. Do you know a John Hawkins? He is . . . like us. May I ask what your line of work is?"

The strange sensation from earlier in the bathroom is re-kindled in my mind. "I don't know a John, and I just met you. There are no other vampires in my life."

He takes a step closer to me. There is an urgency in his en-ergy; it's frenetic. The only sparks I receive from him feel like the ticking of a clock. "I'm not here to hassle you. I'm here to tell you that you could be in grave danger."

I brush this off with a chuckle. "It's been over five hundred years and I've managed just fine. And if you must know, I am in antiquities."

Alexander's eyes shift to the right of me. Colin is by my side again. He studies this strange man in front of me as if he is try-ing to make out if he is human or not, and if he's encroaching on *his* territory. "Ready to head to the Swan to meet my friend?" Colin says to me.

I turn from Colin to look at Alexander. This vampire has my full attention, and if I'm honest, my attraction to him was im-mediate. I should have ditched Colin long before.

"It was nice meeting you, maybe . . ." I say, hoping to give him the feeling of wanting to know more.

"I'm sure we will meet again. London is a small city, really. There is a shop, Lost in Time. Stop by if you need to. I would like you to."

"We aren't staying here long," Colin interjects without any warmth.

Alexander doesn't look at him but instead keeps his gaze on me and smiles.

I turn to walk with Colin. When I look back, Alexander has melted into the shadows and music.

The entire time at the pub I sit with the sound of Colin's laughter and voice next to me, but it's as distant as the waves in the Gulf of Mexico. My thoughts are solely on Alexander, on his scent, his movements. How did he know about my name? And never did I feel the desire to be close to another vampire until now.

My thoughts about him are just as obsessive as my hunger for blood when I was first made a vampire. Thousands of tiny bites gnawed on my stomach and then fluttered like monarchs taking to flight. I want to know more about him. One more day, and I will find him, somehow.

Colin leans over to me when his friend excuses himself to go to the toilet. "I know this might be boring for you. You don't exactly drink. You mind one more round?"

I would love to just leave him there, but now I know there are vampires close, I'm not sure it's safe. I don't think Alexander would harm a human, I could sense that, but what about others? And what about this grave danger Alexander said I was in?

"Just one. I have some work to do."

His one other round is a double whiskey and a beer.

It's just before midnight when Colin has become a little worse for the wear after downing his drinks. I'm ready to leave. I no longer feel in the mood to party. And I really do want to get work done tonight. I'm falling behind on my work again, and it shows in the emails I am receiving. "Hey, why don't we head back? You look a bit tired. You've had your one round," I say when his friend starts chatting with a group of women at a bachelorette party.

With heavy eyelids he nods. "And I'm a little tipsy."

We leave his friend still drinking in the pub. As small as my frame is, my vampire strength helps me bundle him into a black taxi then into the flat when we arrive. He's mumbling and laughing to himself. I toss him on the bed to remove his shoes, and without warning he pulls me next to him.

His eyes meet mine. "You know, I'm not the marrying kind. I won't ever commit like that because I would never want to hurt you like that. I've fucked over so many women in my time. Don't ever want that for you, or us. But, Mali, I will fucking love you forever. And you are going to make me a fortune. Thank you."

I'm glad he can finally be honest with me, even if he won't remember any of it in the morning. "It's okay, Colin, your companionship has been fun. But we need to talk about the book."

He smiles and lays his head on my chest. In a slurred voice he says, "Yeah, sure thing. Also, and it has been on my mind. Thought about it when you left, but I don't want to be a vampire. It doesn't bother me that you are; it's sexy. But not what I see for my life. Even if I'm bleeding and dying. Not for me. I hope that's okay. I've been meaning to tell you that. And we could always adopt a kid." He moves his head to the pillow. It doesn't take long before his heavy breathing turns into snoring.

I'd be lying if I said this misadventure in love doesn't hurt me. But I already had my children. I don't want more.

I leave him in bed to work on my laptop in the other room. I look at the mess in the kitchen from his baking and random items strewn across the flat. The butler-serviced luxury suite I booked in the Dorchester Hotel calls out to me. If only I could call reception for someone to clean this up. The mess can wait, as I want to get back to work. Colin can clean it up. The reason I am in London is to reclaim Chantico's crystal and turquoise skulls and nothing else.

The following evening I will meet with Horatio. It's unusual to do business with so little information about the seller, considering they knew so much about me. When I tried to go through back channels with friends in the business, nothing could be dug up. Some sellers do like a certain degree of anonymity. That is the nature of the antiquities market—there are far more secrets being kept in the shadows than most people know. The circle of who owns the most valuable treasures known to man is very small. But even so, until now I had never experienced any bad or dangerous deals. I mean, this was no Indiana Jones movie, and I am hardly Lara Croft.

Then there was my meeting Alex.

I shut my laptop before dawn to close my eyes in meditation to rest, hoping that in my meditation I will drift upon sparks of information about the vampires in London. When I close my eyes I am taken back to when the skulls were stolen from Chantico and me. And when my maker, the dethroned emperor with an already bruised heart, completely crumbled to ash.

He too had gone through a transformation of blood and solitude.

I left Chantico sleeping, as I did so many other nights, to visit my daughter. A new moon made my path darker than usual, but with my powers I could still see clearly without the light.

When I arrived at the edge of the property Patli was waiting for me. Her hands twisted over each other. "You have to go. Something is happening, but I don't know what. Juan has been conducting his business behind closed doors with guards. The entire household kept away as to not spy. We know nothing. He is not here. I would not have heard him leave if I had not been waiting for you. I watched in the shadows."

My mind scanned my time with my husband for any clues. His strongest personality trait was his devotion not only to the greatness of Spain but also to saving his own wretched skin. That's what gave him his ambition. I was merely a convenient means to those ends. Our people "had to be good for something," as I recall once hearing him say.

Since being in the hut with my weaving, I did not follow the local politics as closely as I once did. Then it hit me: Chantico mentioned Cuauhtémoc would not be around. He was too busy planning something . . . It had to be some sort of attack.

"Patli, have there been any executions lately or any talk of a rebellion?" In that moment we heard gunshots followed by shouts in the distance. "Go! Go to my daughter!"

She ran back to the house without hesitation. I stood there, torn. Do I watch over the hacienda or go back to the hut? My heart could only make one choice. Knowing what happens to women and girls in times of war . . . I waited. Not just for my daughter but for the others, including Patli, who lived in the hacienda. My vampire ears could hear everything in the hacienda even from this great distance. I fell to my knees. There was no breeze, but still the air was heavy with the scent of charred flesh and blood.

I resolved not to cry: No, I had to remain alert in the event the hacienda came under attack. I hardened myself for a fight.

It was just before dawn when I saw Juan ride back with soldiers. By the look of it, they had been victorious. Their armor was sprayed with blood. "Anyone practicing any religion besides the true faith will be burned like those things . . . demons. Savages!" I heard him say.

The immediate threat to the hacienda was over. I slid back into the forest until I turned to run to the hut. The sun was rising so I could not only see the smoke billowing into the clear sky but also smell the burned flesh. In my fear I counted on Chantico being hidden enough to escape any attack.

My legs refused to budge any farther upon the sight of Chantico's hut. Our woven baskets were strewn across the clearing and torn to pieces. Chantico lay dead next to fresh horse hoofprints in the dirt. They most likely thought her a witch, or she fought back.

I kneeled next to her with a sorrow even deeper than I felt when I thought I would die from disease. This woman was the mother I never had. She never wavered in her support of me, even though I came to her as a stranger whom she only knew by reputation. My heart wanted to wail, but it could not—it was rendered numb from the nonstop pain that was too much for one woman to endure in one lifetime.

Even my anger lacked any will to flare. I felt only the rain of Tlaloc pummeling my soul, drowning all my emotions. Chantico was no longer there. Her spirit had already fled somewhere safe. Part of me hoped she remained so I could apologize, so I could feel her comforting presence one last time. I took her crumpled and already rigid brown hand into my own. The pain of the moment burned straight through me.

I made a choice. I could only be in one place at a time. She would be buried with the two skulls, as much as I loved them. It seemed like the right thing to do. I squeezed her dead hand before throwing my head back and screaming for every loss up to now. Birds fled from the trees in a rush, but nothing else moved. There I was, completely alone for the first time since I could remember from childhood.

Then, as I had always done, it was time to carry on.

The hut was a mess when I entered. They had destroyed it as a final act of humiliation. All the valuable items she possessed were gone, including the skulls. "Thieves," I whispered at the rising sun as I dropped to my knees. A rustle from the thick interior of the forest made my body tense. My instinct to attack was very strong, even though I had never fought anyone in my life. Whenever we encountered hostility, Cortés shouted, "Protect her at all costs!" I knew some of his men resented this, but I could give him what ten of them could not. I was valuable to him without having any value in the kind of world he was creating.

The noise in the forest was closer. I whipped my head around as I switched to a crouched position. A growl clawed at the base of my throat. Through the trees I could see it was Cuauhtémoc, accompanied by a man and a woman appearing like the most pious of papas in black cloaks. Their hair fell to their waists in matted knots of blood. Both fingers and teeth were stained crimson nearly as black as their hair. I could see rage and hunger in their eyes as they scanned the scene of destruction. The two vampires shrieked to the sky next to Chantico's body. I could feel their anguish, a thick tree sap covering us all, hardening around our souls. As if enough had not befallen our people.

"What happened? I know you had to be there. I was watching over my daughter at the hacienda when this occurred; otherwise, it would be the limbs and heads of soldiers and not reeds covering the ground."

Cuauhtémoc shook his head. "This is all because of my arrogance. I might have made more of us with superhuman abilities, but I should have taken the time for them to develop their skills."

"You mean to tell me your band of creatures was defeated?"

His face twisted in darkness with the shadows cast by the

trees. "Yes. I thought only a few of us would be needed. It would have been enough if I had waited just a little longer, or made more of us. Their senses and bodies still needed more nurturing to realize their full lethal potential. At least we managed to cleanse the land of a few of them. Maybe they will say this land is cursed with demons and leave. Their superstitious god has to be good for something."

"You're living a fool's dream, Cuauhtémoc. I have known many of them intimately. I know how their minds operate. They are going nowhere and will only increase their grip here and elsewhere. Except for Chantico and Patli, I have never met an unsoiled heart, including my own. We get what we deserve. I have no energy for even this blood life you have given me. What is the point to any of it? I really thought Chantico might have answers. So what now? Chantico also had a treasure trove of valuable items from our people, and now they are gone."

Cuauhtémoc shifted his eyes from me to the charred remains of Chantico. To my surprise his eyes welled with red tears. He kneeled in the ground next to her and hung his head. His hair, caked in blood, clung to his shoulders and the sides of his face. Blots of red dripped upon her corpse. The woman next to him placed a hand on his shoulder without speaking. She looked like a rag dipped in viscera.

"First my child and now her. You are not the only one who has lost it all," Cuauhtémoc muttered.

"Who was Chantico to you?"

"She was my grandmother. I kept her just alive with small drops of my blood. In small doses it can work like a tonic to humans. The ones who did this will pay with their lives. All of them."

His voice became a growl as he said this. He wiped the tears from his face, smearing them like paint. If I didn't know any better, I would think he was what the Christians considered a demon or even Satan himself. Only hate and oblivion emanated from his entire being. I didn't want to ask more about him giving his blood to her. She never asked me for a drop of mine, but I would have drained half of my body if it had meant more time with her.

"Don't tell me you are going to start another rebellion. So soon? They will expect it and take their revenge on everyone to establish their power."

Cuauhtémoc rose and stood to his full height with his back straight. "No. Lesson learned. Maybe I should have paid more attention to what she tried to teach me with weaving. I will start again, spend more time training an elite group of us. Like warriors training for a great battle. We will be the deadliest of beasts. We are made from the darkness of all the horror we have witnessed. We are destined for greatness. Are you ready to do your part?"

I could see the pain in his eyes. But I also saw a determination that had the potential to turn to pure chaos and cruelty. It frightened me. What could he become with the dark power we both possessed? Our existence was a piece of flint with just enough of a point to be very lethal if crafted in the right way.

Part of me understood him: I hated every human who enslaved another. I looked to the sky for some unknown reason. A quetzal whizzed above my head in a bolt of red and green. A single green feather fell to the ground not far from where I stood. It floated with the ease of a whispered prayer. It had to be Chantico giving me a sign. I could feel it inside of me. My heart responded to the sight with tears in my eyes.

I can't deny it, his offer was tempting. He could offer me security. Be a mentor. But that is all I had ever known: standing behind a man who could give me some sense of protection and a place in the world determined by his wealth and status. What if I could have those things on my own?

It might be a dangerous, lonely existence; however, how could I begrudge my lovers and husbands if I perpetuated the pattern long after leaving them? I needed to create a hut of my own before sharing it with another. Who says only men can possess and express power? My mind couldn't conceive how it would be possible. But something deeper still told me to hang on and go after what I wanted.

"No. I must stay here, restore this hut, watch over my daughter before she is sent to Spain. Especially now. Chantico is dead because I left to see her as I have done for many nights."

He looked at me with mild shock and anger that I would not follow him.

"What else will you do? Just sit here? You might as well still be their slave."

I stepped closer to him to look him in the eye. The feather remained in my peripheral vision. I remembered the great headdress of Montezuma and how it was taken like a prize when he was captured. "Wrong again. I will take back every last treasure that has been stolen from us. Then I will take what is theirs. If it is the last thing I do, I will find those skulls to honor Chantico. Bloodshed for revenge is not my way, but I won't stand in your way if we cross paths again. Any bodies you find in my wake are for sustenance or protection. Deal?"

He remained silent, searching my face for any sign of hesitation. There was none. I knew my own mind and would now fully express it without fear. No more masters or lords. He shook his head and extended a hand with blood-ringed sharpened nails.

"Deal. We will bury her together, then we leave each other in peace. Probably the only peace any of us will experience for a very long time."

Chantico would remain in her hut beneath the dirt floor. Nothing was left to bury her with except a few of the torn baskets and gourds she used. The four of us smoothed out the mound of dirt above her buried body to preserve the space as it was when she was alive. I prayed she would guide me back to the skulls one day. Cuauhtémoc's companions remained silent until it was time to leave. They tried to speak to me; however, their tongues had been removed. I tried to contain my horror at such cruelty, as I know this was not done by Cuauhtémoc. It was probably why they joined his fight, being born of the same rage as he.

"Cuauhtémoc, how do you communicate with them?"

He placed a sharp-nailed fingertip between my eyebrows. "Here. We are connected. Perhaps you will learn this one day. We all can do it. Just practice. Information like whispers, flash visions, heightened senses, are part of this existence.

"Perhaps we will meet again."

I nodded with more on my mind. I knew I had to ask before missing an opportunity that might not arise again.

"The two skulls. There is really nothing you can tell me about them?"

Cuauhtémoc looked taken aback by this question.

"What do you mean? Those skulls were crafted by Chantico's husband. He had insight and talent beyond what any human I have ever encountered possessed. The skull was from their child who died, and she found the quartz. Together they created both skulls. They were bound together by sharing a soul . . . at least that is what it seemed like. Together they created beauty and love in their art at our temples. Then he died at a respectable old age."

I didn't know what to say. My heart broke for Chantico. No wonder she could not utter the words to this tale and opted for a lie. The truth of her dead child and lost love were too much to take in her old age.

"Thank you. Be well."

"And you. May we never be enemies."

I watched them turn and leave, then spent the rest of the daylight cleaning up the mess from her murder. Whatever palms could be salvaged I piled in the corner of the hut. I swept everything twice, wanting to wipe away any traces of blood or footprints to make it appear as if she had just gone for a moment, a short journey until I would see her again.

Then I sat in the center of the hut, staring at the forest with the quetzal feather in hand until the sun set into the darkness. Never had I experienced being alone in such a way. Yes, I was desperately alone in all my so-called relationships, but now I was physically alone, without a soul in sight. With no clue what to do with myself, I began to weave.

Sure, I had this grand idea of taking back the treasures, as I told Cuauhtémoc, but I had no inkling how to even begin to accomplish any of it. The monumental task of it made my heart break. I wanted to rush into this noble cause yet had nothing and no one at my disposal to make it happen. In that moment I felt abandoned by all except the moon. No god and no one, not even myself, was there to comfort me or show me a way forward. My entire being was suspended in amber, frozen in sadness and despair. I continued to weave baskets and bowls to distract myself. I surrendered to the moment of not knowing how any of the rest of my immortal life would turn out. The not knowing was worse than any wound to the body. It plays tricks on the mind.

After Chantico's death I sat in my hut with the growing knowledge it was safe to be alone without a husband or children or anyone, including the protection of Cuauhtémoc. I could not be one of his followers in a pack of the undead slaughtering with teeth and claws. Did the Spanish invaders deserve to die by my hand? Yes. But I deserved to be free for once in my life.

I had spent years going through the motions of motherhood without a real chance to experience love with my babies. I had to watch everyone else go by, leapfrogging off my back. I had been tethered to lovers and to having their children as a way of securing safety and power. Here I had to cultivate it for myself.

What freedom I experienced in Chantico's hut under the moon, even while barely moving.

13

Hernán sat in the lobby of the Dorchester Hotel with over-priced tea he couldn't drink watching humans walking in and out. Malinalli was supposed to have been here already, as this was the day she was meant to arrive.

His agitation was beginning to rise. Horatio had promised him she was staying here. John wasn't answering his phone either. It had already been a few hours. That George was more cumbersome than helpful at times. Hernán despised not getting his way, and Horatio would receive an unexpected visit after dark if she didn't show.

Hernán looked at his IWC watch again. It was five P.M. Why wait any longer? He stood up to catch a black cab in front of the hotel to confront Horatio. A phone call would not suffice to intimidate him enough. As he knew from his human life, you get more out of people when their hide is on the line.

Horatio was leaving his office when Hernán moved out of the shadows in silence. He yanked Horatio toward him by his left arm.

"I hope you haven't lied to me. Malinalli did not show at her hotel. Are you playing games with me because you are under her feminine spell?"

A startled Horatio stammered with a wobbling chin, "What? No, not at all. In fact, I was going to tell you but haven't had the chance. She changed where she is staying last minute, but she didn't say where. I tried to get it out of her."

"And you didn't bother to let me know the very instant you knew?"

"Look, I'm sorry. I must work as well. I've done everything you've asked. If it helps, she said she wanted to visit the museums tomorrow."

A sneer spread across Hernán's face. Knowing Malinalli from his extensive research of her new life and from his life with her before, there was only one place he could be certain she would be at. This would be a job for John.

Horatio fumbled with his briefcase. "Can I go now? Please don't hurt my family."

"You may go now, but I'm not done with you just yet. Your primary concern right now is serving me." Hernán flashed him a fanged grin and dug his nails into Horatio's forearm to reinforce his point.

Horatio nodded. "Understood."

Just as hard as Hernán had pulled Horatio to him, he thrust him away before slipping into the shadows again.

After all Hernán had accomplished for Christ and crown, nearing the end of his life, he did not want to lose his position as a man who did what others could not or would not do. At sixty years of age he had severe bouts of illnesses, but still he fought to keep his name in good standing, and he always desired more wealth.

Despite not being the man he was when he first sailed to the shores of the New World, he decided he would try one more campaign for glory. Not God. God had enough. He would find glory, or he would be met with death. He was going to die soon anyway from the cough that would not end.

It was time to ask himself: How did he want to be remembered?

He arrived back in the New World with no fanfare in what had once been the capital under Montezuma. A captain named Fernando who spoke like he came from a decent family greeted him with respect. He knew of Hernán, but as a figure from the past. Fernando was half his age.

"Señor, it is good to meet you. Your exploits made our path easier. But you should be retired with your feet up and drinking good wine."

Hernán didn't know how to explain to a young man the restlessness of old age and facing one's mortality. At one time he was young, and he'd thought he could have it all. "Well, once an explorer, always an explorer. I wanted to leave this world with one more memory."

Fernando gave him a warm, if not condescending, smile. "These savages still do not know their place. A few have become animalistic. The stories I have heard . . . We leave at dawn for a raid. You are welcome to come, though at your age . . ."

Hernán hated aging. It was a frustrating fact of life. He wanted another lifetime to accomplish more. "No, I have done this for more years than you have been alive. Wake me and I will come along."

"As you wish."

Fernando led him to a clean place to sleep. If he wanted a slave, they were at his disposal. When Fernando left, Hernán looked around at his small hut, amazed how time passed and cared little for men. He was no one now.

The raid, like so many others, turned bloody. In the heat of battle he noticed a native man. This warrior was not just any man—he drank blood. In the fury of the fight, he watched as this man tore into the necks of the Spanish soldiers, then pulled their bodies out of sight. He ate and drank like an animal.

Hernán could not believe the sheer power of this man. His muscles glistened with beaded red sweat, and his eyes were furious enough to scare anyone into running in the opposite direction. And the soldiers did.

As the warrior was distracted in consuming a soldier, he was shot multiple times in the chest and head. He tried to flee into the jungle. Cortés followed him, shouting at the pursuing soldiers to leave *him* to find the warrior. Hernán could hear the ragged breathing of the man, who crouched in the dirt. As the young warrior, who couldn't be more than sixteen, attacked him, Hernán thrust his sword into his chest. The youngster bared sharp teeth as Hernán attempted to pull out the sword.

"Tell me your secret! What are you?" screamed Hernán before bursting into a coughing fit.

The young warrior let out a howl through gritted teeth, "Eztli!"

Hernán knew that word. Blood. Sangre. He touched his lips. Maybe these people had other secrets besides gold. They were heathens and not brothers in faith.

Hernán knew he was dying anyway. He pulled the sword out of the warrior's heart. The large wound released a flood of rich, blackish-red blood. Hernán scooped a mouthful in his hands and drank as the vampire warrior crumpled to the ground. Hernán's body stiffened as he felt his muscles tense and convulse. Urine covered his trousers before he felt himself falling next to the warrior in a fit of excruciating pain. Then the world he knew as a human man went black.

He woke up as something else, not believing how good he felt. His muscle tone seemed revived without effort. Although he was sixty-two and had faced ill health, he could have been a man in his twenties. His ability to breathe without difficulty had returned.

That was in 1547. Immediately after awaking, he returned to Spain to fake his death and become someone else, to start again on his journey to riches.

But being in business with John Hawkins meant Hernán couldn't just do what he wanted all the time. He missed the freedom of savagery, the freedom he'd felt when he watched villages and temples burn because of the power he wielded. These days he needed to suppress his true nature while he reclaimed his wealth. But that nature needed a release, and desire roared between his temples.

If Malinalli's blood wasn't as pure as he suspected, he would not have bothered to go through all the trouble of luring her to London. He also could have gone after Cuauhtémoc, who still walked the earth in Mexico; however, he was a big shot and heavily protected, with eyes and ears everywhere. And Hernán knew he would not come out alive if he attempted to attack

Cuauhtémoc, considering their history—Cuauhtémoc would see to it that he would be skinned alive.

No, it had to be Malinalli. She was a loner, without the kind of protection that made Cuauhtémoc a hard target. It was clear from his reconnaissance that Malinalli did not associate with other vampires. Her only real companions were her work and herself. And killing other vampires to sell their bodies wasn't just about the money; the hunt made it all the more delicious. He enjoyed his work. And that is why he'd created his perfect plan. Now that he couldn't sail the oceans in exploration anymore, stalking was his own reward.

When he first began gathering more information about her, he stumbled across the rare skulls that Malinalli had been searching for in the antiquities market, making it very easy to set this trap for her. At the beginning of his plan, the hand of fate seemed to be working in his favor. Not only did Malinalli possess an emotional tie to these objects he couldn't care less about, she trusted Horatio Hutchings, the English broker she dealt with. It wasn't difficult to find Horatio, and he was all too chatty with him once he'd heard the amount of money Hernán was putting on the table.

As soon as Horatio offered the skulls to Malinalli, she'd jumped at the chance to buy them. Once again so very eager to make the sale, Horatio told Hernán of Malinalli's travel plans. Horatio didn't want the opportunity to pass any of them by. Once she finished her holiday in Ireland, she would then go straight to London to personally verify and collect the skulls. And in London was also the equipment and facility needed for the extraction. It had taken six months and a small fortune to set up the operating room in the basement of a large semi-detached terraced home. John purchased it in the nineties and renovated it over years. George thought it was an Airbnb property.

Besides the city being John's birthplace, many vampires passed through London, so it was a logical choice to set up their facility there. Later they bought a property in Budapest as their European place of operations.

Hernán knew nothing of love, even as a human. It was lost on him what people did for love or how they tore themselves apart for it. But John would often say this about George: "Not sure why that man loves me, probably because he thinks I'm not rotten to the core. Doesn't care much for history, thank God. He thinks his nice things are paid for through antique dealing and patents for anti-aging products. Let him live in bliss. He is my angel I don't deserve."

So what he felt for Malinalli wasn't desire or love. He didn't want Malinalli's beauty or companionship. Hernán had had his way with Malinalli in his human life, and now he would have her as a vampire. He would drill deep into her flesh and bone until nothing was left.

Hernán returned to John Hawkins's clinic to ensure everything was in place for Malinalli's dismemberment. It was quiet and dark. John hadn't been there recently, as his scent was almost nonexistent.

Hernán couldn't stop thinking about the two women he'd ripped apart in Ireland. The frenzy of it intoxicated him in a way being a respectable businessman and the work of dismembering vampires did not. He dismantled both female and male vampires with great care. Every step had to be precise for the line of serums John offered to his human clients. They called the product Immortalis. They kept the environment pristinely sterile to ensure no contamination. It was only one room with an electronic lock separate from the alarm system for the upper rooms of the property.

He was fighting back the urge to roam the streets to kill and feed, but the worries of the hypervigilant and all-recording modern world made him pause.

In his human life he had done as he pleased, buying and selling, keeping the native people submissive with the constant threat of death or starvation. He was surprised vampires remained known only in fiction still. They possessed so much power and could eventually overrun the humans, but he supposed total conquest was a long way away. Too many vampires and the supply of human blood would run out.

He and John had created a product yet to be released that could change everything when the time was right.

Up to now he'd maintained a sense of control over his impulsive bloodlust and desire to kill both vampire and human. He could strike a vampire target, get what he needed, and leave without getting distracted, and that had been enough for him, until the next time. But there was something about Malinalli that stoked his fire.

The empty clinic made his restlessness grow. He wasn't hungry, because he had an entire refrigerator filled with blood, yet his hunger only grew. A black hoodie hung on a hook behind the door. He wanted to hunt—he was a natural explorer. But he had to get John to start pulling his weight again. He sent him a message.

John. You must lure Malinalli to me. Stop playing with your food. I know where she will be tomorrow. Call me ASAP.

With the message sent, he could wander the streets to feed.

14

The following day, Colin and I walk the streets without holding hands. I'm still processing, needing space. Colin will have to go back to Ireland without me now that I feel certain about his intentions and my own feelings.

And I want to see Alexander. To be with him alone.

I turn my energy back to the skulls as well. When you are so close to a dream that has been out of your grasp for so long, the fear of it being snatched away is unrelenting. I even called Horatio twice to change the time of our meeting for sooner rather than later, but he didn't respond.

Surprisingly, Colin isn't hungover, and we don't speak of his half-asleep declaration. Instead, the day will be filled with museum visits. Ireland excited me because of the landscape, whereas it was the museums of London that gave me heart palpitations of pure joy.

Before entering the Victoria and Albert Museum, Colin stops at the newsagent stall on the sidewalk. The headline on one of the tabloid papers is about a gruesome murder in London. Alexander's words, *grave danger,* whisper in my ear.

"Is one of you on the loose?" Colin chuckles. I shoot him a look, feeling a jolt of anger, though from his expression he seems to be joking.

But something inside of me wonders: Perhaps I should go to the shop Alexander mentioned once I get Colin out of London. According to the short article, whoever did it knew the area well. The murder occurred in an abandoned shop on an alley with no CCTV and very little foot traffic. No forensic evidence of the perpetrator could be found. There had not been a murder with such viciousness in a very long time. The article appealed to any witnesses in the area to report anything out of the ordinary. This isn't my fight, but there were similar murders when I was in Ireland too. I shake it off, because senseless violence seems to be a way of life in the modern world, and the murders might not be related to Alexander's warning. Colin casually wraps his arm around my shoulders and kisses my cheek. "You know I'm just kidding."

I shirk his touch. "It will be a long day. Let's go." I walk ahead of him to avoid his affection. He doesn't seem to notice.

I save my heart's desire for last: the British Museum. I have many mixed feelings about it. It has the power to take me to places and meet cultures I might not otherwise encounter, especially humans with their short lives. I also know how important these items are to the people they come from, if those cultures still exist. Many of the items were collected by open robbery. They deserve to go back to their homelands. I've been trying to get our artifacts back—it is only fair others be allowed to do the same. The loan program has to improve somehow. Perhaps that could become the next phase of my mission.

The building is flooded with bright light with an oculus in

the center of the ceiling just like the Pantheon in Rome. Here you can visit every corner of the world and a large span of civilizations in a day. For me it's pure heaven: The visit fills my imagination with stories even if most of the objects in the museum belong in their respective countries, or should at least be owned by them.

I move from civilization to civilization until I find myself in the room of death. Canopic jars and mummies line every wall. The utensils by which these humans were prepared for the afterlife are on show as rusted and fragmented instruments. Wood coffins are beautifully painted with images of their inhabitants and intricate hieroglyphs. Poor Cleopatra lies behind glass, her fake eyes staring at nothing. She has been there since 1832. Seeing her small body wrapped in cloth and her painted face sent a shiver down my back. I thank the heavens I escaped that fate. My own history is still alive and biting. If only Cleopatra could have lived, with her power allowed to continue to grow and flourish. So many women in history had their lives cut short. Such a shame.

Colin doesn't seem as interested to linger over the explanations attached to each object. I want to take my time with every different part of the world found in each room. Their deities, treasures, practices, and histories spread out for me like an intellectual feast. The sheer enormity of the beauty of it all brings tears to my eyes.

Eventually Colin ventures to the café for coffee and cake. There are also more calls about his book. I can only give him a distracted, "Yeah, see you soon." Somewhere in the room that houses mummy after mummy, an unease beyond being surrounded by shrouded death creeps over me.

I feel watched and scared, even though very little scares me anymore. I've killed more than once, albeit out of necessity. I search the thick crowd of tourists snapping selfies. No one sticks out to me, but I do detect the faintest scent of dried blood and decay. I inhale and glance around more slowly. I dismiss the feeling: It just has to be my emotions and thoughts jumbled together like a mass grave. After all, my life has been very simple until now.

But as I turn to leave, a copper tang hits me, and a man stands before me. He smells like me, not human. I don't know what to say or do.

"What a beautiful surprise to find you here today. I often wander this museum reminiscing on days past, considering I am also a relic of the past. Not in a very long time have I met another. What brings you to my city and this fantastic institution today?"

I open my mouth to speak but pause, feeling suspicious. He is a decently handsome white man with green eyes and light brown hair swept neatly across his forehead. If I had to give him a human age, I would predict at least forty based on the creases on his forehead, at the corners of his eyes, and around his mouth. His fingernails are cut short and clean, and his hands appear soft. Based on the way he speaks I assume he is, as Horatio would say, *very posh* and educated. His Barbour jacket and Church's shoes appear to be in pristine condition. I knew of these things from Horatio, whom I met a few times during his business trips to New York City.

All of these details I evaluate like I would an artifact to gauge its worth and authenticity. I still don't trust him, especially after my encounter with Alexander. None of it makes sense. Why would anyone want to kill me? And I've never seen this man before. All these years I kept to myself to avoid more violence. "It's nice to make your acquaintance, Mr. . . ."

"None of that, please." He leans in closer to my ear to prevent anyone near us from listening in. "We are extended family bound by blood and marrow. You can't get much deeper than that. Call me John."

I remembered Alexander asked me if I knew a John Hawkins. My guard is up, but I can't exude panic. "Call me Mali."

"That is a unique name. Have you been to the lower floors with the Mesoamerican art? I'm sure you could write the descriptions better than any of the historians here."

"How did you guess?"

"Come now, we have years of practice sussing out who is who. And there are not many like you here. Call it an educated guess, with that turquoise-and-gold pendant hanging around your neck. It doesn't appear to be something you could buy at Camden Market."

I clutch at my neck. He is educated and very good at paying attention to detail. It is true the pendant is one of the treasures I salvaged. I had the back reinforced with platinum so it could be strung as a necklace. "You have a very good eye."

He crooks his arm for me to come closer to him. "Would you join me for a stroll?"

I look around the room, trying to detect any other vampires or Colin. John notices my reluctance to fully engage with him. "Don't worry, I can smell human on your skin. I have no desire to bed you . . . I just wish to enjoy the pleasure of meeting another one like us."

I smile to be charming. "I know. I can smell a male human on your skin."

He matches my charm and offers his arm again with a friendly nod.

To not alarm him, I take his arm. This is obviously his home. He has to know I don't mean to encroach on whatever he has going on in London and am just passing through. There is no need for a fight. Perhaps he will reveal his intentions.

"I suppose it could be a treat exploring this museum with someone who might have been alive when it was being built?"

He throws his head back and laughs. "Not far off. The doors opened in 1759. I'd never ask a lady her age; however, I suspect you go even further back than that."

I give him a smile and allow myself to walk with him. I also feel the need to give him a very small warning. "I am older than you, with perhaps more experience in bloodshed. I'm not here to cause any trouble, but if it should find its way to me, I am more than prepared."

He continues to look into the mummy-filled glass cases with a smug smile on his lips. Goddamn vampires can be hard to read, but small sparks of information filter through my senses.

"Noted. Do you like the Egyptian room? It makes me feel closer to God when I am here. Here *we* are, two of Osiris's children. We are the resurrection. Isn't that the most amazing thing? It saddens me we have lost the art of ritual and death."

He is right. Ancient civilizations always captured my imagination over more modern history or art.

"Yes, in my line of work I have returned many items to their rightful places or at least to collectors with some connection to ancient objects or works of art. It is very gratifying and lucrative. I have a wonderful post-resurrection life. At least now. It wasn't always easy," I say.

We stop when we arrive at the mezzanine with the staircase leading down.

"I'd very much like to hear more about it. I know you are entertaining a human, or at least feeding from him in some kind of mutual transaction. But would you like to join me tonight?"

"Thank you for the invitation. I am also here on business. As I said before, I do not mean to interfere with your territory."

"If you change your mind, then take this. May I ask where you are staying?"

He reaches inside his jacket and pulls out a white card with a phone number embossed in black. I take it to not be rude.

"Thank you. I will consider it." I ignore his last question.

He pauses, hoping for an answer. When none is given, he takes my hand that's holding the card and gives it a gentle kiss. The coldness of his lips makes my hand jerk away slightly as if his saliva has permeated my skin and frozen inside my veins. It's not so much the temperature as the energy between us. He might be younger but has killed more than me, has watched others die. He makes me feel seasick. Was he a sailor?

"May this not be goodbye, Mali."

He turns and walks into the selfie-taking crowd.

That is the last thing I expected to happen on this journey. Another vampire encounter? But when I was home I'd become so out of the loop with vampire dealings on the other side of the ocean. Of course, I will not go to meet him. He gave me the creeps despite appearing perfectly normal on the surface. And having had very little exposure to other vampires, I don't want to risk a fight.

I continue my walk through the rest of the rooms, looking over my shoulder without any reason—there is no longer any trace of his presence or scent. When I reach the end of my wandering, I stand in front of the Lindow Man. In life he was a poor human who fell into a bog with all his time, thoughts, and energy coming to an abrupt end as he curled into a fetal position. But that was not the end of his story or his time in history, because now he lies forever preserved as a petrified sack of leathery skin behind a case with millions of people looking upon him at his moment of death. If I hadn't taken the chance to emerge from hiding through the centuries, I would have become a walking, talking Lindow Man. For a human he is a reminder of what awaits beyond this life and the cost of not living. It reminds me there is no time to waste leaving Colin and finding Alexander, especially after meeting John.

When I finish the top floor, I meet Colin at the café before leaving at sunset. He wants something fresh for his dinner, so we plan to stop at the corner shop near the flat. The entire journey is uncomfortable. Colin is rambling on about his career while I try to still myself to discern what is real and what is in my mind.

Something is off: I felt it first in Ireland when I walked away from the park after my feed, and then here I am, meeting a very friendly vampire in the museum. It makes no sense. Horatio's silence also makes no sense. For weeks he has been hot and heavy for this deal and now nothing from him but crickets.

After a long ride on a tourist-packed double-decker red bus, we are back in Notting Hill. We step into a corner shop to grab Colin some food, and I browse the aisles trying to consider what steps to take next. When the food is purchased we head back to the apartment in silence; at least I am silent. Colin tries to kiss me. "I'm thinking maybe after dinner we could go straight to bed," he says.

But I pull away to avoid him again. "You can go to bed if you like. I have work to do before my meeting tomorrow." I feel too distracted for sex and no longer want to have sex with him ever again. The spell he'd cast over me has been broken, the spark of lust as hot as a wet match.

Without looking at his face I can see his disappointment.

They all feel jilted when the hot-and-heavy lover starts to be a real person. For the rest of the evening we are like the two proverbial ships passing in the night. He works in the bedroom on his writing and I in the living room taking care of my business. So much for his fantasy of me being a demon or ever having to face them in real life.

15

receive a text from the broker Horatio that the skulls have arrived from the safe deposit box and could I meet him at the office later in the evening than planned. It feels somewhat odd meeting well after hours. But Horatio has always been hungry to seal the deal. He might have been a vampire in a previous life.

And this will be our largest transaction to date for him. I spent money on what I wanted and used it to make any inconvenience or time-wasting go away. Catherine taught me the value of that. In any event, my mind needs clearing away from Colin. When I tell Colin I have to head out to meet my broker, he tosses his laptop aside, wide-eyed.

"I want to go with you," he says.

"Are you sure?" I ask, puzzled. I'm not sure why he would want to be bothered with things he had shown no interest in. The museum seemed to bore him to death.

"Absolutely. It's great material for another book."

This angers me, yet I'm glad he has said it openly. Now I know I must end things for sure in the morning. There will be no tears or love songs. We are no Dolly Parton and Kenny Rogers. It would be more like me singing "The Gambler"—that tune had always spoken to me.

However, I possess no ill will toward Colin. It has been fun while it lasted. Lessons learned, and isn't learning one of the reasons we are here on this Earth? I do my best not to show my emotions. Flippantly I add, "All right. I don't know how long this will take."

"You won't even know I'm there." Before grabbing his jacket, he takes a pencil and notepad from his backpack.

We arrive at Horatio's office, which is located on a cobbled side street near Berkeley Square. From the sidewalk, only a very faint light can be seen escaping the blinds from a single window inside the old building.

I buzz the office on an intercom box next to the door. Horatio doesn't bother to say anything, and the door emits a loud ring as it unlocks. The building is quiet as we enter. The air feels thick with lingering tension. From the bottom of the stairs I sense Horatio should not be emitting so much sweat, or fear. I don't like it. I'm about to turn and leave when Horatio calls from the second floor of the winding staircase.

I can only see his head peering down at us. "Malinalli, please come up. I have plans tonight, and I'm eager to leave for the evening. Who is your friend? I thought you would be here alone? I mean, not that it is a problem . . . uh, just not usual business."

"Hiya. I'm Colin. I'd love to ask you a few questions if I may?"

This is bad. I really don't like it. Horatio told me to meet him later and now he has plans? And what happened to Colin not making his presence felt in my meeting?

Horatio waves to Colin to come closer. "Yes, of course, but come quick; as I said, I must leave soon."

Colin is racing up the stairs. I glance around, trying to detect any other scents and looking for out-of-the-ordinary clues. My gut is telling me otherwise, however; I feel obligated to follow Colin. If something is lying in wait, he will have no chance.

I try to further brush off my worry with my thinking mind, hoping for logic to rescue me from my dark intuitions. Horatio's voice doesn't sound alarmed. But still multiple warnings sound inside of me: I can sense that his pulse is elevated, and the scent of his sweat remains strong in my nostrils. I know these are signs of deep fear because my previous victims emitted the same physical reactions when I stalked them.

Perhaps a closer look at him will alleviate my worry. I walk slowly up the stairs, still concentrating on sensing anything that would not be perceived by a human. Colin is stomping loudly and breathing heavily. Both men's heartbeats are high.

When I enter the office, Horatio is sitting at his desk, perfectly still. Immediately I know something is wrong. Although I can't see it, I can smell fresh sweat around the collar of his shirt. There is more soaking beneath his arms under his suit. His laptop is closed, and the shades are drawn. Only a small side lamp is on.

I can also feel the skulls are near. There is no mistaking their energy. I'm torn. My desire is so strong for these lost items I ignore my fear.

"Malinalli, thank you for coming. Please sit," Horatio says.

"I'm fine. Can you please show me the skulls? I want to finish my business in London as soon as possible. You know I'm good for the money. It will be in your account within the hour."

"Take a seat, please." His eyes are quivering, as are his hands. Something isn't right, and I know I have to get out. I have to let the skulls go. Centuries of searching have come to an end. But why would anyone want to harm me?

I try to give him my best smile despite a sinking feeling in my soul. I want the skulls so very badly; however, they aren't worth risking my skin for. "You know, I've had a change of heart. The seller is asking too much for something that is not theirs to begin with." I turn to leave, keeping my composure even though I want to fall to my knees and cry. "Colin, we have to go now."

"Wait! Here. They are here." Panic-stricken, Horatio reaches inside a desk drawer and pulls out a black felt bag. He opens the top of the drawstring sack and pulls it down. Both skulls stare back at me. They are exquisite enough to stop me from leaving despite knowing I should run. The emotions I experienced during my time with Chantico and my transformation come flooding back. And by some miracle the skulls are in the same perfect condition as the last time I saw them.

In a flash, I see Chantico's soft face smile at me in my mind. Then she looks off to something I can't see, raises a finger.

I catch Horatio glancing nervously toward the door, then back at me again. His eyes are wild. No longer pulled by strings of mere panic, he is filled with terror. I sense more sweat. I don't care about appearances anymore. I hate the idea of leaving the skulls, but I have to. As I move to leave, grabbing Colin hard by the wrist, I can smell a vampire before he appears in the doorway. It's a familiar scent.

A man with the darkest eyes I have ever seen stares back at me. His eyes aren't human; they are something so much darker than what inhabits a vampire. They are the color of brutality.

Hernán Cortés stands before me. He looks like something I don't think even the underworld would care to invite in.

Hernán glances at Horatio. "You can go now, meatball."

Horatio doesn't look at me twice before scrambling away. I can't move—I feel frozen in time. My brain can scarcely comprehend what my eyes and senses know is true. Many times I'd wondered how Cortés had died. But it turns out he never did.

"La Malinche, you are just as ravishing as a vampire as you were as a human."

"Fuck you, Hernán."

Hernán looks at Colin with narrowed eyes. He shows the tips of his fangs.

Colin's heartbeat races in my ears as he stands just behind me. His heart rate is dangerously high, yet I also sense curiosity and excitement. I hope it doesn't make him say or do anything stupid, because Hernán will go for the easy target first, and I know Colin would not stand a chance against him.

The only thing keeping me from attacking Hernán is that Colin is in the way, again. I don't want innocent human blood on my hands.

"What do you want? Have you not already used me enough?" I say, still struggling to understand this twist of history.

He takes a step closer, and I move my right hand behind me to force Colin to move farther away. We are trapped in the office with Hernán blockading the door. I could survive the fall out the window; however, Colin would not fall without serious injury or death.

Despite the bloody rage in his eyes, Hernán is good-looking and most likely charismatic in his day-to-day life, which has no doubt helped him go undetected as a vampire for all this time. His clothes are very expensive by the look of the fabric. A Swiss-made watch shines on his left wrist.

"I just want you, my dear. Come with me. I need your assistance, and it doesn't involve betraying your own people. After we are through you can go on with your life. Everything worked out for you. I only want a sample of your blood. C'mon now. Aren't you used to giving it up?"

His arrogance enrages me. I've been on the receiving end of countless lies in my lifetime, and I can see that this man is lying.

"What do you want with me? A sample of blood? I won't ask again. I'm no fool and I don't have to consider you a master. Why all the theatrics?"

Hernán pauses before answering me. "First, tell me who created you. I have an inkling, but I'm dying to know."

"No. When we were human I had to do what you invaders told me to do. All of us did. I don't owe you shit now. Fuck you."

Hernán is angry with impatience. I can feel the heat emanating from those pits he has for eyes. He doesn't like to be challenged. I steady myself for a fight because this won't end any other way. He must die. The Hernán I knew when we were human went to every ruthless extreme to get what he wanted. Why would he change now that he is a vampire? As a vampire I suspect he is worse.

His façade drops, and he morphs to Mr. Hyde–level wild. The thready veins around his eyes grow and throb like maggots fattened on blood. Fangs spurt saliva as he screams, "Fine! I want what is inside of your bones! I want what makes you a vampire so I can sell it to those who can pay. And I will enjoy flaying you alive."

His eyes look like a place where everything dies. They are full of all-consuming greed and hate. As I gaze into them, I detect a twitch in one of them as it glances toward Colin. I know I must react without hesitation. I lunge for Hernán as he makes a move to attack Colin. I anticipate him going for the neck like any other vampire out for blood or a fast kill, because a torn jugular will bleed out quickly. He could also decapitate him with one swift movement of the hands. But he ducks to jab a needle into Colin's thigh. I didn't anticipate that.

Colin falls to the floor and begins choking for air, his body convulsing. The cords in his neck turn bright red.

I roar without hiding any of the monstrous rage within. My fangs grow longer, and my fingers are more clawlike. "What did you do to him?"

Hernán says, "If you want your lover to survive, then you will come with me now. I will keep my word. Did I not spare your life and give you land when you married Juan? Was I not generous? He will live . . . as one of us. But his hunger for blood will be more savage. If you don't, I will kill you both."

I twist behind me to grab the crystal skull. With one swing of it, I hit Hernán on his left temple with all I have in my entire body. The unexpected blow sends him reeling, and he crashes against the window on the right side of the wall. The glass shatters upon impact. He looks bewildered by my blow.

Hernán scrambles to his feet even angrier than before. If he didn't want to kill me before, he wants to now. "I will carve you like I do to all my victims. All the people in our time together who dared resist me. People cowered and whispered my name. They still talk about me.

"But you are nothing. No one knows your history or story. History doesn't care about women like you. I am more than you could ever hope to be."

"You're right. My story has been left on a dusty shelf, but only because of people like you, small and easily threatened. And only spineless cowards murder women and children the way you did. You're a butcher! Let me show how much more of a man I am than you are."

I drop the skull and leap toward him and he in my direction. We are at each other's necks. As we grapple, the room shakes with the force of it. Furniture turns over. Frames fall from the wall. I finally have his throat. I don't just see a monster with black eyes; I see the invader, Cortés, and all the others who dared to make me call them master.

A shadow passes on the wall behind Hernán. Another vampire is here, smelling like jasmine and soil. I know that scent as well, and my eyes dart toward Alexander.

"You," I whisper.

He holds my gaze longer than I would expect in this type of situation. Finally he speaks. "I need him alive. And I will help your friend."

I am still entranced by this stranger—that is, not so much a stranger. His scent, his eyes and hair. The attraction I felt before has returned, as inconvenient as that is during a fight to the death with a man from my past and the man I wanted to drop as my lover.

Hernán uses this moment of distraction to break free from my grip. Using his body weight, he knocks past me. Alex gives me an angry look for letting Hernán go before chasing him out the door. My legs move to run—I know I could catch Hernán because I am jaguar-fast—but I hear Colin groaning on the floor. So instead of running, I kneel next to him.

Colin's eyes are rolling into the back of his head. I will have to watch him die to respect his wish not to become a vampire. The photos of his family in his office flash in my mind. My guilt hurts me like a belly that's been empty for days.

I grab a cushion from an armchair in the corner of the room to prop his head up as I turn him to his side. This is why I can't be with a human. I will always outlive them, won't experience illness or face the same dangers. In this moment I am helpless when it comes to life or death because Colin has made it very clear he doesn't want to be a vampire even in extreme circumstances.

There is stomping on the stairs outside the office, but I don't sense Hernán's scent. My head whips around to see Alex walking back into the room. The same feeling I got when I first saw him returns. My body feels hot, and I want to be close to him. I want to hear his voice, feel his ancient vampire energy. The scent of blood on his lips from his last feed is irresistible. It doesn't seem like he feels the same.

"He got away." His eyes meet mine. There is anger, bordering on rage, but this anger is not like Hernán's murderous wrath. That Alexander was unable to capture Hernán worms its way through him like a slippery eel. Every evasion and missed opportunity causes the eel to grow larger. It chips away at his confidence about ever capturing him, of good being more powerful than the true evils of the world. I feel it in his energy and see it in his eyes. This would only be experienced by another vampire. The magnetism between us is strong. Somehow fate has decided to put us in the same room.

A groan from Colin's lips brings me back from reading Alex and taking in his mysterious predator-like beauty.

"Let me have a look." Alex redirects his attention from me to the syringe still stuck in Colin's thigh. He kneels next to Colin and rips it out. He smells the needle before sticking his tongue out to taste its tip. Then he reaches into a pocket on the inside of his black trench coat and pulls out another syringe, takes the cap off, and plunges it into Colin's neck.

Colin's muscle spasms stop, but his eyes close. He looks like he is in a deep, peaceful sleep. "That should do it." As Alexander pulls his hand away, it brushes my arm. The back of his hand lingers for a moment before he fumbles to put the syringe back into his coat. His skin on mine felt cool and delicate. He is looking around like he doesn't know what to say or do next. I touch his knee. "You okay?"

He pauses before looking into my eyes. His Adam's apple moves from swallowing hard. "I am usually doing this alone and not with another . . . um, or a . . ."

I flash him a smile. "That's it?" He is still looking into my eyes when he nods with pursed lips. There is more, but he won't say it. But that is okay. I have other questions. "What just happened? Hernán Cortés is alive? What is any of this? And who are you really?" I ask.

He holds my gaze, studying me. "Why did you hesitate when I entered the room? Why did you just sit there staring at me? We had him."

I couldn't believe my ears. "Me? You were looking at me too!"

We hold each other's black-eyed gazes like when he first entered the room. In the silence, I shook off the magnetic attraction even though I was happy to see him again. I wanted to. With his face close to mine in the stillness of the office, I can see a hardness in him.

"Anyway, we need to get him out of here," says Alex, intently searching my face.

I continue to wonder about Alex and my attraction to him while also trying to understand how the hell Hernán is still alive. That is as cold as it sounds—that is where my thoughts are, even with my ex-lover lying on the floor unconscious. I try to shake off the strangeness of this unexpected collision with this vampire and pay attention to Colin. "What can I expect to happen next with Colin? What is all this?"

Alex shifts his attention as well. Our mutual spell upon each other is broken for a moment. "John and Hernán use vampire blood, plasma, and anything else to create products for humans to increase their longevity and reduce the appearance of aging. There are also concoctions they use to create vampires and harm us. I have interested clients wanting to stop their business. Also, I have a specific client who has a long-standing grudge against John."

"So what does that mean for Colin?" I ask again, not liking anything I just heard except that there were others that didn't want Hernán around.

"He should be fine. They gave him VX24—a type of venom that can produce vampire-like effects—in time. He will be sick for a few days, so take him home and make him stay in bed. Everyone reacts to VX24 differently, just like how all our vampire transitions are different."

"And you? What are you going to do?"

"I have to get back to hunting Hernán and his business partner, John. This is bigger than your history together."

"Well, you can't do it alone. He wants to kill me. I didn't live this long to be hunted and dissected by Hernán Cortés. He's mine to destroy, and I want to know who made him. It couldn't be Cuauhtémoc."

"Can't help you with that one, and I fly solo. Besides, this doesn't seem like your line of work."

I can tell Alex either wants to get rid of me or to see how quickly I will abandon him.

"No, I am not a bounty hunter, and I don't do anything like whatever it is you do, but I have connections in London with my business. He was the one selling those two skulls. Maybe I can find an electronic trail. My broker, Horatio, left his laptop behind. I will try to contact him first to make sure he is okay, then get whatever information he has."

"*If* Horatio is still alive. I would bet money that he will be dead by morning if he isn't already."

He glances back at Colin then me. "You want some help getting him back home? I'll steal a car and we can grab whatever we can from here and bundle him in the back. Then I'm off."

I nod. There is more to know about this enigmatic man. The crystal skull lies on the floor, covered in Hernán's blood. I take both skulls, considering he has zero interest in such priceless treasures. I crawl over and pick up the crystal skull. Tears sting my eyes to finally have it in hand. But what a price. Colin almost became a vampire, something he didn't want for himself. It has hardened my resolve: no more mixing with humans so intimately. I wish Chantico were here to give me her advice. The spark of her spirit alerted me to danger during the fight, and I was grateful. Perhaps holding the skulls when I am alone will give me some clarity, as it once had in Chantico's hut.

"That is an incredible piece of art." Alex's voice breaks into my nostalgia and helps me see clearly what is right in front of me. It brings me back into the present, and I remember: the blood on the skull. Hernán's blood.

"Alex, you might want to find something to collect this sample. I have his blood here. Could be good for tracking?"

Alex glances at the skull then at me. "That is an excellent idea. In fact, I was thinking the other day how much easier it would be to sniff him out if I had something tangible to work with during the hunt. He is one paranoid vampire. His business partner, John Hawkins, does a lot of the work with the human world alongside John's lover, George."

I smile at Alex, feeling slightly smug. That would show him to not underestimate me. "I guess I might not be bad to have on your side after all. I've spent a few years doing a lot of tracking myself, albeit of rare objects and not vampires. Many years I spent with Hernán. I know him."

He gives me an expression of curiosity. I even think I detect a hint of a smile, but he is too cool for that. His apprehension at completely opening up to me gives me the feeling he doesn't presume too much about people until he has tangible proof about their intentions.

"All right, get whatever you need from Horatio's office while I fetch a car. I'll be waiting outside. Be ready. You gave Hernán a good hit with the skull, so I know you're strong enough to handle your boyfriend's body."

"He's not my . . . Never mind. It's a complicated story. I'd intended to end things before all this happened. Just go. I'll see you in a minute."

Alex stood up and rushed out the door. Why did I feel the need to tell him Colin wasn't my boyfriend? I push away confusing thoughts and bundle whatever I can into Horatio's laptop carrier, including both skulls, which I carefully wrap in the black bag on the desk. I hoist Colin over one shoulder and put the laptop carrier on the other. Hopefully Alex will already be waiting outside. And he is. Seeing him gives me a sense of comfort despite the fact that we only just met.

When we arrive back at the flat, Colin moans with eyes half open. Alex and I agree to carry him in and make it look as if we are just taking care of a friend who's had too much to drink. The streets in Notting Hill are never fully empty, so we have to make the scene appear as normal as possible. Once inside the building, we carry him up the three flights of stairs. As we carry him, my hand brushes Alex's forearm, then lingers there for a moment. I don't bother to say anything. I let the touch do the talking. He glances at his arm. This time there really is the faintest hint of a smile, though it quickly straightens back to a neutral expression. Then I hurry to unlock the door. "Largest bedroom is just in the back."

Alex wordlessly takes Colin to the master bedroom to sleep

off the antidote. I slump into the sofa, my entire body and mind aching from fatigue. The sensation of my muscles' weakness creeps over me as my brain scrambles over the events of the last few hours.

Hernán Cortés is alive: the man who had kept me in captivity, used me, traded me. It is all hitting me now, and I know there is no way both of us can exist on this planet at the same time. I had once thought him dead—and I need him to stay dead.

"Have you fed?"

I look up from my daze to Alex. The last time I had fed was this past morning on Colin. All the commotion has made me forget my hunger.

"No, not recently."

"Well, I suggest you don't feed from him this entire week. I know a guy who can help you with that. Come with me."

Now that he mentions it, I realize I do want to feed. My stomach aches at the very thought of blood. "Feeding from Colin is over anyway, so it won't be an issue. Is it safe for him to be left alone?"

"He will be fine. Most likely he will be out cold until at least noon tomorrow."

"What about Hernán? That man is out to get me. It's personal with him. He won't stop until he gets what he wants."

"Hernán will regroup with John to come up with their next moves. That will keep him busy. He thought you would be an easy target. He will strike again eventually. He is a calculating control freak who likes to take his time because he knows he has time on his hands. And you injured him. If he comes for you again you need to be ready, and you can't do that in a starved state."

He is right. My body needs to be looked after while we have

this brief moment of relative safety. I take out my phone and send Colin a message on the small chance he wakes up before we return. Before leaving I double-check all the windows are locked and place his phone next to the bed along with a glass of water.

The streets are still busy at this hour as we walk deeper into Notting Hill. "Thanks for everything, Alex."

"No problem. It's my job."

"May I ask, what's your story? I know you're ancient. I can sense it."

He gives me more than a confident half smile. "You could say that. I'm just keeping my word to an old friend and weeding out the bad apples. Fulfilling my destiny while earning what I need to in order to get along in this world. And you? Just trading and selling artifacts? Sounds lucrative."

"You knew about me before?"

"Not until recently. I don't have extensive information on people unless you're a threat to others or someone wants you dead. My target was John Hawkins and his business partner, who I now know is Hernán Cortés."

"I've stayed away from violence and chaos in all forms on purpose. Now I am reclaiming my history. And yes, I've also been giving myself and others a good life."

"Hey, what I do know about you. I think . . . Well, I admire what you have accomplished. After what you experienced during the Spanish invasion, you deserve a good life."

I give him a wicked smirk. "I know."

We walk through the dark streets side by side. It somehow already feels natural being next to Alex. It reminds me of how I felt when I ran next to the jaguar. It's such a cliché, but I feel like I have always known him, as if our bodies have walked side by side before. It is the most comfortable I have felt next to someone besides Chantico. I don't know what any of this could mean; however, it was clearly meant to happen. When you have lived as long as I have, you begin to see how all events are strung together in a pattern that often creates a design you could never have imagined. Just as the moon and sun move across the sky inexorably, so do our lives move in their own patterns.

"This is the place." The small shop has one window with *Lost in Time* in gold lettering across it. Alex buzzes the doorbell. While we wait in silence our eyes naturally gravitate to each other again. As dizzy as my mind is, I enjoy looking at him and wondering about the stories he could tell me about his human and vampire lives. He is also simply beautiful to me, with his sharp jawline and disheveled black hair. Even just standing there next to him I can easily imagine being in his arms, our fangs caught in each other's shoulders because neither of us can bear letting the other go.

Before either of us speaks, the door unlocks. A friendly-looking human man in his seventies with sparse brown hair and tortoiseshell spectacles greets us. He wears the clothes of a vicar. "Is it late at night or is it very early morning?" he asks.

The two men give each other a warm embrace and pat each other on the shoulder.

"Does it matter, Maximilian?"

The man gives me a sincere smile. "This is the first time you have brought a guest, Ju . . . Alexander." His eyes quiver at both corners as he corrects what he is about to say.

If I don't know better, I think I see Alex blush as his eyes dart around the ground, not wanting to look at me or his friend. "Maximilian, this is Malinalli. We need breakfast for two."

"Sure thing. Come inside." He gives me a smile. We enter, and Maximilian walks behind the counter and through a black-curtained doorway.

"It is so nice to meet you, Malinalli. Alexander needs . . . female vampire company, in my opinion. I hope this is the start of something good for you both."

Alex looks away with a shy, boyish expression. "Waiting for the right one at the right time. Plus, I don't exactly have a fixed address anywhere." His eyes glance toward me, but I don't want to embarrass him or press. I'd rather he open up to me in his own way, so I change the subject.

"So how do you two know each other?" I ask them.

"There are a few sympathetic humans who know about us and help us out in our endeavors, especially when it comes to protecting humans from us. Maximilian was a contact I made when the previous owner of Lost in Time passed away. It's one of the few places we have around the world where humans and vampires work together to keep some sort of balance for those not wanting to drink straight from humans. Paddy was here before Max and created this space for his wife, who was turned by a rogue vampire. When he died, she took her own life."

My ears hear what he says, yet I cannot help being distracted by my surroundings. The shop is full of clocks from different eras and countries, and in eclectic styles. Some hang from two walls and from the ceiling to four feet from the floor. There is a wall of metal shelves with smaller clocks. Another wall is lined with antique grandfather clocks made from solid wood. Clocks have never intrigued me—after all, time and I have a complicated relationship—however, there are so many of them I can't stop looking at them.

As grateful as I am for all the wonderful experiences I've had as a vampire, time is what separates me from the mortal world.

Surrendering to the concerto of time and circumstance is both infuriating and humbling—and of all the lessons time teaches, letting go is the hardest. And harder yet, time sometimes just asks you to be still—to sit with your pain, regret, sadness, rage. Without this stillness, you will never be able to open your hand and release whatever you clutch too tightly.

I stand in this room with every type of instrument to tell time, and they all tell me a different hour. The numbers are a jumble. But for the man next to me, I just might be able to forget the passing of time altogether and learn true patience.

"Interesting place," I mutter.

"I know. I find it very comforting. When I'm here I feel less lost in the world. Time is everywhere in here, yet time also doesn't matter here, because it's impossible to know which clock is right. You just have to sit here and breathe." Alex has a calm expression on his face. It's as if we hadn't been in a brawl with a vampire conquistador hours before this. "Very true. I was think-ing something similar."

He holds my gaze, his lips curling to a soft half smile. "Glad I brought you here then. You are actually the first person I have ever brought here or introduced to Max."

My stomach grumbles. Now I am even more keenly aware of my hunger even though I like what he just said.

"I'm a bit confused. Do the clocks bleed? I thought this was a dinner date?"

Alex shakes his head and laughs. The distant sparkle in his eyes is so very enticing to me. "I don't date. Never have and never will. I only believe in forever."

My breath involuntarily stops in my throat when he says this. I don't want throwaway encounters anymore, and it sounds like that isn't what he is about. I want a love who believes in forever, because that is what we have as vampires. He also seems open to the possibility of lasting love. My weakened state from hunger, processing seeing Hernán again, and his words are all giving me vertigo. Could we have an impossible connection, even though we've been separated for centuries by an entire ocean, only to meet here at the exact right time?

I have to change the subject or else I'll get swept away in the churn of my thoughts. "Do you have another name? It sounded like Maximilian was about to say something besides Alexander."

"What do you mean?" He tries to play it off, but the tension in his face at my remark reveals his lie. I don't say anything else. He knows I know. "So you are one of *those* vampires? Extra senses and all. You don't miss a thing," he says.

I wag my finger at him playfully. "Don't change the subject." He wants to tell me, but the years have hardened him against vulnerability. I know what that's like so well. Behind this I sense a yearning for someone to open the door to welcome him home.

I place my hand on his hand. In my left ear I can hear Maximilian's stomach sloshing and his breathing as he stands behind the curtain listening to us. From what he said when we met, I wonder if he is hoping for there to be a spark between Alex and me.

"Please tell me. I want to know you."

He pauses. His eyes dart toward the curtain, sensing Maximilian. "You can come out now," Alexander says.

Maximilian shuffles out with two silver pouches of blood in each hand. "You don't get it until you answer the lady's question. Let someone besides me get to know you. I like this woman."

Alex shakes his head, but he looks relieved at the prospect of laying down whatever he's been hiding from me. He pauses with his lips slightly parted before he confesses, "My real name is Judas."

"As in . . . from the Bible? Judas Iscariot?" I ask. He sips on his blood pouch as he glances at a beaming Maximilian.

"I am indeed the one. Every story needs a 'villain,' and it rarely covers their perspective."

I was not expecting that. This day could not be more of a mindfuck. "Wow. I remember when I first heard about you from the Spanish missionaries who forced us to convert. The ones who wanted us to feel the flames of hell because we had different beliefs and were considered savage. I secretly thought all the damnation and self-loathing we were forced to learn through the invader's religion was all bullshit."

"There is a lot in that 'holy' book that was twisted and told in a way to serve the ones who used it like a sword."

"Well, I am called La Malinche. I know how you feel. People call me a traitor without knowing what it was like to be traded."

"When we met in Horatio's office I knew the name Malinalli from history." He leans closer to me and touches my arm. His gaze sinks into me like a bite. "I'm sorry for what happened to you and your people. Everyone that happened to. It's sick manipulation of free will exerted. I am happy you are still here and not left in the past."

"I appreciate the sentiment. Thank you. But what is your true story? I want to know."

I can feel Maximilian staring and smiling at us. "I will leave you two kids to enjoy your meal."

We don't notice him leave. Alex takes a deep drink from the paper straw in the blood-filled pouch and I do the same before stopping. I remember a tarot reader at Woodstock who showed me the Two of Cups card. She was so confident in her reading and what she told me despite my misgivings. But it stayed with me because leaving Mexico for the first time to explore the world was such a significant period in my life as a vampire. Out of curiosity, I looked up the interpretation: It means harmonious union or partnership based on deep understanding. This partnership is not always romantic; however, the reader made it clear that for me it would be. The reading had not come true until now: because there we were, sharing our cups of blood, sharing our stories. He turns to face me while placing his blood pouch down.

"I only did what had to be done. My duty—what he asked me to do himself—was to give him over to his fate. This was over a last supper of his *own* blood in a chalice.

"I pleaded with him. When he did not waver, I had to sit alone for days in utter stillness until I could surrender to my fate. And surrender I did, for love. For the teaching of time-defying love so humanity would be less heinous and people would treat others better, with real kindness.

"But unlike the story, I didn't hang myself. Instead, I became what I am now. There is an entire other Bible that could be written about the days leading up to when I was supposed to be the betrayer. Let me just say this: People shouldn't wonder why his tomb was empty when searched. How did the large boulder too heavy for a human to move get rolled away? You draw your own conclusions. Humans don't really understand life after death."

I sit there in utter rapture as my vampire companion tells me these secrets of his past. Our past—because these are the secrets behind the stories that had been brought over to my part of the world and then used to tell us that we were less worthy than our paler *Christian* counterparts. "If *he*, the one crucified then risen because he was one of us, is out there somewhere . . . Keep going, I want to know more."

"After his 'death' I traveled to a place Jesus instructed me to find, called Akeldama, which translates as 'The Field of Blood.' There I met a stranger. He said he had been waiting for me. His name was Hamish. Hamish offered me eternal life blood to carry on the work of benevolence and justice.

"I remember it so clearly: The man sat alone looking at nothing at all, but with a gentle smile on his face. It was a look of tranquility like nothing I had ever seen. He made me a vampire, then once my transformation was complete, I saw him preparing to leave.

"I had thought Hamish was going to be my new teacher after Jesus, so I asked, 'Where do we go now?'

"He laughed and said, 'Where we are going, we are not going together. You must learn to follow yourself for a time. You do not need to follow another right now.'

"After everything that had happened, the thought of being alone was a bit of a gut punch. But then Hamish told me I would eventually understand why—and ended by saying something profound that has always stayed with me:

" 'If it was not important for you to embark on this journey alone at the start, you would have done something different along the way. You are the map now.'

"I watched Hamish take up his wineskin filled with animal and human blood mixed with a dash of his own to prevent the animal blood from coagulating. Then he got up and left. Some teacher. How would I know how to access this so-called inner map? There was nothing I could do but walk and see where my steps led me.

"And so when Hamish left me, I wandered through the desert in despair with nothing but the clothes on my back. Loneliness ate at my soul. Part of me wanted to not drink blood and simply die, until I stumbled upon a Bedouin camp.

"At last I was not alone! My thirst was great, but there was no way I would drink from any of them. The words that kept replaying in my mind were 'Drink from me. My blood is in this cup.' But still I would not drink from them. I hesitated, licking my lips as I could hear their heartbeats in the distance like a drum calling to me. I didn't know what to do, fearing what I was and my thirst for blood.

"Then a miracle occurred. Before entering their camp, before anyone spotted me, a camel not tied with the rest in the camp wandered toward me. It kneeled, with its neck outstretched. I looked around to see if anyone was nearby. Then I drank from it. It helped clear my mind of my aching thirst.

"And it wasn't just the blood—it was that the camel had given it to me as an offering. When I had enough, the camel got up and wandered back to the camp. This stirred the inhabitants.

"Upon seeing me, they welcomed me, even though they could see I had nothing to offer them. My heart stirred with a blazing joy at their generosity after feeling alone for so long. That night, we laughed and chatted in the firelight. Because the camel had quenched my thirst, I had no instinct to harm them. Being alone in the desert made me appreciate these strangers even more.

"That night they offered me my own tent. I lay there, trying to figure out where I would go next. It occurred to me perhaps I should ask to stay with them, but that was not the divine purpose for my meeting them, as I would discover. It was a preparation for something else—like so many things we experience in life.

"Early in the morning, before dawn, the animals began to make noises. Then there were screams of both animal and human. I jumped to my feet. The camp was under attack. I tried to find where the attackers were until one stood before me, blood splattered across his clothing and face.

"He was just a mortal, yet the sight of him filled me with fear because of the blades in his hands. I had never killed anyone before or even thrown a single punch. The rest of the Bedouins had already fled in the dark. And I couldn't quite see well in the darkness—my vampire vision had not kicked in yet.

"I opened my mouth to cry out, which must have revealed my protruding fangs. After seeing my transformation, the man ran, but I did not chase him. What would be the point with the damage already done? When dawn broke, I assessed the slaughter. Streaks of blood led away from the camp then stopped. At the end of the trail, I found no corpses.

"I burned the Bedouins' possessions and said a prayer. At that point, my path was set: I would chase down anyone doing dark work, like the men who attacked the camp. And I was also resolved to find the dark side of what we are, and what happens to our gifts when corrupted. Like Hernán and John.

"And I have also made sure I am never caught off guard again. That is why I have been alone and in solitude. I also never imagined anyone would understand what I do or who I am.

"Now you know my story and my true name. But please call me Alex or Alexander."

They say when you know you have met the one, you just know. Once Alexander has finished his story, I know. Here is the love of my life.

Everything I had been searching for now stands before me, but it's come to me in the most unexpected, and nearly tragic, way. After all, to say the least, the circumstances of our meeting could have been better. I think of Colin, and I'm thankful that he's alive, but also that I met him: Had I not been open to our brief affair, I might not have been open enough for this.

I never wanted to be a vampire. Having myself be the love of my life for centuries has made me more guarded than I should have been, and way-station lovers have made my heart grow yet colder. I don't want to say these affairs, most especially the one with Colin, gave me nothing, because now I feel prepared to . . . at least to not fuck up what might be possible with Alexander.

I've hunted treasures my whole life, and now I've learned that the greatest treasure in my life is another vampire. My heart burns brighter and dances to the winds of love stirring inside of me. I wonder if he feels it too. The glances, touches, the energy only another vampire would feel because they are so subtle. I would see if he would stay with me. I think that would tell me what I want to know.

Then I have to catch myself: When I think more closely about it, I can barely stop from gasping at the realization we are both misunderstood, solitary, and mysterious figures from history. We've been called many names. We are one and the same. Maybe we can understand each other with a silent recognition. Stardust brought together. Time will tell.

I wonder if he knew about Cuauhtémoc or encountered him before. If I had followed him I could have been the type of vampire Alexander hunted. My maker had turned to the dark side of our gifts. History made him cruel and callous. His benevolence transformed to greed. This is part of Alex's mission.

Max returns to the front room, beaming. I know he has been listening the entire time. "Here is a little something for the road. Now I must get you two out of here. I need my beauty rest." He hands us two more pouches of blood.

"Got it. Thanks, Max. See you tomorrow." Before we leave the shop, I look around one more time and realize: None of the clocks work. Every single one is frozen.

As we leave the cluttered shop where time stands still, I know I don't want this to be goodbye even for the night. Not giving a damn how thirsty I will appear, I blurt, "You've got a place to stay in London? I guess you don't crash with Max."

He opens the door for me. "No. I usually stay elsewhere for his own protection in the event someone wants to harm me. Something always presents itself when I need it."

I look up, feeling a light rain hitting my cheeks and lips. It's perfect. "You can't wander the streets in this weather. Why don't you stay with me?"

He doesn't look surprised at my offer, and I know he will say yes. "I don't want to break up your romantic getaway with Colin."

"It isn't. Not anymore. Just friends."

I want to add, *You and I are just friends, but I want to see if we can be something more.*

He steps closer and shakes his head as he pulls a small retractable umbrella from his pocket. It's one of those cheap ones you find outside tourist shops with low-quality printed images of Big Ben and red phone booths. He also gives me a playful smile. "You work fast, Malinalli. You already broke that human's heart. Bet you eat them for breakfast."

I lick my lips. "No. I just know what I want and what I don't want. I was looking for something and snatched the first thing on the shelf that looked like it would satisfy."

"What were you looking for?" His voice is deeper, softer. As he says this, I can sense his soul swimming just behind them. It pulls me to him. He is the siren in the sea calling me to jump in headfirst. My feet take a step closer to him as the rain finds its way to us.

I want to say, *You. Every damn inch of you. Right down to all the flyaway hairs on your head blowing in the night breeze.* Not a damn thing has made sense on this trip except this moment.

"We should go," I say instead. Without pressing for an answer to the question he just asked, he nods in agreement and brushes away hair that has flown around my face from the wind. We begin to walk back to the flat. "How did you get involved with antiquities? I'm guessing that is how Hernán found you."

Now that is something I don't mind telling him. "We will need a lot of time for that."

A genuine smile crosses his face, and there are lovely creases at the corners of his eyes from the desert sun when he was human. I want to touch them and kiss them. But I can't do that now. Not yet.

"It's a good thing we have pretty long lives and the walk back isn't exactly short."

This is the first time I can be honest with anyone since Chantico died. I won't leave out details I never talked about to anyone. It doesn't feel like oversharing. In my heart I know if anyone can understand me it is Alex.

16

Without anywhere to be or anything to do, I remained in silence in Chantico's hut. I simply watched the sun rise until it was time for the moon to take its place in the sky. The weaving kept my mind from wandering needlessly, tormenting me with questions and cursing all the wrong I had done and had witnessed.

Most of the time I felt robbed of both my sanity and joy, even though I tried at the very least to be grateful I was still alive. But the grief had to be felt until it passed. Chantico's quetzal feather grounded me. With my fingertips I caressed its softness and placed it behind my ear. My soul needed faith, and so I said a prayer in my mind for stillness. When I detected humans passing by the hut, I hid in the trees, but otherwise I did not move during the day.

Only at night did I venture out to catch glimpses of my daughter. It wouldn't be long until, like Martin, she would be sent to Spain to marry. I snuck into the rooms of sleeping Spanish soldiers and fed upon them.

I would sit on their backs so they could not see me, and with one hand hold their windpipes tight enough to restrict their ability to scream. But unlike them, I showed mercy to my victims: I drank from them, but I didn't kill them. Well, it was not exactly mercy. If too many died the villagers would be blamed and executed, so I held back from killing them in order to keep some semblance of peace.

During one of my excursions, I happened to stumble upon a death that would change my fate forever.

The scent hit me first. It was the aroma of rich blood freely flowing. My belly ached while my teeth grew in response to the scent of blood. I had to follow it. As the scent became stronger so did my desire; it consumed me. The smell of blood was so much more intoxicating than a beating heart and sweaty skin.

Under a crescent moon I saw six bodies moaning, slurping with the occasional loud croak and gurgle. Blood filled the atmosphere with a savory precipitation. The bodies parted, sensing my presence. I gasped at the sight before me. It was Cuauhtémoc, the two vampires I previously met, and three new ones. Hanging by their wrists from a tree were three Spanish soldiers, their heads slumped to their chests. Gaping, oozing holes could be seen where their hearts should have been. Seeing the mouths of the vampires stained red, I didn't have to imagine what had happened to the soldiers.

Cuauhtémoc gave me a welcoming grin that did not match the gruesomeness of that scene.

"Have you had a change of heart, Malinalli? I can feel your hunger . . . how it burns inside. Come and take sustenance. You will grow very weak soon."

The glistening blood smeared across his mouth and his tur-quoise septum ring and dripping down his bare chest whetted my appetite and stirred my anger. But I didn't move.

"I have not been looking for you, if that is what you are asking."

"Malinalli, we are creatures of lust now, the very thing their priests talk endlessly about, yet here we are greater than them or their god. Kill them all you want. They have given us nothing less. Why not return the favor in kind?"

My dry mouth attempted to swallow. "You don't have to tell me any of this. I know that book they call the Bible and the empty words and promises it gave us. All I want is to see my daughter. And are you trying to get them to start a hunt for us? These soldiers will be missed."

"Come and drink first. Then we can discuss. And I've learned my lesson. I wait now until the transformation of these new blood drinkers is complete, and each one can realize their true radical power in our vicious appetite."

His eyes sparkled as he said this. His eyes flared with a fervor no different from that of the Spanish priests talking about hell and Judas's betrayal of Christ.

"I said no."

Cuauhtémoc walked closer to me. A serene rage had taken over his eyes, a permanent intention to inflict indescribable pain on others.

"Why are you so stubborn? Why still hold on to your human-ity? Let it go. You will find happiness and peace."

"But my daughter . . ."

"What about her? Did you give yourself freely to any of those men, including her father? I had a child once. How cruelly he was taken from me by the disease. *Their* disease. But death spared him all of this, and I can move forward as something great to honor him. To avenge him. And I know you can't truly hold an attachment to a child you did not choose to have.

"You know the time will come when you have to hide all you are. Once you step foot out from that hut and into the real world of humans you will need to be one of them, operate like them. Embrace the monster inside you, and you can be free."

"Is it so bad I want to carve my own space and not be a follower?"

His eyes narrowed. "I don't want to live not actively fighting. You make your own choices."

"Why did you save me? Was I the child you couldn't save from disease?"

A slice of moonlight hit his eyes long enough that I could see him soften. He said, "Just go, but I will give you another gift. It will keep you out of our way and from preventing us from reaching our goals."

He walked back to the hanging bodies being consumed by the other five vampires. He kneeled on the ground to retrieve something I could not see from a leather satchel. Then he stood and reached into the chest of one of the bound humans and ripped out the heart. As he walked closer, I could see the item from the satchel looked like a map.

"Here, take this heart and another priceless item." With his other hand he held a map with notes. "I left other treasures from our people before they could be stolen or destroyed. Find those skulls too. They belong to us. And then I want you to eat the heart. You will die otherwise. He died by my hand and not yours. This is my last gift of blood to you. But if you should call in the future, I will answer as long as you have not made an enemy of me."

I felt in my hands the folded amate with the map drawn on it. This alone was a treasure. "Thank you. I will do my best."

For a moment I hesitated before taking the heart as well. If I left the hunger unchecked, it would overwhelm me and cause me to do something stupid. "Thank you for the sustenance. May we never be enemies even if we do not agree."

The thick muscle released a swell of blood into my mouth, and I instantly felt a wave of calm energy throughout my body.

He nodded before I walked away. I glanced at the bodies one last time, my hunger causing tears to form in my eyes, because if he continued to kill like this they would send out search parties. I still feared the conquerors more than I believed in my own power or worth. I turned from Cuauhtémoc and walked in the opposite direction.

I spent years alone in the hut away from everyone. My longest journey was to the secluded stream. I lay in the water, allowing the flow of the current to tug at my body, lick it clean. How it made me moan with joy. There was nothing else I could do but allow the current to keep my mood somewhat buoyant. Not a worry or thought crossed my mind as I allowed the water to befriend me in its luscious embrace.

At the age of six my daughter was sent back to Spain like Martin, to be married off eventually into an aristocratic family who could supply Juan with a large dowry he would inevitably squander. Despite having immense physical power, I felt powerless to help her in the way that mattered in our world at that time.

I did not find out what happened to her until I showed up at the hacienda one night, and Patli embraced me without saying a word. I knew the time had come. There was no way I could see her again without doing something I would regret, so I thanked Patli and walked back into the forest. Except for the map, the tiny hut, and myself, I had nothing.

It had to be enough. I prayed to the glowing moon, gray as a rabbit skin: *Please let me be enough on this road.*

For a space of time no one bothered me, not even the priests.

Knowing them, I made sure to place a large, roughly made crucifix in front of the hut so they would not mistake me for what they called a savage bruja. My appearance was unkempt, so no one would mistake me for a woman to be used for pleasure. Though my outer appearance matched my inside, it was also a cocoon as I continued to discover more about myself alone as a woman and a vampire.

There were larger villages for slaves to be taken from, and when I sensed any Spanish in my vicinity I hid. I stayed at the hut until I had no other choice but to flee to the Petén Basin.

Because one day, despite my precautions, the Spanish ransacked my hut. From the trees I could see them approaching with a string of slaves tied together with sisal ropes. The slaves' bodies were full of pumping blood, but there was no soul behind their eyes. Their souls died when they became captives. Unfortunately, there were also more soldiers than I could take on alone.

As I watched them destroy Chantico's hut, did I feel animosity or the deepest of sorrows that no words in any language could articulate? My fury silenced me so completely it was as if my tongue had been removed.

For a moment I even doubted my decision to rebuff Cuauhtémoc. This was a clear reason to take up arms—in that moment, I truly understood him. But part of me also felt completely defeated as I clutched tightly to my chest the map that revealed Cuauhtémoc's hidden treasures. The world was in a putrid imbalance: It always seemed to hold more soldiers and masters than those who could make a real difference.

At the same time, the paper in my hands felt more real to me than what their flesh would feel like as I ripped them to pieces. I made my decision: I would retreat and do what I could in silence. But also: no more holding back my hunger.

If my enemies crossed my path, they would all die.

And so I made my way to the Yucatan, the Petén Basin.

It was one of the last places the Spanish couldn't conquer right away. The people there fought hard from their base inside the thick and dark jungle. It was there I lost the last of my shyness when it came to consuming every and any Spanish who made their way into the darkness of the trees. Villagers and warriors never saw me, but they did hear the screams of the soldiers and knew to stay away. *Was it a jaguar or some other beast sent by the gods stalking the jungles?* they asked themselves, even though, by the looks on their faces when finding the bodies, it didn't matter to them. They feared what they couldn't see and left it at that.

I gave up the solitary life of weaving for the solitary hunt. In those instances when I needed sustenance or I could kill invaders without harm to myself, I allowed myself to feed the way Cuauhtémoc had been teaching his disciples. The map Cuauhtémoc gave me I hid in a cave next to a cenote I would dive into after my kills to wash myself. I let the light of the full moon be absorbed into my bare flesh as I floated on the surface of the water. All the guilt, loneliness, and hunger I felt were released into the night.

Beneath the new moon I drew the darkness closer to me. The new moon reflected what I harbored inside, and I felt at home there in its light. Again I spent that time in stillness, in darkness, with myself, as Chantico had taught me. I found how to be good and happy in my light and shadow.

Not far from the cenote and far from the villagers, I built a small hut. It soothed me to have a space similar to the one I had shared with Chantico. When the priests or soldiers were asleep, I would hover over them like a dream and take their blood.

Some I did leave for dead, and others I allowed to live. Whatever wealth my victims had on them I buried with the map. Their bodies I discarded for the animals to finish off or for someone else to find. It really depended on how benevolent I felt that day. I also took some less valuable items I found on my victims and stored them for reasons I did not know. I just knew in the pit of my soul I didn't want them to take everything from us. Eventually, however, even the Petén Basin was conquered by the Spanish.

Our world had finally been taken in its entirety.

Time passed, and I wandered to the more crowded villages that turned into towns. As the times changed, so did the style of dress. I wasn't a complete hermit. When I ventured out I attempted to blend in. There were shoes, ribbons, and clothing that caught my eye. Despite not interacting with many, at times it felt good to be part of a community, at least part of the Indigenous community that remained.

It was around the nineteenth century I first heard the tale of the Chupacabra. I had to laugh because it was probably based on me or perhaps even Cuauhtémoc and his band of vampires killing in the night. If it wasn't, then I wanted to see this creature with my own eyes.

In 1846 it all changed again. There had been civil wars, through which I had been able to remain in my own space and world, but this war was different: It was the Mexican–American War. The United States had annexed part of Mexico. This would not have stirred anything inside of me, except Mexico had only just become free from Spain in 1821. I had witnessed the huge losses our people suffered in the fight for independence from

Spain, and now this: Were there new conquerors looking for a conquest and coming to our land?

My old fears resurfaced. *Not again,* I thought. I couldn't live through another invasion or more slaughter, or see more of our valuables, more of our culture, stolen. I didn't know what I could do, so I did what Chantico would have done. She would have danced or prayed beneath the moon. And there was one I knew I wanted to visit me again because she had guided me to Chantico.

And so I prayed to the goddess Malinalxochitl to send me another dream or vision.

The first night there was nothing. The following morning, I wandered through nearby villages and towns to hear whatever news I could about the war and America. As usual, I passed through with the invisibility of a ghost as I kept to the shadows of the buildings and trees and didn't interact with anyone unless I had to. I made no eye contact.

It was always a strange experience to walk among humans like this. I had watched them live and die as their society evolved. There were shopkeepers in local towns I saw from afar age over the years, yet I stayed the same. We looked alike, human, but were very different because they were my prey, and the things that made them vulnerable physically no longer concerned me. Another invasion did concern me. Being enslaved or hunted again made me feel on edge. The one thing I did know for sure was that I needed to learn the language of that place called America. I could read and write Spanish with ease because of my position with Cortés, although I learned how to read during my pregnancies when their fathers left me alone. Then I would coax the priests back then to teach me how to write.

When I returned from town I settled next to the English-language newspapers I had taken to read later. I lay in front of the small fire I built in front of my hut, wondering what new cycle this burgeoning war was beginning. My gaze fixed on the jumping flames and the smoke rising to the moon. Without realizing it, I closed my eyes at some point.

"Malinalli," someone said.

I could feel myself jolt upright, hearing a voice not my own or human. Sitting across the fire were the goddess Malinalxochitl and Chantico. I looked around then back at them. Tears began to well in my eyes at seeing Chantico. I had missed her company so very much. "I know I don't sleep, so this can't be a dream. Are you really here?"

She gave me her familiar comforting smile. The goddess stood behind her with her hands on Chantico's shoulders. Both looked the same as I remembered them.

"This is me reaching out to you for a moment in time thanks to the energy of the blessed Malinalxochitl here. So I am here in spirit, but not in flesh."

"Someone took your skulls. I'm sorry."

"They are no longer mine, my dear. I have no need for such things. But that is not why you have been trying to summon us."

"What should I do? I am afraid of this war. Is it happening again? More people invading the land?"

Ever so patient, Chantico gave me her warm tone as she spoke and smiled. "I don't know what is happening with the goings on of men, but you should do what you were gifted at doing."

"Being passed around? Used? Or bleeding them dry?"

"You know that is not true. That is your doubt and fear speaking. You have been in hiding for a long time, truly dead to the world. If you want a change, then get to your feet and find it."

"But what? I'm so lost!" I hung my head because none of this made sense. And in some ways I wanted her to tell me what to do with exact directions and coordinates. As if she could read my mind, Chantico spoke again. "Many things have been lost. Maybe it is time they are found. But start with your soul. You began the process. Now finish it. You are also gifted with languages."

I raised my head and thought of the skulls: The skulls were out there somewhere. But Chantico's words also made me remember how the Americans had sparked my interest. I didn't know who or what they were, and they spoke a new language. I could find out more about them, just as I had with every other new people I encountered when I was human. After all, the world I was born into and the world in 1846 were completely different.

Chantico helped me realize that all I needed I already had on my person and inside. Before our conversation I might have looked out at my world and said, *What a barren land, how scarce everything seems.* But now I knew better: Treasure by treasure I would regain my people's wealth. When enough was heavy on my back, I would trade it for the rewards that awaited me. Hidden wealth—not just material, but the richness of my culture, the treasures inside me—was everywhere. I only had to allow myself to search for it to flow into my satchel until it was bursting at the seams.

I could already envision my plan: I'd have to move with stealth using Cuauhtémoc's map and all the places the Spanish buried the treasures they didn't carry off. And their churches— I would walk straight in and take it all. For so long I had been betrayed by many. No longer would I allow others to betray me. And no longer would I betray my own soul.

Chantico and the goddess Malinalxochitl stood and walked toward me. "You have so very long to go before you are like us, because you have much to give to this world. There are many places and experiences that wait for you. Don't be afraid of that."

Chantico had a piece of burning palo santo that glowed red in her hand. The charred wood took on the appearance of the bones of a severed finger. It seemed to be pointing in the direction of my destiny. It was time to go and chase it.

I stood to embrace Chantico—so real was her presence to me—but remembered it was not possible. "Thank you, both of you."

"We are never far away."

And with that they were gone.

I put out the fire, then lay down in the dirt, facing the sky. There were so many stars. In the morning I would begin the new chapter of my life. I remembered how Cuauhtémoc moved too soon and suffered a huge defeat. I wouldn't forget Chantico's lessons or step out before the time was right.

But that right time was now. Everything that had happened to me had been preparation for this moment. At that point if I never had another lover in my life I couldn't care less. I had become a new seed placed into the ground, and I had to burst through the soil on my own to reach the sun and rain.

And only then, perhaps, if a bee perched upon my petals one day, I'd accept.

For the following two years during the Mexican–American War, I remained in the disputed lands on what is now considered the Texas–Mexico border. In the heat of war I fed well and took many valuable items from the wealthy and the church's missions. As it turned out, the fight between Mexico and America over the disputed land was none of my business. There was no intention by the Americans to go farther south. But it was an opportunity to learn English. There I encountered Black men and women, Indigenous like me, but from America, and more pale white men from other countries.

It is also when I took a lover of my choosing for the first time. He was a beautiful man from the Comanche tribe. His skin was as brown as mine, hair as silky and black, and his spirit stronger than any man I had ever met. We had both witnessed our people die, yet we somehow survived. Unlike me, he was mortal.

I remember so well how we met: It was in the middle of the night as I rested in an abandoned mission I had found when I heard shouting and horses. There was also a faint scent of blood. My eyesight sharpened, as did my fangs. I jumped to my feet, expecting a fight. But all I saw was a single man, a Brown man with the same skin tone as mine, with straight black hair to his shoulders flying in the wind behind him. He was being chased by two others. All three were on horseback. The scent of blood was heavy in the humid air once I was outside.

A shot rang out, and the horse belonging to the man being pursued fell to the ground. The rider cried out as he hit the ground. He was already wounded, and the wound opened to release a gush of blood. The two other men, who were speaking English, stopped, and I could see their guns as they dismounted. The shot man shouted out in a language I did not understand.

My anger was triggered instantly at seeing these white men on horses, because it made me think of the conquistadors' treatment of my own people. My fangs yearned to crush muscle and bone. Faster than even I could process, I leaped toward them with my arms outstretched. As soon as my long nails made contact with their necks, I crossed my arms once to slash their throats. I moved so quickly they never saw what had ripped open their throats. Instead, they dropped to their knees as they choked on their own blood. They also never saw my face as I hovered over them and drank their blood.

When I'd had my fill, I walked over to the groaning man who'd fallen from his horse. I pulled him from beneath the dead horse, then hoisted him over my shoulders and carried him to the abandoned, half-burnt mission where I had been hiding out.

I propped him against the wall in the dark before making a small fire. All the while he looked at me with exhausted fear. There had to be blood soaking my cloth tunic and still on my chin and hands. This man had already seen more than his young life deserved to see.

I ripped off the portion of his leather trousers that hid the wound on his thigh. It was so deep the muscle was exposed. He also smelled delicious. But he was not for me to consume. He was an Indigenous man trying to escape. We were from different countries, but I felt a kinship to him because I had seen this happen when the Spanish arrived. Instead, I would heal him as best I could. And I wouldn't be honest if I didn't say I found his face and body so very beautiful in the firelight.

When I moved his leg to further inspect the extent of the damage, he spasmed in pain. With slow, long licks I cleaned the gash. His sweat coated my tongue. When I raised my eyes to look at him, he had a look of terror but also gratitude. There was no mistaking he knew I was not human. To put him at ease I touched his thigh so he would know I did not mean any harm. The tension in his entire body released.

With his wound clean, I gave him a smile and left to fetch him water and kill a small animal. He would need to eat. I also intended to search the two dead men to scavenge what they had on them.

He was asleep when I returned. I'd found skins for water, a blanket, and guns, and had captured a small hare to roast. For the next few days, we would stay there in the mission. Anyone who approached with malicious intent would die immediately.

With a soft touch I shook his shoulder. His drowsy eyes squeezed and opened. He had to be in pain. I brought the water-skin to his mouth. His lips quivered, and he winced as he tried to drink. The skin was emptied in a few difficult gulps. I raised the hare to show him he had to eat as well. He nodded and smiled as best he could.

Inside my own satchel I carried with me small things to aid humans I liked. It was wartime. There was no shortage of wounded humans or those about to die. Among those items were coca leaves from home and a small medical kit taken from a victim. He looked at the leaves in my hand without fear. His people also knew the power of plant healing.

I placed a few coca leaves in my mouth and chewed to soften them with my saliva. With my fangs I bit the inside of my lip to extract the smallest amount of blood to further aid his healing. In such a small dose, it would do so without turning him into a vampire. Then I brought my lips to his. He didn't fight my fingertips gently opening his mouth, and he received my pain-relieving kiss.

My saliva and tongue mingled with his so he could experience the full effect as quickly as possible. A soft moan escaped from him the deeper I kissed him. He lifted one hand and touched my cheek, kissing me back. His full lips searched mine as his fingertips trailed to my face, to my breast. I kissed him one more time before pulling back from him to skin and cook his meal. After the coca leaves took effect I would stitch his wound.

Two days later, after he'd had some time to heal, I made love for the first time in centuries.

It could not have been with a better soul. His touch was as soft as Chantico's feather, which I still kept with me. It began when I was again feeding him coca leaves. My mouth took his full lips in. Then he pulled me on top of him as he sat propped up. I could feel him harden between my legs as I straddled his muscular thighs. We didn't need to say a word for me to know what he wanted, what I wanted from him. His cock slipped in with ease, as I had been wet since kissing him that first night and watching him while he slept. He feasted on my neck and breasts while I straddled him until we both orgasmed. Other times I leaned back as I straddled him with one hand on his cock and my other hand between my legs. His beautiful brown eyes looked upon me with desire.

For five days we made love while he recovered. When he could finally stand, I knew the time had come. I ran in the night to steal a horse and supplies for him. He kissed me one last time and rode off to be with his people. Returning to them was an important part of his own story. If he had truly wanted to become a vampire too—if that was to be his story—he would have stayed. As he left, I found myself hoping that perhaps we would cross paths again to be brethren in blood—and that the history of his people would be different from mine. But for now, what we had shared was just a beautiful affair. A fleeting moment in that Spanish mission that had been burned to the ground, and then brought back to life with our blood, cries of ecstasy, pain, and sweat from the sex that had satisfied to the hot cores of our souls.

I stayed one last night in the dark and empty mission feeling my loneliness smolder. It hurt. But it was time for me to go back to Tulum with all the treasures I had collected in Texas.

I settled in a quiet corner in Tulum. There I found a rundown, abandoned hacienda that would be perfect for me—so perfect I was surprised no one had claimed it. I was thankful for my luck in always finding those abandoned solitary spaces.

So I decided I'd stay in the hacienda while looking for items I also didn't dare store in my home. The ransacked hut after Chantico's death was a lesson learned. Cuauhtémoc's map had faded, so I made a fresh copy of it, but also while creating my own: With no one watching I had buried treasure in an above-ground cave system connected to a nearby cenote.

As I searched for treasure, with every silent raid I hoped I'd find the skulls. But they never turned up. I knew that most likely they had been put on a boat and shipped away, but I held on to the hope I would hold them in my hands one day.

To take care of the small daily needs of life, I sold or traded woven baskets at local markets. The skills from Chantico came in handy as tourists poured in over time and wanted my "quaint" souvenirs. It didn't matter to me what they thought of my crafts as long as they paid. Little by little I gathered a hoard of treasure, but it turned out to be just the beginning: During that time I used all my knowledge to find and hide stolen treasures that were not on my original map in and around Mexico and South America.

I remained in the hacienda in Tulum until 1969. When I finally left, my luggage was a single bag with a few Spanish relics, gold items from their churches, and jewelry I could sell in a pinch. I doubted woven baskets would get me far outside of Mexico.

But this time it wasn't war or treasure that dragged me away; it was music—I'd heard the music from north of the border and wanted more. Live music seemed to be everywhere in America. It was too tempting not to explore. There were also lots of bodies I could feed on at concerts. Richie Havens belting out "Freedom" and Carlos Santana with "Soul Sacrifice" made me want to dance again. By accident I also discovered too much drug- and alcohol-saturated blood made me violently ill. As a human servant, drinking large quantities of pulque was prohibited. I could not be inebriated. I could watch the Spanish become belligerent on their wine, but they never offered it to me. Until now small traces hadn't affected me. There had been victims with some alcohol in their blood. I had even drunk from a shaman on peyote. Neither left me ill, just a little fuzzy-headed.

Concerts in the sixties and seventies were flush with blood tainted with alcohol and drugs. It didn't occur to me it would be a problem until I drank from a man very high on LSD. He seemed like an easy target, and he would never know what was real or not. I'd be a bad trip. I couldn't stop vomiting his blood until my body was empty. I stayed away from anyone very out of it on drugs; however, the same effect occurred from another young man with a bottle of Jack Daniel's in his hands. He could barely speak or walk; he was sitting against a tree. But he was alone, and it was dark. I could be shaken off as a nightmare. It burned my throat and belly when it came up. I had to venture into town and try to find someone completely sober. It only took those two times to make me observe my meals before consuming. If someone could barely talk or walk, then it was a no. This was a new experience of being a vampire I would have to navigate.

Then I heard about the concert of all concerts, an explosion of free love and sound—Woodstock.

At Woodstock I found myself sitting in the mud again, just as in Chantico's hut; however, this time it was on my own terms. I braided Chantico's feather into my hair. My hips moved in ecstatic trance-like abandon to the music. So deep was my trance it didn't feel as if there were other people around while I wandered through the crowds without fear. I took small nips of blood here and there from people too high to notice me. Usually, I drew blood from good-looking males who would at the same time caress my legs and arms in the dark, thinking my bites would lead to something more.

When Richie Havens took the stage, his music made me cry uncontrollably. Before that moment, I thought I'd purged all my grief in my periods of solitude. But I discovered that I had not. Because I cried for the mother I didn't know. I cried for all the times I was abandoned yet didn't recognize that the abandonment had nothing to do with me and my value. But even after this bout of deep grief, the end of the day found me still standing once more to watch the sun rise and fall. And I knew that even after all my pain it was something no one could take away from me.

One evening near the end of Woodstock, I sat next to a bonfire as I watched a young woman pull cards from a tarot deck for another querent. I'd taken psychotropics, and it was hard to see clearly, but the young woman's friendly smile drew me closer. She had freckles on her nose and cheeks, and strawberry blond hair in need of a good washing hung just below her shoulders.

As she drew the cards, I could see that the images on them seemed to recall images from my past. The Tower was the temple of Tenochtitlán as it burned. Cuauhtémoc was the Devil. Cortés was the King of Swords, Chantico the High Priestess. And I was beautiful Death but also the Empress.

On the verge of tears, I crawled closer to examine the cards in more detail. The tarot reader was speaking to someone else, but I continued to stare at the cards that seemed to portray all the players in my life, including myself. Someone pounded a drum in the distance, or it could have been close for all I knew. She caught my eye as I looked at the images. She asked, "Do you want me to pull for you?"

"Yes. I need something."

She swayed to the beat of the drum as she shuffled. Her placid smile told me she didn't have a care in the world. Either her mom and dad took care of everything, or she had blind faith that what she needed would be provided for. Cards flipped out of her hand and onto the dirt, some face up and others down. "I'll do a three-card spread for you," she said.

"The Tower is your past. The Queen of Swords is your present. And . . . well, there are two cards that have flipped out." She turned them over. "You have Two of Cups and the Lovers. Bottom of the deck is Three of Swords. That means you've been through a lot of hurt. But fear not, the Two of Cups and the Lovers mean you will experience soul love."

I stared at her. Did vampires experience lasting love; could they? Did I want to love a human who would die? My Indigenous warrior in Texas recovered with my help, but he was still more vulnerable than I ever would be. The idea sent my thoughts into a tailspin. Up to that point I could not have imagined my maker settling down and forgetting the past. My heart clammed up. "I already have that kind of love with myself. Not sure who the lover will be or who will share my cup. But thank you."

"Wait . . . the lover . . . You will be searching for him, but without knowing it's he who you search for. He is currently . . . tied up. Not for long."

"Like I said, thank you, but I don't know. Guess only time will tell."

She smiled again with her eyes closed and rocked to the drums. I stood and scanned the carpet of bodies still enjoying themselves and lost in this collective musical moment. After bursts of self-imposed isolation as a vampire over the years, it was good to be part of this, to experience life beyond drinking blood or being bitter about the past and taking for granted that I had so much time. Life, after all, was meant to be lived, and this concert reminded me of that. But I did hear a saying that all good things come to an end, and sometimes you need to leave things on a high note. I decided to leave for my next destination before the mass exodus of all these people. The concert had been an amazing experience, but there were other destinations to visit. In the distance the music still boomed. One last glance, and I knew I'd always remember that place for the rest of my existence.

The time had arrived for me to make my way to New York City: I had read about it in newspapers and heard snippets in passing from concertgoers. It seemed more famous than the other cities and destinations in America. I wanted to see what the hype was about. And it wasn't too far from where I was.

Times Square in the fall of 1969 and into 1970. This was back when New York was a dangerous and sleazy place for women who didn't know the city well to be wandering around alone. In Times Square there were live sex shows but also go-go dancing and sex workers walking down the street without any sort of protection as they looked to earn a living. But after hearing the different types of music and watching people from a myriad of places, Woodstock made me want to explore. And I could walk without fear through Times Square because I had the strength of ten men and a hunger for blood to match.

I found a small bar to sit in and try to detox my blood with a head swimming with memories. Those tarot cards had me fucked up. The only way I could manage and clean out my system was through a steady stream of clean blood. I figured a splash of whiskey and water would take the edge off after days of drinking tainted blood. Not everyone I drank from was completely off their heads, but it was still enough to build up in my body. My hands shook as I handled my glass.

There were a few dancers on a small stage behind me, but I just wanted to rid myself of these psychedelics. The bartender was a young, pretty girl wearing next to nothing. The air conditioning was blasting high because it was a hot day at the end of summer, with the kind of humidity that makes the humans crazy. Her nipples were showing through her thin polyester top, and her arms were covered with gooseflesh, and I just wanted to wrap the little lamb in a thick cardigan.

Then the door burst open to admit a group of loud guys. There were only four of them, but they made enough noise for ten. "What can I get you fellas?"

They all ordered cheap beer and didn't leave a tip. I made a mental note to leave the waitress a hefty tip. My throbbing head hung toward the glass.

The door opened again. The scent struck me with an immediate straight-to-the-vein impact: It was another vampire.

Cuauhtémoc had been the last vampire I'd encountered, and that was now more than a hundred years ago. I turned and made eye contact with the beautiful creature who swanned in, surrounded by a handful of humans. One of them broke from the group to order bottles of liquor and champagne. She had to have sensed my vampiric nature, because she kept her eyes on me as she walked past to the back of the bar to the largest table. Half of me wanted to run in her direction and ask a million questions, and the other half was too exhausted for a fight or god knows what else could happen as the result of encountering another vampire. I turned back to my glass and finished the watered-down whiskey.

As I got up to leave, a voice in a British accent called out. "Please don't leave. Join us."

She sat like royalty in the middle of her small human entourage. I didn't detect anything suspicious in her demeanor or voice. Her eyes were bright jade with jet-black mascara and eyeliner that made them the first feature of her face you noticed. Parted in the center and straight like the current fashion, her silky blond hair fell just past her shoulders. Her lipstick was a light frosty pink to complement the single dash of blush on her cheeks.

She seemed pleasant, and I was curious about who else like me existed. My moment of hesitation fled, sensing she was not a threat: After all, this woman couldn't be looking for a fight, not dressed like that.

I joined the strange white female vampire at her table. Her entourage consisted of four men and four women who chatted with each other as they drank the full bottles the waitress brought them. I assumed the vampire had purchased these for them. Her clothing was far more expensive than her companions', who dressed for trendiness instead of high fashion and status. She wore a white satin, low scoop neck minidress with bell sleeves. Her jewelry was made from real stones and precious metals, and it appeared genuinely old. The emerald earrings complemented her eyes.

"What's your name?" she asked.

"You first."

"I can see we are going to be good friends. That is exactly what I would say to someone like me. It's good to be a little guarded." Her laughter was light. It made me feel at ease with this new situation.

"I'm Catherine," she finally said.

"Malinalli."

"Where are you staying in this city? Please don't say this neighborhood. The motels are shit. Scratchy sheets, stained mattresses. I only come here for the atmosphere . . . and the blood."

"Haven't gotten as far as finding a place to stay yet. I just arrived in town."

"Well, you can't stay here. I've got the penthouse at the Waldorf Astoria and a supply of fresh, clean blood. You look like you've indulged in a little too much tainted blood. I have been there myself."

"Just came from Woodstock, and it was a trip. Still recovering from blood with what I thought would not affect me as much. I tried to stick to the half-sober humans," I said.

"I enjoy mind-altering elements sometimes, but it can be hard on our systems. Sit back and relax. We will leave when my friends have emptied their bottles, and you can crash in a beautiful bed for a few days while you detox."

I sat there with my hands on my lap, not knowing what else to say. She knew what I was thinking, though.

"Am I the first vampire you have met?" she asked.

My eyes darted to the humans talking among themselves, drinking, or singing along to the music. She followed my gaze. Without a word, she moved to the table next to the others. I joined her and leaned in to the table, keeping my voice low.

"Yes. In a very long time."

"We will have a lot to talk about then. You said you were at Woodstock. Let me take you somewhere tomorrow night I think you'll enjoy."

I didn't bother resisting because I didn't care where I went next. Let the adventure begin. It was nice to meet a possible friend who didn't seem to want anything from me.

Catherine and I walked out of that bar together an hour later and into a years-long friendship. Because we did become good friends even though there was a lot left unsaid between us, so much we couldn't reveal to each other. At least she didn't take the time to reveal it to me. I came to love her generosity—which I'd later hear was as great as her cruelty, which, fortunately, I never experienced firsthand. From what I heard: If you were in with Catherine, then you were in. But catch the tip of her tooth, and you would either be dead or never forget her wrath.

The following day I woke up in a bed larger than I had slept in before. Catherine warned me she slept late, even though vampires don't really sleep. We only need a few hours to recover and rejuvenate. Her "sleep" consisted of a long, hot bath, a skin care routine—despite not aging like a human she loved the ritual and scents of the products—sometimes a massage by a lover, and resting longer than a vampire needed for complete rejuvenation. But still I didn't expect to be sitting there reading the same fashion magazines multiple times until she finally arose at four P.M.

"Are we going out now?" I asked.

She let out her unmistakable laugh. "We won't go out until after ten P.M. I'm taking you shopping."

I looked at my high-waisted bell bottoms and T-shirt that had a lot of wear and tear from Woodstock.

"This isn't nice enough?"

She gave me a playful smile with her eyes running the length of my body. "This is New York City, and you are an exquisite woman, like me. There is nothing wrong with your look, but let me show you how to do this city right."

Catherine took two emerald rings off her fingers and placed them on my hand. "Take these as a gift from me. A gift that for once doesn't require anything in return."

I liked that. "Okay, I will accept, but where are you taking me tonight?"

She took a long drag from her cigarette and rubbed the love bite on her neck.

"Broadway and Fifty-second Street. A little jazz club."

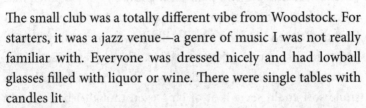

The small club was a totally different vibe from Woodstock. For starters, it was a jazz venue—a genre of music I was not really familiar with. Everyone was dressed nicely and had lowball glasses filled with liquor or wine. There were single tables with candles lit.

We sat at a reserved corner booth with alcohol and Catherine's human friends seated. Catherine outstretched her arms to greet them in her fur coat that was too warm for the summer heat. But as a vampire, she didn't feel the heat, and she didn't give two fucks what anyone thought of her. She loved the feel of the black mink on her skin. The diamond tennis bracelets stacked on both of her wrists looked like magical cuffs. She'd paid for them herself and gotten them specially sized for her wrists. I wanted the opportunity to have my life filled with whatever I wanted and paid for by myself. My life story could be crafted by my own vision.

I sat in the booth, not noticing the people around me. I couldn't wait for the music to begin. There was drum set with a musician ready to start, stands for sheet music, and stools for the musicians. One held a trumpet and the other a standing double bass. Three spotlights illuminated the stage about a foot off the floor. The lights went low, and the musicians began to play in perfect harmony. The sound of their music was pure emotion. They were life itself being expressed in front of my eyes, which were burning from cigarette smoke.

I didn't hesitate to drink when Catherine handed me a wine-glass full of blood. It felt almost like a celebration, a joyful party to toast still being here after all these centuries and the pain of my human existence. I wanted to stay drunk in the moment of this new life in an unexplored part of the world.

After the first set, still high on the music, I could smell that unmistakable scent again: There were more vampires. Two smartly dressed Black men and a Black woman holding instruments in cases approached our table. They greeted Catherine warmly before looking intently at me. The woman flashed me a smile so I could see a hint of fang even though I had already noticed the faint scent of blood on their lips.

"Hello, I'm Mary. This is Winston and Mark. Nice to meet you," the woman said.

Dumbfounded, I opened my mouth but couldn't speak. I looked back at Catherine as if for affirmation before turning my attention back to the trio. "Hello, wow. More of us. It has been a very long time."

Mary took my glass of blood and finished the contents. "I can tell. The three of us are usually on the road from gig to gig or recording. Not a lot of time to settle down. Plus, making music is what we love. We were backstage but should have joined you. How long are you in New York for?"

"I don't know yet."

"Well, we are here for a few days. Let's have fun before we leave," said Mark.

Mark touched Mary's elbow. She nodded before blowing a bright red lipstick kiss toward Catherine. "We will see you after the show."

The rest of the night was fantastic. After the musicians had finished their last set, we went back to Catherine's penthouse to feast all night, with the exception of Mary and Catherine. They continued the party alone in her room with the door closed. Mark, Winston, and I drank blood while I asked them questions about life on the road as vampire musicians. "Have you ever slept with a vampire, Malinalli?" asked Mark.

"No. The opportunity hasn't presented itself. Should I try it?"

Winston laughed. "Only if you want your heart broken. Vampires stay on the move. And you can't feed on other vampires."

"What about Mary and Catherine?"

"Those two do whatever the hell they want. Their hearts are so cold there is no chance of heartbreak. They know the score. They love themselves above all else, which is both good and bad for them."

Winston shook his head while chuckling. "Yeah, they may be cold-hearted but they're also so hot they can burn down a town."

"Mary's voice *is* pure fire. And you two?" I said.

"We love to feed and fuck at the same time," said Mark.

I thought of my Comanche lover, and how satisfying it had been to do both with him. They were also right that I didn't need more heartbreak, didn't need to be yearning for a body I couldn't feed from. Part of the allure of my human lover was that because I could drink his blood I could truly taste every part of him. But at the same time, his being human was a barrier that could keep us from growing too dangerously close. After all, my heart remained tender and wounded from the past.

On a different night out, it was Catherine who dragged me onto the dance floor, and on another weekend took me shopping for my first pair of stilettos. One cold New York City New Year's Eve, she rented out a club for a hundred of her closest friends who were, like us, without family, religion, duty, tears, or any fucks to give. We only had each other. I spread my black wings that night and took a human man who couldn't have been more than twenty and let him pleasure me for hours using only his lips and tongue. I thought of no one but myself for the first time in my life. I was in control. I've never sucked so much blood in one night. My Halston dress clung to my chest and thighs after being saturated with other people's blood and sweat. I ate and fucked all night with abandon before discarding my lovers as easily as I might an empty soda bottle.

We danced beneath a silver ball with the aggression and vigor of alley cats fucking between dumpsters. Everything was fair game if it caught our eye or claws.

Catherine was not always a good human or a good vampire. She helped many women, but she also tore many people to pieces just for sport. A few times I found her in her large bathtub smoking a cigarette drenched in blood as she stared at the wall with a vacant expression. Red footprints covered the floor, and all you could see beyond her wet, bloody face were those dead green eyes. She simply said, "When you find me like this, turn and walk away." And I did. Her generosity to some was as great as her cruelty to others. However, she truly was a great friend to me.

Every night with Catherine began with us lounging in the back of the club in a booth. However, even on our nights out, I always saw a distance in her eyes. Behind them was a lake of tears and pain that she seemed determined to keep dammed for all eternity.

We were driving to her beachfront home in the Hamptons when I asked about her origins. She brushed me off. "The thirteenth century in England was a shitty time to be a woman. And that is the past. I live for now."

"Have you ever been in love?" I asked her. There was a part of me that relished my freedom as I healed, but I wondered if there would be a time when there would be enough space to invite in true love. Catherine had lived long enough to perhaps have an answer.

Her eyes stared at the road intently as she increased her speed in her cherry-red Porsche convertible. A tear rolled down one cheek. "Will you be a lamb and wipe my face and put my sunglasses on? I think a bit of dirt caught my eye."

I removed the pale streak of crimson from her face and replaced her oversize Chanel sunglasses.

"If I'm a lamb, does that make you a lion?" I quipped.

"I am the king of the jungle. Don't ever forget that. We vampires all are!" She placed a hand on mine like a loving sister would, then brought it back to the steering wheel.

"And to answer your question about love. Why would I do something like that? I only have enough to love myself, and sometimes I question that. I don't know how you had children . . ."

"I didn't have a choice to have them."

She placed one hand on mine again after shifting gears. "I know. Being a parent isn't something vampires are meant to do. It's a complicated, shitty job. That's why there are so many fucked-up people walking around. So many adults masking as children bringing more children into the world. Most of the time people have children without any thought. You won't catch me taking care of anyone."

"But you've been there for me. Kinda like a mom."

Another streak of red. Must have been a lot of dust in the air.

"Well, you can wipe your own nose and ass, don't go simpering and whining your demands to me every five seconds, then change your mind when I give it to you, and our adult parties are so much more delightful than kids' birthday parties. No damn clowns."

I didn't press because I had seen my own share of atrocity. Her anger and wounds were her own. If she wanted to reveal them to me, then she would in time.

Her thoughts on love would stay with me as I continued to learn about this vampire life. And deep in the pit of my belly a small pocket of humanity remained. I wanted love in some small way. I had a feeling that it would present itself to me even if I couldn't understand it at first. At least I hoped. I longed for something more tender, something given with patience, if such a thing existed. Who would show me what real love was, challenge me to grow?

Another question I didn't press Catherine on was the source of her wealth. Did I really want to know? But it was because of Catherine that I hit the big time with my business, as she introduced me to someone from Sotheby's who attended one of her infamous Hamptons beach parties. Catherine asked him to do her a favor, and the gentleman in question, Ethan Morris, claimed he would do anything for her.

"If you will do anything, then set up a meeting with Malinalli here to discuss her new business."

My head whipped toward her. "My new business?"

"Yes, you know, you have all that cool old stuff you keep in those safety deposit boxes of yours."

"But she is a woman, Catherine. There are not many in our line of work, and it has to be more than just cool stuff. I need rare, extraordinary things."

I didn't like his dismissiveness. "There are artifacts ranging from the sixteenth century to the twentieth. Gold, illuminated prayer books, jewels, weapons . . . and those are only to name a few."

Ethan sat upright. "Their origins or owners?"

I flashed him a smile. "Dead. I own them, and their origins are from the history I have lived. That is all you need to know."

He nodded as he remained silent in thought. Catherine slinked next to him in her see-through chiffon robe with the fluffy white feather trim. She then sat on his lap and traced the cleft in his chin with the long tip of her fingernail. "I thought you would do anything for me. This is but a small task. It's just one meeting."

His face appeared pained at the thought of being on the receiving end of her cold shoulder. He looked at her, then me. I could see he probably didn't think my treasures could really be worth anything. "Fine. I'll see her at Monday at nine A.M."

"Great. Now . . . Do you want me to rip into your thigh or neck?"

With those words he melted into her arms with a look of total detached contentment. Nothing existed for him outside of her fleshy fortress. I knew that was my cue to leave.

Her Hamptons house was filled with people, as this was the last party of the summer. They called it an Indian summer here in New York, that last blast of warmth and light before fall settled in. Funny how Indigenous culture is romanticized and idealized when it is non-threatening to the dominant culture. When it can be controlled.

Through the large speakers one of my favorite songs, "One of These Nights" by the Eagles, played. I shuffled outside to the patio, where burning torches illuminated the perimeter. I liked this. Fire is required on a full moon when reaching out to the spirit realm, the ancestors, whatever ancient deities watched from the void of the universe. Filled with blood, I couldn't help swaying with the rhythm of the soft waves hitting the shore and Don Henley's cashmere voice. I danced with a lonely ecstasy, but also with freedom. All the while my emotions ranged from joy to bewildering sadness. I found myself thinking of the Lovers card the tarot reader had pulled at Woodstock. I didn't know who the Lover was the card had promised or if it was even real. But I liked the fantasy.

People have always judged me by everything except the contents of my soul. My hope was that there would be a mysterious Lover who would see my soul, that he'd *feel* it.

Until this man arrived—if he even existed—there would be only the moans of short-term lovers, the blood of my victims. And I would *buy* my own home with a view, even if I didn't know the details and only had a few grand saved from small-time private deals. After all, though the hacienda in Tulum had served me well enough, I was there out of necessity. It wasn't a home of my choosing or creation.

The following week I met with Ethan, who appeared to have trouble crossing his legs after his weekend with Catherine and wore a turtleneck despite it still being too warm. "I've never had . . . one of you in here before. A . . . bloodsucker. It makes me a little nervous to mix the two worlds, to be honest. And please do not be disappointed if I can't do anything for your business."

I opened the briefcase Catherine had bought me. It had my name embossed in gold on the front.

His eyes widened when he saw the briefcase's contents. He took out a white glove from a drawer on the right side of his desk. "May I?"

"Be my guest and have a look."

He ran his fingers across a gold crucifix on a gold chain. It was embellished with pearls and precious jewels. There was also a string of beads made into a necklace. They were not precious jade, but the ones the Spanish used to barter with us. It held no value to my heart.

"You are going to be a very rich woman after these go up for auction, even after I take my ten percent."

"I know. And I only trust you because Catherine is very discerning."

"Just give me one minute while I tell my secretary to clear my schedule. We can start appraising these now if you like. And I'd offer you tea or coffee, but I know . . ."

"We start today. If not now, then when? I've waited long enough. Time to come out of hiding."

After that I walked around like I was hot shit, because I was. I flew back to Mexico to bring back to New York City more of my hidden Spanish treasure. While there, I shipped ten Spanish and Portuguese suits of armor and five swords.

When I secured my first million, I went on an entire weekend bender of fucking anyone I wanted and afterward drinking from those who allowed me to even if I didn't feel hunger. And when you get a taste for that first hit, you naturally want more. I did, and I got it—as if anything could stop me from getting what I wanted. The first purchase was a piece of property, even though Catherine tried to persuade me to buy a car and clothes instead. I knew I needed a beach property, and within months I found a place where I could retreat to conduct business and just be me. The river in Mexico that I once bathed in was no longer in a forest, which had been cut down. But I wanted to be near water as a reminder of that time. There was plenty of space near the ocean for a home, a space of my own not controlled by anyone else. All my beautiful antiquities from my people decorated the rooms and walls. It was everything I never had, nor anything the women before me could have dreamed of. I looked at the water and sobbed uncontrollably. My mother had sold me. Who knew what my daughter had endured. Yet here I still stood on this shore centuries later.

Freedom at last. I had wanted freedom, but it had come at a cost. I knew wealth would give me the power to live without worry, and the ability to move as I pleased. Money is power because it is also freedom. Power is changing your own circumstances so you can change the circumstances of others. And freedom is the power to choose, to say no, to beat the tyrants at their own game.

I earned every last penny of my fortune, and I didn't take a single cent for granted. I accomplished what so many could not through the centuries I lived through. My thoughts dwelled on the woman I had watched be cut into slices so her fat could be used as a salve.

Eventually I had to walk away from Catherine. She never wanted the party to end, and I was growing more serious about my career. I also wanted to find Chantico's skulls with my new connections and expanding business. Catherine had a thirst for pleasure and experience that could never be quenched. She wanted to cross the pond to Europe. The night before she left was the rare night we stayed in to enjoy a liquid supper together in her penthouse. She wanted to pack, but also was planning to take a few empty suitcases to fill with the newest fashions out of Paris. Her bed was a mess of clothing, some so new they still had price tags on.

"Come with me! We will drain every city from Barcelona to Madrid. I have told an old friend about you. She owns an ancient vineyard. She is curious and will spare no expense hosting us. Think of the treasures you can steal. Think of those gorgeous Spanish . . ." She stopped herself before she could say "men."

"I'm sorry. That last part was insensitive."

There was genuine hurt in her eyes. "I know. You don't have to worry. You are my dear friend with good intentions when it comes to us. But I want to build something first for myself. The time is now."

She threw her arms around me. "I will send you postcards from all my locations in case you change your mind about robbing the continent blind. Mary will be in Paris singing, so I won't be totally alone."

"Have fun, Catherine. I know we will see each other again."

As time went on, I would visit my secret hoards in Mexico to sell pieces to collectors or museums. I sold back to the descendants of the conquerors the crosses they made from our gold with precious gems. I sold them their ancestors' blood-spattered swords and their jewelry and other priceless items they'd brought from Spain that were now all mine. The Europeans had taken everything from me, and I took all I could from them.

Catherine sent me postcards for a year before they stopped.

When I finish telling Alexander one of the stories about my past, we are back at the flat in Notting Hill. Once inside, I can hear light snoring coming from the master bedroom where Colin is recovering. I toss my bag on the dining table before allowing my body to sink into the sofa. Alex sits next to me.

"Both of us had a birth of sorrow and came out spiritually breech. And antiquities? It's very different from translating like you did when you were human?"

"They are related. My ability to speak many languages allowed me to procure the Spanish treasures I wanted and take back what was ours. My travels with Cortés showed me the vastness of the land. Secret pockets I could use to my advantage for hiding as much as possible. And it enabled me to learn other languages quickly and expand into different countries once the internet became a thing."

"You're so resourceful. And you know, the Vikings buried their treasures too, for the afterlife."

"Are we, as vampires, not a manifestation of the afterlife? We are the living possibility that existence continues in some form even if we do not want to believe it or can't see it."

His black eyes soften until they look like jaguar fur. I want to rest my head against the beast inside of him.

"I never had the chance to have children, a family," he said.

Without thinking I blurt, "And what about love?"

He turns his beautiful face toward me. The cracks in his pupils show me heartache but also the hidden radiance he possesses inside. I want to cover his body with my kisses, coat him in my saliva like a shield—I want my love to be a shield from all his self-doubt, hurt. The lingering scent of my mouth would be a constant reminder for him of the love that is always within reach if only you let it happen without fear.

"When? I'm married to my mission," he said.

"So was I. But then the yearning became too much. And that mission is making me less happy year by year. It's time for a change. Time for me to find someone like me . . . like you, Alexander."

There. I say it out loud. Fuck hiding behind fear. I didn't want to seem weak by uttering those words. But even a vampire as old as me wants love from another no matter how hard I loved myself. He continues to look at me. I can see in his eyes that he feels it too. His eyes are mirrors that reflect my own love back at me. Many times, I had seen myself looking as he does now. "I would like to see Mexico one day, Malinalli. I have never been across the ocean."

Again, my mouth moves before I can think. "I guess when I

go back you will have to come with me. I won't take no for an answer."

A little light chuckle from him. "You are a wonder. You know that?" His laughter infects me. I tease, "What? Besides all this craziness, it was the right decision to cross the ocean to come here. But I have one more question."

"Ask me anything. I will always give you an honest and direct answer."

"Catherine. I mentioned a vampire by that name. Do you know anything about her or have you heard that name?"

Alex wouldn't bullshit me, but I can see on his face he measures his words. The name is familiar to him.

"I know of her, not much, so I didn't want to interrupt you. She had a nasty reputation for killing indiscriminately as well as a huge propensity for great charity. Never needed to find her. She went quiet some years ago."

My heart aches. What if she'd gotten in over her head with something or someone? Her confidence was her best quality; however, it was hard to know who would be drawn to that confidence who did not have the best intentions for her.

"Thank you, Alex."

"Sorry I don't know more. I only deal in immediate threats."

Through the blinds I can see the sky becoming lighter. My favorite time of day. The sun is about to rise. Alex must notice it too.

"Hey, I have an idea." His eyes brighten with an easy smile appearing on his face. He is angelic when he smiles. I give him a look like he's about to ask me to jump off a building. "All right, you have my attention. What is it now?"

"Let's go to the rooftop to watch the sun rise over the city. Is there a fire escape or other way out?"

"There is. And I'm game." I grab a spare throw off the sofa

and head toward the front door. From this floor there is one flight of stairs that leads to the roof. There are keys hanging from hooks on a mirror by the front door. I grab the keys and flash Alex a smile before leaving the flat. I'm looking forward to whatever he has in mind and what vampire magic awaits, because he already has me spellbound.

I open the metal door that opens to an informal terrace. It's nothing special, with a few empty wine bottles, beer cans, and bird poop. I lay the blanket on the ground directly in front of where the sun is beginning her ascent. Through the clouds, rays of sunlight pour through. But the light looks like a deluge of water flowing off rocks. A waterfall in the sky.

"Take off your shoes," he says as he removes his leather combat boots before sitting down. I slip off my Vans then sit with my legs crossed like him. From this vantage point you can see high above the streets of London. Only a few double-decker buses pass. Very few people are on the streets. Pigeons coo before taking flight. "This is . . . different," I say.

"I love doing this. The silence of that world below us telling us who we should be when we can only be what we are. The sun seems to burn through all the shit we internalize. It sets it ablaze like an offering so we can just be worthy without any labels. Vampire, human, rich or poor. I've seen it all."

His words make my pulse quicken with the fresh blood in my body singing to life. As the sun rises, I place both my hands palms up on my knees, as to catch all the golden, syrupy light the sun offers. He does the same with a smile. Our knees are barely touching when the first rays hit our faces. "Now close your eyes."

He doesn't need to say this because they already are. This is a ritual I enjoy myself. To share it with him feels nothing short of divine. I sit there, absorbing the warmth, allowing my thoughts to melt like the winter snow, allowing blossoms of flowers and small mushrooms to break through the frost. All the radiation seeps beneath my skin, swims luxuriously in my veins like blood. And like blood the sun is life. For most humans it is eternal even though one day in the distant future she too will die, but not before exploding and releasing beauty into space to create something new we can't even fathom. We have no concept how far or deep any of it goes.

I can hear his breathing. It has slowed down. The blood from his last meal is swishing inside him with all the speed of a calm brook. He moves, and I can feel his knuckles brush against mine. I have a deep desire to hook four of my fingers with his.

And then, as if the energy in my body desires to connect with the energy in his, I feel my hand move in his direction. Four of my fingers latch on to the pads of his fingertips. The warmth between us hits me like a solar flare. It feels like the current of something so familiar it's scary. I can feel him wanting to pull away, afraid of this, but he doesn't.

We sit there until a typical London cloud crosses the sun, breaking us from the source. We turn to each other at the same time, not knowing what just happened. The cloud moves again, and I can see the world, his history, his love, and his pain reflected in the light of his eyes. We are in a cloud of crackling heat. I'm not sure how long we bask in this sensation until he pulls away.

"Maybe we should go check on your friend." I nod wordlessly, even though this is clearly an excuse.

When we return, the flat is quiet, and Colin is still resting. My attention turns to the skulls. Centuries and lifetimes have gone by since they were in my possession.

I open the bag and hold one in each hand. They feel different than they did when I first held them in Chantico's hut. Before I had sensed there was magic in them that brought out so many memories and mixed emotions in me. Now, after all I have been through on my own, they are merely beautiful objects that happen to be a part of my history long ago. They will go to a museum for the rest of the world to enjoy and learn from.

Flush with blood, bright red tears cover my cheeks. Alex steps close to me with a napkin and wipes my face. "You all right? Hope you don't mind. Your hands are full."

I look at him in deep appreciation for his kindness. He knows just what I need in that moment. "Thank you. It feels like I am experiencing the past, present, and future all at once." More tears stream from my eyes. Alex is there to catch them again.

"Feel it, Malinalli. We all go through that at some point. After, we can move forward again. And it seems like maybe you need this before we attempt to stop Hernán. You're too wonderful to not be in this world."

"They are home, Chantico," I say to myself and to the skulls before turning to Alex. "You're right. I'm ready to do this." I place the skulls back in their bag until this is over.

I retrieve stolen memory and history as my job. Maybe it's the way I have tried to piece together my own soul, to retell my story that has been passed down and then muddled by everyone but me. That is who I have become. Who I am down to my atoms. The skulls held significance because they were tied to Chantico. Cuauhtémoc and Chantico helped me birth a new life. If I held them once again, I felt I could have some grasp on my existence. It happened while searching for them, not when I possessed them.

17

Hernán sat in the dark clinic, cleaning the wound on the side of his head inflicted by that cunt Malinalli.

For years Hernán had avoided problems, and his enemies had never lasted long before. But he had underestimated Malinalli. And though he had killed Horatio to avoid any unnecessary complications in the future, Alexander J was now involved. And on top of it all, even John had let him down.

John had done as Hernán requested and met her at the museum; however, that was the extent of his involvement. John was treating this stay in London as a holiday instead of work. After leaving Malinalli, John sent him a message that took his blood to the boiling point.

> *Hernán, in all our years we have never encountered so*
> *many problems. Let this one go. She is more trouble than*
> *she is worth. Get a grip and stop this obsession. It will get*
> *us caught or killed. —J*

This time he would obviously have to do everything himself, no matter the cost.

Until recently John and Hernán had had a great business partnership. With every new discovery he made about existence as a vampire, Hernán had found himself wanting to learn even more about his anatomy and how it differed from humans'. John felt the same. Hernán's natural curiosity drove him to experiment, even if it did seem cruel to the unsuspecting vampires. All the while John never questioned his methods; he simply stayed in the shadows and observed.

Hernán made his most significant discovery when, in the nineteenth century, John had taken him to an opium den in an area in London called the Docklands. John said they'd find easy feeding there, and drinking the blood of the humans who'd imbibed opium would even give them a little high.

There Hernán happened to see a vampire using his blood as a salve to heal a human with infected vampire wounds on her arms and neck. Hernán thought nothing of it until the following day the same human woman healed again spontaneously after the vampire fed from her. But when he considered it, the strange sight made sense: He remembered the effect of turning John, who had been dying, and the rejuvenating effect on himself from consuming the blood of the warrior vampire all those years ago. It had never occurred to Hernán to use vampire blood in small doses. For the right price vampire blood could be a treasure, a sort of opium that could stave off humans' inevitable decay without transforming them into full-fledged vampires.

Realizing this had sparked images of the future in his mind. The powerful potential of such a product excited him. Creating it would give him a new purpose, because in the depths of his soul, he had never stopped wondering how being a vampire fit into the Christian worldview he had been born into. Did heaven or hell even exist in the way he was taught in the Catholic church? The church would surely denounce what he was and consider what he did sinful. He killed others to survive and profited from death, even though the church in the sixteenth century profited from the death of thousands of Indigenous people. It all made his head spin at first, but the longer he was a vampire, the less he cared about any notion of God, because he felt like a god.

After leaving the clinic, Hernán made his way to Highgate. Since coming back to London sporadically over the years to set up the extraction clinic, he'd always found it a pleasure to walk through Highgate Cemetery. He did so most evenings and early mornings before the gates opened.

On rainy days, he enjoyed how the rain would fall in sheets through the hundred-year-old trees; on brighter days, the sunshine would seem to uncover the graves hidden beneath shade and ivy. Wild, unpruned rose bushes grew in clusters. Small droplets clinging to the curve of rose petals reminded him of the tears on the faces of his victims as they begged for their lives in the moonlight.

The cemetery also reminded him what it had felt like before this vampire life, when he knew he was dying from years of ill health. He had felt like a leaf suspended in midair, hanging by a single cobweb. So did his existence twirl and sway, in danger of falling at any moment. He saw a wild fox in the brush and stopped. They were everywhere in London with the plethora of garbage to scavenge from. This one had trapped a mouse underfoot, and the fox tore at the mouse's flesh as it consumed it. The sight of its sharp teeth stained with blood and fur made him think of the job at hand.

Hernán needed a plan, and quickly. This time he had to end Judas once and for all and take what he wanted from both Malinalli and Alexander. At this very moment they were probably trying to come up with their own plan for how to trap him. Alexander had gained a reputation as a tracker and bounty hunter. It had taken some time for him and John to figure out Alex's true identity, but once they did, for the sake of their business they never went after him outright. Alex had too many powerful friends. But there was no running away now—this was the final game of chase, and it was going to leave someone dead.

And it wouldn't be Hernán.

First, he needed John to fall back in line. He picked up his phone and opened a new message.

> Hello, George
> I have a private matter I need your help with. If done correctly it might sway John to allow you to join us. Meet me at the Highgate house in three hours.

George was eager to become immortal so he might never part from John. Hernán had always resented his presence and did not want George to be transformed: There was no room in their partnership for a permanent third wheel. So far John had been reluctant to go through with transforming George; however, when Hernán watched them together, it gave him a deep sense that John's mind was changing.

It was high time the power in their partnership shifted back into his hands.

18

As the day wears on, while we try to come up with a plan to deal with Hernán, I can't stop thinking about Alex. Even the way he touched my cheeks replays in my mind.

Yes, I thought of Colin a lot after our first meeting, but the way I think about Alex is like nothing I have ever experienced. Colin is also very attractive, but I found it easy to let go of him when the signs presented themselves that our relationship was not meant to be.

I already know I don't feel the same way about Alex. I want him to be mine—he feels like he could perhaps be an unexpected gift of everything I hadn't known I needed in this lifetime. I'm glad I found the path to heal myself first and be truly open to the prospect of love, because otherwise I might not have appreciated the magnificence of Alex when we first met. I would have been too afraid to take the leap of faith to be vulnerable with a partner. When I became a vampire, I could feel my soul rising to fill out my flesh, and for so long I didn't think I could be fuller in spirit.

Alex changed that. I could share myself and experience the world and love with another without fear. Our first interaction was not one of sex. It was deeper. To this point in time our movements around each other still feel like a tango, where he is the double bass, deep and brooding, and I the piano. We are different in where we come from and the experiences that have shaped us. But together we create harmony. Our differences complement each other to create a beautiful sound.

Colin begins to stir around midnight. Alex and I look at the clock.

"I think it is better we all stick together. You should continue to crash here with me," I say.

"Thank you. I will," says Alex in his luxuriously deep voice.

I get up from my seat, staring at his mouth all the while, and hesitate before placing a hand on Alex's shoulder.

I then check on Colin. He doesn't respond, only rolls over, still in deep sleep. The rest of the night Alex and I study the skulls together. Both of us make notes of our observations, trying to discern the many scents left on both objects to see if we can catch any clues about Hernán. We take in the scent of his blood so we will recognize it when he's been to a place recently or if he's close to us. If we can't get to Hernán, then we will go after John.

As we stand side by side, I can still feel the magnetic energy between us that I sensed on the rooftop. My heart wants to know if he feels the same. His exposed neck gives me visions of kissing him, undressing him where he stands. I can't stop thinking about how he would feel inside of me.

I check for responses to emails I sent for any information from my sources while Alex scours Horatio's computer. The only lead is Horatio's WhatsApp. There were calls to a number that has been disconnected. No emails. It's smart to use an encrypted way to communicate. Other times Alex sits alone on the roof to meditate when trying to gather his thoughts on Hernán, allowing his mind to get creative with the few clues we have. Meanwhile I meditate on my wrath. Because there is no question in my mind that I will kill him.

A full day later, Colin shuffles from the kitchen back to bed with mugs of tea and plain toast. He looks at Alex, then me, without saying a word. His eyes when he looks at Alexander say it all. He knows Alexander is a vampire and stays away from him.

I bring him dinner when he can stomach food again. "Thank you" and a smile is all I receive, which I am fine with. Most of the time when I check in on him, he is sleeping. As the days go by, his face slowly begins to regain its color. But I suspect that the entire ordeal has scared the soul out of his body. I hope it will return so he can live out the rest of his life in joy.

And Alex was right about what he said in Horatio's office. Hernán never left witnesses, and we consider Horatio a dead man.

And I soon receive an email that makes my heart break: It's from Horatio's business partner. Horatio was found dead on the sidewalk on his way home the night I saw him last. The email said the police believed the murder was a mugging gone wrong. I can't help but cry for my dear friend dying for nothing. And for his family.

But another friend has emerged from all this tragedy— Alexander. A friend who doesn't like to see people like Hernán get away with literal murder. We are both resolved: Hernán will be found one way or another and stopped for good.

"It never gets easier. I've tried being numb; maybe that's why

I work alone. It never stops hurting when people close to us are taken away." Alex's hand on my hand gives me comfort. He knows how to read my heart. Working with him makes me feel like he is my male counterpart. It is as if our souls were separated during a supernova back before creation and are now at long last reunited—though not as humans but something else, and brought together for some purpose I can't see just yet. But I don't need to see it yet: Either that destiny will blossom, or we will go our separate ways.

When the sun refuses to shine and heavy rain lasts all day, Alex and I take our pouches of blood to the rooftop, where we sit beneath umbrellas, watching the humans mill around at their daily lives, oblivious to our existence. It feels strange to be literally above it all, the two of us silent observers of a world moving to a different, and human, drumbeat. We are two loners together, learning not to be afraid of the dark, because we have the light within each other to guide the way. For hundreds of years, we existed under the same sun, might even have stood beneath the same clouds.

And it was beneath the moonlight we met. The moon brought us together, and by the moon we will live. To hunt. To be just as we are. This is my heart's desire.

How sweet that moment of blood and rain. To feel content in the present moment with another.

19

George arrived right on time, and Hernán greeted him inside, trying to seem jovial. The wound on his head had healed already.

"Thank you so very much for your help, George. John and I have worked together for so long, and I wanted to give him a break," Hernán said.

"I appreciate that. He feels like he might need a long vacation or even an early retirement," George said.

Hernán internally grumbled. He knew it. The words *vacation* or *retirement* had never entered John's vocabulary until meeting this young man.

"Precisely! That is why I must find a replacement for him so he can have his well-deserved rest. Perhaps you can help? I need you to keep it quiet, though. Don't tell John just now."

George embraced Hernán with both arms. "This means so much to us. Whatever you need I will do."

Hernán broke away as quickly as possible. He loathed human affection. Humans were nothing more than meals to him.

"Wonderful. I have someone waiting. They are currently going through the process of becoming a vampire in a crypt in Highgate Cemetery. Will you help me get them through the final few hours? Then I will truly have someone to replace John, and he is all yours."

"Of course."

"Let's head out. Everything we need is already there."

Later that day in the crypt, the scent of wet earth filled Hernán's nostrils. He loved the smell of fresh soil. In the crypt were decaying and broken coffins lining the long tunnel, with smaller rooms housing more bodies and coffins. This crypt was in one of the forgotten parts of the Victorian cemetery, not suitable for tours, and it was here that rotting coffins were stored. Hernán felt at home here because this was what his mind felt like: made up of tunnels and tunnels of decay.

Even as he walked through the crypt, all he wanted was to hunt and feed on his prey as they screamed and their limbs struggled in his grip. He shook this thought off. *Control yourself,* he reminded himself. He had to regain control over this impulse to finish the work at hand.

The solitude of Highgate Cemetery gave him the quiet he needed to calculate his next moves in killing both Malinalli and Judas.

Now he looked at the body of the young, handsome George he'd stuffed into this crypt. As a mortal, George would have died someday anyway. Hernán needed John to step up and stop being a sniveling, love-struck child. And what better way than to blame his lover's death on that bitch Malinalli. That would light a fire under John's ass.

He took George's phone and sent John a message. A woman and man are after me! Help! I'm hiding in the cemetery. Please come quick.

After sending the text, he smashed George's phone with the heel of his boot. As he left the scene he swept his boot prints out of the dirt. The scent of George's body made him want to feed, but he couldn't. John would smell George's blood on him, so he made sure that he killed him without even getting the tiniest of specks on him. Instead he injected one of John's concoctions that would cause immediate death straight into his neck. This turn of events Hernán had orchestrated should move things along. Now to turn his attention back to killing Malinalli without mercy.

He returned to the clinic for one last power move. In the very back of the operating room was a safe where they kept their products that were in various stages of experimentation before being released. There was one that Hernán wanted to try on himself.

This new product was nearly complete, and it was intended for vampires' use, not humans'. He and John called it *The Hyde*. He looked at the red liquid inside. The Hyde gave its users increased strength, but also increased the worst of a vampire's urges.

John hadn't allowed the vampires they experimented with to live beyond the research period. He'd then labeled the product unstable and urged Hernán to continue his research before using it. But Hernán didn't want to wait: He wanted to feel the savagery and strength he'd seen in the others they'd experimented on. He took all five syringes out of their holders.

He uncapped one syringe and jabbed it into his neck. Now he would wait for the real monster to emerge.

20

We spend another routine day looking for Hernán and finding nothing but dead ends. Alex leaves the flat mid-morning for our food stashed at the clock shop. When the door shuts, Colin joins me at the dining table. He appears to be back to his normal human self. I'm glad his recovery hasn't taken more than a couple of days. "Hey, mind if we talk? I finally feel like my head is clear enough."

Here comes the talk I didn't get to have with Colin thanks to Hernán. It was bound to happen at some point. "Sure. Good to see you have regained your strength. You look well."

"That was like the worst trip ever. And I have never tried LSD in my life. Nightmares, sweats, the weakness. My jeans are really loose around the waist."

"But all of that is gone now?"

"Yes. Thank God. But, Malinalli, what the hell was any of that?" His soft blue eyes possess a sadness I have not seen in him before. If only I had answers even for myself.

"This has all been . . . an unexpected complication. Alex and I have been working on finding out more the last few days."

"Yeah, nearly losing my life could be considered 'an unexpected complication.'"

We both know what comes next now that the varnish of lust has worn off, even in ordinary circumstances without the complications of the events of the past week. Who will pull the blinds open to the morning light first? His heartbeat flutters, and his cheeks turn pink. Here it is:

"I don't think your vampire world is for me. I'm sorry," he says.

I stand and kiss him on the cheek to reassure him I am not angry and don't wish him any ill will. Words can only convey so much. He needs to feel that I only want the best for him after our tryst. But I do say, "And your human life is not one I can be part of, no matter how hard I might try. That part of my life is over. I will forever live on the fringes of humanity with my business being the only way I interact with you all. Even then I will have a middleman to do my business for me. This is my destiny. I thought you were my reintroduction to the world, but it served to push me toward the truth I sought."

"Alex? Is he the truth you've been looking for?"

"What?" My eyes shift around, making my feelings transparent; I can't seem to help myself. I withdraw my hand to my lap. The boyish, playful look returns to his eyes. "C'mon. I've seen how you two move together. It's like magic. There is something there. Don't fight it."

This is an awkward conversation. But I would be lying if it didn't make me feel better to get third-party confirmation about what I've been feeling inside of me.

"And I don't know if he said anything to you, but I told him the same thing when he checked in on me last," Colin says.

I can feel what little blood from my last feed is swirling in my body go straight to my face. I don't want to ask because it will truly give away how I'm feeling more than I already have. Yet I have to ask. "What did he say to that?"

"He looked at me the same way as you do right now. That says it all, in my book."

"Speaking of books . . . good luck with yours. Don't make me out to be a huge she-devil. Everyone knows vampires don't exist." I chuckle and give him a friendly smile so he knows there are no hard feelings and we can be happy about how we parted ways.

"What? Never. Your secret is safe with me. I write these stories for a living, so no one would believe me anyway. I'll send you a copy when it's out. Friends?"

I smile. "Friends. It was a good time, Colin. Thank you for your blood too."

"I think I'm going to head back home and start another book, plus I have the bookstore to attend to. I booked a flight from bed last night."

"I understand." I stand up and give him a hug and kiss on the cheek. An hour later he is off to where he belongs in the world until the next adventure meant just for him. He has his own stories to write. And I sit alone in the apartment, taking stock of all that has happened since I left Tulum not long ago.

21

The daylight turns to night as I continue to sit on the sofa without switching on any lights. My heart and mind are in a standoff over who will win. Should I wait for Alex to return or go to him?

A police siren outside the window breaks my mood. I look at the clock. A feeling of nostalgia for that first night in the clock shop makes me dizzy, fills me with longing to see Alex and hear his voice. He still has not returned. I'm only slightly worried because I know he can handle himself, but I send him a text. He messages me back immediately with a location, a pub not far away.

Alex sits at the end of the bar, looking into a glass of club soda with lime. His shaggy black hair hangs over his eyes and his sharp jaw leading down to his exposed neck. The yellow light above his head illuminates his face, casting shadows. He looks like a dark fallen angel. How I want to fall into his wings, to allow the feathers to cushion me for a moment from the world. But I sense he's the one who needs some sort of comfort in this moment. I know that look; I can feel it in my bones.

"Lookin' for Love" by Johnny Lee plays from the speakers overhead. What an odd song to hear in a pub in London. God, this song—the lyrics could have been inspired by the many one-night stands in my life. The bartender turns to me as I approach. "Please tell me you will order something besides a club soda. He's on his third."

I smile at him. "Sorry, friend. I'll have the same. But here." I throw down a fifty-pound note. "Hope this settles it." The bartender gives me a short nod before leaving to fetch my drink. I sit on the stool next to Alex. "Need some company? I thought you were returning with lunch. Not that I am upset. Just want to know you are all right."

He appears surprised to see me. He stares at me with cold metal in his eyes. If only I could penetrate that chain mail. It's hard to be vulnerable. So I decide to try to be vulnerable for both of us. "I've been thinking all day. Thinking of you . . . us. Maybe we can work together. What do you have to lose? We want the same things."

He turns from me and back to his club soda. "You let your pet Colin go?"

"He wasn't my pet. And yes. I told you it was a short-term thing."

"So why do you want to hang around with me? I can't feed off you and you can't feed off me. And I don't have time for messy breakups or heartbreak. Like I said, solo."

When he says this, I am struck with a comet to my heart. It reminds me of the first time I stood knee-deep in snow, the flakes falling upon me like ash spewed from a volcano. I allowed it to cover me until my sodden hair lay flat against my face. I cried out in joy toward the white sky for this freedom to experience this new wonder. My arms rose to receive the abundance of my life. I could feel the gratitude flowing from me like the snow from the clouds. It made me think of the lengths I had gone to, feel the strength I mustered to endure when I thought all was lost. Of how I had become my own friend and befriended my own loneliness.

Then I saw the large black creature staring at me. His fur was thick, with an oily sheen. I faced him, a great black bear. We stood face-to-face, two predators looking at each other in recognition. He was so beautiful I wanted to touch him. With slow, deliberate steps I approached. He stood to his full height. His strength could easily have caused me a lot of pain if he had chosen to. But I did not fear. I opened my mouth and showed him my teeth while looking into his eyes. He lowered himself to all fours and walked toward me. Once he was within reach, I stretched out my hand and stroked his head, our black eyes still locked on each other. He allowed me to feel his strength. And this took strength on his part, because he was very vulnerable in his way—humans are the greatest threat to his existence. "Go in peace, my friend," I whispered. He roared before turning to return to the woods. As he left, all I could think of was how I wanted to walk by that bear's side.

I reach out to place my hand on Alex's forearm, not expecting anything to happen. The nearer my fingertips approach him, the stronger the pull I feel toward him. His body feels like a sacred place. He slowly rears his head toward me. The wildness in his eyes is now bewilderment. He can feel it too.

I don't stop myself from touching him, despite my fear of not knowing what is occurring between us. My fear of this indescribable force that ignited when our atoms greeted each other in recognition, of this energy that then burst forth to bring us closer together for some reason.

And with the most unexpected person, another vampire. I can't believe the extraordinary events that occurred to bring me to this pub halfway around the world to meet a person I would not have met otherwise in any other time in history.

Now is the right time.

He stands from his stool as if he wants to walk away from whatever this is. But still his eyes never leave mine, and then both of his hands reach for my waist and pull me close. His jaw tightens before he says, "You know, I've been sitting here for hours contemplating what to do next. Kept telling myself I should leave without a word once Hernán is dealt with. That I should just keep things simple . . . because the thought of spending another second with you is too complicated for me."

I want to cry at the thought of never seeing him again, at even the idea that he might have left just like that without any explanation. "Have you changed your mind? Will you leave the next time my back is turned?"

"As much as I might want to, I find that I can't. Meeting you is like when I received that first vampire bite—it's changed me forever. And now I know: I must be by your side until the flesh falls off my bones. I'll never forget the way you make me feel about life, myself. The way you look at me. The way you've given my world new meaning. All I have to say now is that you are my goddess incarnate and I have found you at last." His dark eyes reflect vampire lust, so up close they look like flames. Like the eternal fire of the heavens that never dies, and only transforms to something new and beautiful after every cycle.

He is my torchbearer. My light.

"What do you want from me, Alex?"

He steps closer to me. "More. I want more of you. I'm hungry.

That thirst for it all is strong when I think of you. I want to be more than acquaintances or business partners or friends. Do you?"

I run my fingers through the hair on the back of his neck. "Good, because I want it all too, from now until the very end of me. You are everything that was ever lost, stolen, or denied to me."

He leans in to kiss me with trembling lips. But they soon find their confidence and crush me with predatory hunger. His mouth grants me cosmic amnesia: Suddenly it is as if there were no one before him. And there won't be anyone after him, because this is the start of some adventure neither of us signed up for consciously, but we are now committed to.

He is the one I have been waiting for all my life, with eyes so deep they contain all the moonlight from the beginning of time. He is my destiny. We are the sun and moon, two bodies in perfect harmony that bring light to the world by hunting the darkness. Our kisses bring death, but we are also sources of life.

I pull away from him. "Where do we go from here?"

"You tell me. This is all new. I was not prepared for this."

"Neither was I, but I don't want it any other way. Let's stay alive for starters."

He laughs at this. "Well, Mr. Cortés likes being in control and also being in the shadows. I think he will stay in England. No way he will leave without getting what he wants. He takes obsession to the next level. He likes his blood and his money."

He glances at the necklace and pendant around my neck. The one John recognized. Alex leans closer to me.

"You know I don't have any material wealth to share with you. I hunt other vampires for just enough money that I need to get the jobs done to get by in the modern world. Any more wealth or possessions are pointless for me, since I'm always on the move."

"You don't need any. I have all I need and extra for you. Consider your mission fully funded."

He kisses me, biting my bottom lip. The sensation of the sharp tip of his fang sends snakes the length of my spine. "Take me home, Malinalli, my eternal vampire companion."

I can't wait to get him alone. My body is already responding to my arousal. My clit is a burning candlewick and I need him to come closer to singe his tongue on it.

The flat is dark. It's raining outside, which makes me wish I was making love to him to "Purple Rain" by Prince. I grab my phone from my bag and do a search in my music. It's the first song on my playlist entitled "Bed." I press play and turn the volume all the way up before leaving it on the dining table. Droplets of water stream down the windows.

We both rip off our jackets, discarding them on the floor. Shoes fly everywhere. One of his boots knocks a lamp to the floor. I watch him remove his Black Sabbath T-shirt followed by his black jeans. The streetlights are now streaming across his nude, sculpted six-foot body. A large shadow of a cross from the outline of the windowpane rests in the center of his chest.

Meanwhile, I take my time unbuttoning my cardigan. Each button I undo takes our passion up a degree. His dark eyes hold my own as he approaches me and unbuttons my jeans. Before I can react, he lifts me from the ground. I wrap my legs around his waist. He carries me to the spare bedroom. With a swift and delicate motion Alexander lays me on my back on the bed. Then he pulls my jeans from the ankles and tosses them to the corner of the room. I suddenly recall that during one of our work sessions, I had a specific fantasy as I watched him reading from the corner of my eye. Now I can finally fulfill it. "I want to try something with you, Alexander."

He lies next to me, pushing my long hair away from my breasts. "Anything. I am your apostle. Let me worship you with every part of my body."

I kiss him and look into his eyes. "Sit in the center of the bed." He knows I can't take my eyes off him, nor do I want to. He does as I ask. A devilish half smile forms on his lips.

I crawl to where he is and slide my body onto his erection so we can face each other. My legs wrap around his waist. We are both slippery with excitement, with the wetness of a muggy tropical rain. He shudders as I allow every inch of him to enter me. His mouth is open as he exhales, showing me the sharp points of his teeth. This makes me want him more than before.

He is a beautiful mirror that reflects who I truly am. I don't have to worry about him seeing the real me. And he in turn is revealing himself, both the danger and the tenderness that live side by side in him—just as the monster and the woman in me are both welcome in his arms. I rest my hands around his neck while his arms instinctively close around my back, pulling me close.

We look into each other's eyes. The energy we felt at the pub has returned. The magnetic attraction flares between our connected bodies. The flickering light of our passion burns brighter the deeper he thrusts inside of me. We burn for each other. The heat between us almost creates a light seeping from us like the sweat from our pores and the moans from our mouths.

Making love to him makes me feel like stained glass. His

beauty, his tender soul, the ecstasy of our union feels like a myriad of colored light streaming into a cold chapel, indigo, red, and yellow illuminating me from the inside.

The rain falls harder. I roll my hips back and forth. Alex's hands guide the tempo as we flutter into a world of pure physical joy. Nothing else exists. I ride him harder. The blood goddess is unleashed to give to him and take what she needs.

This intimacy of mind, body, and spirit joining brings tears to my eyes. We are making love. For the first time in my life I make true love without the fear of intimacy. I rest my forehead against his.

One of his hands moves to my ass, telling me to grind harder, so I do. Our breaths escape to the other's mouth. We smile between kisses. Tongues and lips exploring with the wild calm of a jungle at night. The rhythm of this dance sends us into a simultaneous frenzy. My hands are in his hair and his hands in mine. His curved cock thrusts right against my clit. He runs his fingertips down the length of my spine while his tongue simultaneously travels down my neck. I want his mouth on mine again.

Alex is like a Beethoven sonata, rising and falling on top of me with dark emotions.

We rain dance each other to orgasm. Inside I feel like one of those fancy towers of champagne glasses overflowing with the delicious sweet ambrosia that makes life worth living.

I am reminded of the power of being in the present moment. The present is all that matters. Close your eyes in self-defeat or pain for too long and you might miss something. If I had given in to my fear and not ventured so far from home, I might not be right now experiencing the true calling of my body and soul, the fulfillment I never imagined possible only because the human part of my brain was too small to begin to truly understand the universe. But Chantico understood all of this, and that is why she was so calm.

Afterward, I lie in his arms, his hand caressing my forearm, my head on his chest. The deepest part of me is at rest even though we cannot rest much longer. We have real and urgent work to do.

The best part of lying with him is that his body temperature is perfect. He is like that cool stream I bathed in after I became a vampire. I feel at home in my own skin and next to his.

"Alex . . . Judas, tell me about the desert. I too had a period of drought and doubt."

He kisses the crown of my head. "I will tell you what I have not told anyone else."

Judas walked village to village, living on the goodwill of animals he did not slaughter but that instead offered themselves to him. Hamish did warn him he could only feed off animals for so long before he would need human blood.

Meanwhile, he trusted that this walk through the desert would reveal his purpose. Dust clung to his clothing and in his thick black hair. When he encountered those in need, he helped. What else would he do?

But soon the hunger became too much. Still, the only human he could bear draining was a Roman soldier. When he drained the man, the soldier's unwashed flesh melted in his mouth. Sweet viscous blood filled his mouth like the sweetest wine he had ever tasted.

Soon after he killed the soldier and returned to his walk, the atmosphere in the desert changed. It had to be a sandstorm coming. He fell to his knees and stretched out his arms. He screamed to the sky, knowing his voice was nothing in comparison to the wind, "If you want me to live, then I will live. But I can't keep wandering without direction. I can't do this work without sustenance or understanding. What is any of this?" He screamed hoping God or whatever created humans and vampires would hear. Would what he had become be known to all, or would it have to be kept a secret? There was so much uncertainty he wanted answers for.

Judas closed his eyes, hearing the approaching wind. Small granules of sand tapped his face until gusts of it pummeled his entire body. By some miracle his body did not fly away in the raging storm, yet he felt it all. The storm did not go over or around him. It couldn't go through him either. Instead it felt like it slammed directly into his entire being. Not an inch of him was left unscathed by the sensation of being consumed by the sky and earth at the same time. Judas kneeled in the face of the storm until he could no longer remain upright. The desert blew across his face and into his nostrils, the sand filling the cavernous spaces inside his body.

Soon he swayed before falling to the side. A blanket of sand followed by another heaped on top of the other until the sand weighed him down. Under the sand, the darkness was a comfort, as was the silence. Only there did he finally feel freedom from his guilt and the constant uncertainty that gave him no peace.

This is where it ends, he thought. *Underground without sight or sound. Alone.* He drifted into slumber.

Without any sense of time, Judas became aware all at once of a loud banging sound in his mind. A crashing tower of panic struck him. He reached overhead to feel nothing but sand. He wanted to escape the sands. He didn't want to be entombed in the desert.

With no clear way out, he decided there was nothing he could do but try to pull himself through the heavy sand that was holding his body down. The only idea he had to do so was to swim through the sand—despite the desert being the furthest possible thing from an ocean. His arms pushed, as did his feet. *Now. Help me now, God.*

With the strength of five men he fought off the sand.

He could open his eyes. Through blurred vision he could see the storm had passed. Only soft dunes remained. Still there was no heaven-sent sign to give him direction on where to go or what to do next.

But he had survived the storm, and that was enough of a sign that he had to continue on despite his doubt, the obsessive thoughts of wondering about the role of vampires in the world of humans. Jesus was a man. He didn't doubt that. But what would lesser men than Jesus do with vampire power? He had entered the bleak and monotone wasteland of questioning.

When day turned to night over and over again, on those nights he felt like the moon was walking beside him, changing shape as he changed with it. On his long journey, time ceased to exist. He had no idea where he was or how much longer he would go. He surrendered the worry and waited until the desert ended. Each heartbeat was another step into the unknown for an undisclosed time.

That was when he saw the Bedouins.

22

The following morning we make our way to the clock shop. Maximilian drops a newspaper on the counter in front of us. "More people have been found murdered in North London. Two were found in the park next to Highgate Cemetery. I'm willing to bet it's Hernán. Expect him to strike soon."

We sit with Max at the clock shop, drinking pouches of blood, scanning the headlines in front of us. Part of me wishes Hernán would burst through the door so we can just finally have it out and end this stalemate. Someone has to attack first.

And if he is behind the murders—that they happened while he was in London would otherwise be too much of a coincidence—then he must be stopped sooner rather than later.

Before the events of recent weeks, that Hernán was still alive had been unknown to me, even though our work might have meant we should have crossed paths, because my business mostly took me to the southern hemisphere or New York. My

Europe work was over the phone, and much of my work was done online now. We would never have been in the same city before, considering he worked from the UK and Europe. I do have one very old connection I am forever tied to who can possibly give me inside information on Hernán. His previous defeat by the Spanish made him want to know everything about everyone who could be a threat to his survival. He never wanted to experience being a captive ever again or lose what was his.

"There is one thing I can try that I haven't. I'm not close to him, especially now or ever really, but he is very connected to the darker side of the world. His name is Cuauhtémoc. He is the one who made me," I say.

Alexander looks shocked. "Cuauhtémoc is your creator? Part of me expected that when tracking vampires from that part of the world, but I didn't want to assume. You couldn't be more different from him. He is not . . . I can understand why you stay away. You really think he would know about John and Hernán still being alive? Their worlds are completely different. Both those men pride themselves on having this perception of a spotless human life so they can do his dark deeds behind the scenes. Cuauhtémoc, on the other hand . . ."

"Doesn't care. He lost hope long ago. I know. And he leads the most lethal vampire militia in the world. I've never seen loyalty like that. Because of Cuauhtémoc, every country below Mexico is impenetrable to vampires looking for trouble."

"It's worth a try."

I take my phone out and scroll until I find the single letter "C." My index finger hesitates for a moment before I press the contact. There are three rings before a woman answers and asks to know what my business is and how I know this number.

"Just put me through. Tell him it's Malinalli. I promise he will take the call."

After she puts me on hold, I put the phone down and press speaker.

His deep voice sounds the same. "Malinalli. It has been a very long time. I have thought of you a lot. There have been a few . . . incidents here with my business."

"You know me. I only chase my own dreams and money. Don't need yours."

"Then why this call?"

"It's about two other vampires. Bad motherfuckers in life and now in death. John Hawkins and Hernán Cortés."

There was a pause. I could hear a low growl.

"Yes, they use the secrets of vampires for their own gain. They know better than to come my way even though they would love my carcass. I've often considered if it's worth the effort to end their existence; however, they have never made a move against me, and I don't want to draw unnecessary human or vampire attention to myself or my business. Besides, if provoked, Hernán would create all-out war. I would hunt anyone associated with him. I wouldn't care where they were or if they were human or vampire."

"It's anything but quiet now. Hernán is killing humans in London. The papers are reporting the found bodies."

"Are they giving you trouble? Do they want your body?"

My eyes dart toward Alexander. "Yes."

"Hmm. That is a predicament. I guess you should kill them first. Do you want my help? You know I mind my own business and don't interfere with other vampires, so you can't expect me to just jet over there to Europe. Mexico is *my* home and where I stay to defend it. My job is ensuring there will never be another genocide here. If they cross the line here, it's a different story that would not end well for him."

"I only want any information you might have. No muscle needed."

"I never offered you muscle, but information I can do. I may not entangle myself with many of our kind outside of my loyal militia, but that doesn't mean I don't make it my business to keep very detailed tabs on them. Unlike other vampires with scruples, I have no problem extracting information with ruthless precision."

I glance at Alexander again. Cuauhtémoc must have been referring to him when he mentioned vampires with scruples.

"Go on."

"Their main operation is out of L.A., but a few vampires have gone missing in London. He prefers older vampires; however, they are not easily handled, so he takes an increasing number of younger ones for his business."

"Yes, I have heard."

"I will text you the address I have where I believe he may have one of his clinics but only used for the purpose of taking what he needs from vampires. There is also another one in Budapest. Be careful. He is not as kind as I am."

Kind? He was far from kind in his bloody private security business—his militia was composed of the deadliest assassins and bodyguards.

"Thank you, Cuauhtémoc. I would say I owe you one, but I don't think there is anything I could offer."

Without pause or hesitation he answers straightaway. "Actually, there is. I want the Penancho. I want the headdress that belonged to an emperor of our land and should be in the hands of a Brown emperor again. Get it for me from Austria in the delicate way you handle all your business matters and we can call it even."

I almost can't believe my ears and regret making the offer. I personally believe the Penancho should be in a museum for all to enjoy, not in Austria—and not with a private collector.

"You know governments, Cuauhtémoc. I'll see what I can do."

"I do know governments. That is why I have my own kingdom. But there is one other thing. I can hear more than just the blood circulating in your system. Who are you with? You didn't want my company, so I wonder who has caught your attention now. Whoever it is, they are not human."

Alexander and I lock eyes. He nods.

"I'm with another vampire named Alexander J."

There is a pause. "This makes sense why you need my help. Alexander is good at what he does, but he lacks bite in certain areas. He doesn't like to make heads roll. So don't forget the power of *your* instincts when you face John and Hernán. No mercy. They showed none in life. It might save your own."

"Thank you, Cuauhtémoc."

"Goodbye, Malinalli. Don't be a stranger. And Alexander, you are welcome to visit too. An offer I don't extend to many. I would like to know if the stories about you are true. What liars those priests were. We could learn much about each other."

"Noted, Cuauhtémoc."

Before I can say goodbye, the line goes dead. A message pops up on my screen from Cuauhtémoc. It is a London address, for the clinic. I paste the address into Google Maps. It is near Highgate Cemetery. Why am I not surprised? That is where the bodies were found, according to the newspaper.

Alexander and Max look at the map.

"I'll go check out the cemetery and the surrounding area if you like. He won't suspect an old human vicar of being on a vampire hunt," says Max in a calm voice.

Alexander looks up from the phone. "It's too dangerous. I can't let you do that."

"I want to. He needs to be stopped. Maybe this is part of my destiny."

"Fine. Tomorrow you go to Highgate and look around the surrounding area and we will check out the property."

"I don't want to put Max in harm's way, but we need as many eyes on these two men as possible, so there are no surprises. Knowing Hernán still lives is enough. That will end. In the meantime, we should feed a lot over the next twenty-four hours to keep our strength. We can incapacitate him and entomb him in Highgate Cemetery instead of killing him outright."

He touches my cheek with his fingertips. "You will be safe. I know you can take care of yourself, but let me try to keep you safe."

I take a step back. Not a single person in my entire life has ever expressed a desire to take care of me or keep me safe except Chantico. Even Catherine had ulterior motives, mainly to not be alone. This kind of care is so foreign to me. But still I stand my ground. "I want him dead. No one must die because of him any longer."

"I understand."

"This is real now and my life is very much on the line. So how do you plan on subduing these murderers?"

Max reaches beneath the counter and opens a humming refrigerator. He slides a clear plastic case toward Alexander, who opens it. A viscous, pale yellow–tinted liquid fills three syringes.

"A mixture of vampire blood and tranquilizers. Vampire blood consumed by other vampires has the opposite effect of human blood. I guess it's some sort of evolutionary thing to prevent cannibalism? We haven't cracked that mystery yet. Last time I busted the lab John had in Budapest, I grabbed as much as I could before destroying it. Had a few of my contacts analyze it to see how we could use it."

"Gotcha. We can head out to find him just before dawn. Whatever he is doing he probably won't be doing during the daylight. We can catch him coming back."

We wander the neighborhood of the address Cuauhtémoc gave us. From the shops, bicycles, and cars parked on the street, the neighborhood appears inhabited by a mix of families and young people just starting out their adult life. The park leading to Highgate is well maintained with ample benches and playgrounds. There is a sense of peace here. Hernán's so-called clinic is an end-of-terrace house that seems to be the only property not chopped into flats. Alex has the syringe to stab Hernán with at the ready, and I have one too. We are close enough to assess, but not close enough for him to sense us.

Max slowly walks close to the address with a camera attached to the red poppy pin on his black vicar's jacket after the cemetery and surrounding area came up with no sign of Hernán. After, Max will leave and we will check out the property. Alex watches the live feed on his phone.

"Fuck," says Alex.

"What?" I press closer to him. His body is against mine. Our arms touch. I look at his phone and see John leaving the address we were given.

He wears black Hunter Wellington boots and a long blue wool coat with the collar upright. His wool hat is worn low. From the phone we can see Max following behind. Alex texts Max, "Do not follow him. Leave. Please."

The feed is still going. "Dammit," growls Alex.

"Why don't we go in and see what we can find. We can take advantage of this opportunity."

"Yeah, let's go."

We walk up to the front door and look around. There is no one. Alex pulls out from the inside of his trench code a kit with different instruments for picking locks. I stand in front of him in the event of a passerby. Within a few minutes he has it opened.

The entrance is elegantly decorated. A photo of John and another man hangs on the wall. There are hooks lined with hats and coats, including a black hoodie. I can smell the blood on it despite it having been recently washed. Alex glances at me: He smells it as well. I stand there trying to decipher whether we should go up or down. If I was dissecting dead bodies I'd put the laboratory in a basement, especially in a country where almost no residential homes in the city have air conditioning, and the top floors are the hottest in the warm months. I can hear air conditioning beneath my feet and the hum of something else using up a lot of electricity.

"Downstairs?" Alex has the same idea.

We rush down a short flight of stairs to a locked door. Always prepared, Alex also has a handheld device I have never seen before. It connects remotely to the lock, and various numbers blink on and off until it comes up with a code. As if by magic the door opens.

"Wow. Where did you get that? Remind me to never show you my secret caches of artifacts."

"I said I work solo, but I do have friends in pretty cool positions with access to tech many don't even know exists."

I walk in, and the lights turn on automatically. The facility is a single room with one stainless steel operating table with thick cuffs, larger than what would be needed for a human, for wrists and ankles. The bolts on the inside of the cuffs have sharp points. Most likely to go through the bone to keep down the strongest of vampires. There is also another band on a headrest with the same pointed bolts. The top is open, because attached to the edge of the table is a saw thick enough to cut through a skull. A machine similar to a dialysis machine sits next to it. Needles of various sizes are attached to the side. There is a plastic vat beneath that's large enough to hold the blood of two human adults. It smells like bleach and blood. Embedded in the opposite wall is a recess with what looks like a meat slicer behind plexiglass and two holes with gloves attached for using the slicer. The faint smell of bone marrow can be detected coming from that direction. Next to it is a stainless-steel table with various scalpels, saws of all shapes and sizes, glass vessels in the shape of canopic jars. There is a large stainless-steel fridge with glass doors taking up an entire wall. Inside are more glass canopic jars with various floating body parts and organs. Despite the gruesome scene, it's as sterile and clean as a hospital operating room. Not a drop of blood or speck of dust can be seen. There aren't even fingerprints on the steel. On the wall there is a rubber suit and boots, also spotless. Bleach and cleaning agents sting my nostrils and eyes.

Along one wall on the shelves are Hernán's products in simple stylish jars with brief slogans for their use. Some are for anti-aging for the skin, pills to ingest for hair growth, erections, and other various things humans worry about. These must be his products for humans made from vampire parts. On a counter beneath the shelves are three glass canopic jars with a pale pink dust. They appear as if they will be empty soon.

"That must be our bones," I say, feeling full of sorrow for whoever that was.

"He channeled what he was in his human life into his immortal life. Being a vampire amplifies what is inside, then one must choose their path. Not everyone appreciates or uses what they are given for good."

Flashes of Hernán's cruelty as a human make me want to destroy the entire place. "And you are telling me we shouldn't just take him out for good?"

"Malinalli, we are not gods or the hands of fate. The minute we think we are better than humans and act on it, well, game over for them."

He pauses and looks me in the eyes. "But for you I will kill him."

I feel myself shaking. A lover has never wanted to go that far for me. "Do you mean that?"

He still holds my gaze. "Yes. But let's get out of this place. After seeing the security and the state of this house, I don't feel comfortable with what tricks he might have up his sleeves. We could get trapped here."

"Yeah, if it wasn't terraced and attached to an entire street of adjoining houses, I would say burn it down to the ground. Hiding in plain sight and surrounded by innocent humans gives him some level of protection."

This statement makes me think of Catherine and how very rarely she was alone. She had an entourage whenever in public, and if she wanted to sleep alone, then there were humans sleeping in other rooms. It was only when we were together that she didn't mind there not being humans nearby.

"I'm putting trackers in his shoes and in that black bag. We can see where he is going and catch him out if it's safe to do so. Let's go back upstairs."

Alex secures the room again before we walk back up the stairs to the entrance.

The door bursts open. Alex and I stare at the threshold. It's John. There isn't just rage in his expression—there is hatred and grief.

"The only reason Hernán hasn't ripped into you both is because I wanted to get to you first. George is dead. My George. Many centuries ago I knew being a faithful husband to a wife was something I'd never be, and I never thought I'd get to have the kind of love I found with George. And now that love is gone forever. I was going to make him a vampire in just six months . . . Six months until we could spend eternity together!"

Alex and I back into the hall, farther into the house.

"I'm sorry, but I don't know anything about that," says Alex, holding his ground.

John slams the door behind him. "But I know."

I can feel Alex's body relax. *Hernán!* I scream internally. John looks in my direction as if he can hear me. The energy from my own hate must be strong enough for him to sense.

John steps closer to us. "Yes, I know you didn't kill him. I wanted to get to you first before Hernán could kill you both. If you are ready to make a deal, then I am. Hernán killed George. I am sure of it. He didn't know I had been feeding George small droplets of my blood. It increased our connection, at least my psychic connection to him. When I found his body, I didn't feel the sense of panic like his message relayed. The energy I felt was from Hernán . . . his rage. I will help you capture or . . ."

". . . kill him," I blurted. Alex glanced at me before turning back to John.

"I will aid you. Nothing matters now," John said.

"What do you propose?"

"He is obsessed with you, Malinalli. The only solution is to use you as bait, with my help. I can probably hold him back for a day. So a day is how long you have to come up with a plan."

"How do we know we can trust you? Your history isn't exactly what I would call noble."

"When you leave here, go to Highgate; you will smell George's body. I can't bear burying him yet, so I have left him there in the crypt."

John removes from his pocket a cream-colored handkerchief with *George* embroidered in blue. His fingertips run across the stitching. Self-loathing and bitterness shadow his face. "I gave this to him. He never understood my love for old things. I would joke and ask him why it was that if he didn't love old things, he loved me. Take it. It will lead you to his scent."

Alex takes the memento. "You know this doesn't make the contract out on you null and void. You were and are a murderer. Falling in love and having a 'come to Jesus' moment doesn't erase that or the families you tore apart. You enslaved people."

"I know. My sins, my karma has caught up to me. Just go. Hernán goes down with me."

We leave the broken man to sit on his stairs to stare at George's photo hanging on the wall.

We walk through the cemetery. George's scent on the handkerchief is subtle, yet strong enough for us to follow. We wander a catacombs with both walls housing coffins, some with bodies and others empty and rotted. We stop when we stand before the bloated corpse of a young man.

"Should we leave him here? He is innocent."

Alex nods. "Let's call the police anonymously. Hernán will know we are close. We need to end this."

As I look at poor George's corpse, I think, *Never fall in love with a vampire unless you are one.*

Max sits on a stool, tinkering with an antique watch. "Those two are strange vampires. But I am not surprised by this turn of events. John sniffed around me, but then walked away as if my blood wasn't good enough for him. After locking eyes I thought it best to leave. I messaged you!"

"I know. That is when we tried to leave."

"The time has come for me to find him. I can't live like this. This is how I felt as a human, constantly hunted and watched. But I can't understand his level of hate. He is the one who used me," I say.

Max puts the watch down. He possesses the same calmness that Chantico had. "Because he fears you, your power."

"We have to lure him out. He wants to be in control, and he won't stop until he gets what he wants. And that is my head. I know I will have to be the bait. It doesn't scare me considering how intimate I had been with most of my true enemies as a human. And I know I can get a good shot on him."

Alex puts his phone down after responding to a message. "I say we strike first. We will get him in Highgate Cemetery. Based on his killing patterns, he likes that place."

"We get there before sunrise and wait."

"And what shall I do?" says Max.

Alex gives him a warm smile. "You stay safe, my friend. George did nothing wrong but fraternize with vampires, and I don't want to see you in a box."

"I agree. I won't let you die for me," I say.

Max places both of his shaky hands on mine. "You will get him. I know it."

We walk to the Notting Hill flat, not knowing how any of it will play out. Alex and I curl into bed to rest, rejuvenate, and re-group our thoughts. Our not agreeing on Hernán's ultimate fate digs into my thoughts until the comfort of his body sends me drifting into a state of nothingness. Then we both snap our eyes open to the sound of my phone pinging.

It's a text from Horatio. A very dead Horatio. I nudge Alex. "I think something is about to happen." We both sit straight up-right in bed.

The message is only one word—*attached*. There is nothing else but a video attachment. My hand trembles, not wanting to know what it is. My soul knows. My mind flashes back to seeing Chantico's charred body when I returned from the hacienda. I press the attachment. It is a video of Max in an ancient wood coffin. There are mounds of fresh dirt next to him. In the back-ground is a pile of modern possessions that clearly don't belong in a closed-off Victorian cemetery. He is being drained of all his blood with multiple wounds inflicted on his body. They appear to have been made by a scalpel or blade. Hernán is not in the frame. Who else would this be from? And then he speaks.

"Any last words before you meet your nonexistent Christ?"

Max stares off with vacant eyes and a calm I only remember from when I saw the woman murdered for her fat to be used to dress the wounded Spanish. He closes his eyes. "I do. Bless you, my son. I forgive you. And to Judas . . . Malinalli." His eyes open, and he shoots a look toward Hernán, giving him a sinister and smug grin. "Get this motherfucker if it's the last thing you do!"

The video ends, and Alex is out of the bed, dressing.

I throw the phone aside and do the same. This fight will re-quire my sharp-tipped boots from Mexico. "You think John played us?"

Alex rummages through the pockets of his trench to make

sure he has everything to stop Hernán, including two blood pouches for us if we need it for recovery. "I don't know. My senses didn't detect bullshit."

"Same," I say, trying to make sense of what could have occurred. I grab my phone. Nothing from John.

When we are about to leave, Alex grabs me by the waist and pulls me close. He kisses me hard and then a small growl escapes his lips. His dark eyes leave me panting for more despite us being about to run headfirst into a fight. "I would rather see him dying in the dirt than have any chance of you not being by my side. And if there comes a moment when I have to choose between you and me, I will give my life for you, Malinalli. You're my other half who must survive if I don't."

He reaches into the inside of his trench. "If you get a clean shot, then take it. All you need to do is press the bottom. The needle will automatically inject with the tranquilizer at the same time."

I place it in my back pocket and kiss him back with tears running down my cheeks. "I love you, Alex."

"I love you, Malinalli."

My phone pings. It is a message from John.

I promise I knew nothing about Hernán's plans! He is out for everyone now seeing only blood and wanting to only feed. His hate is magnified from the serum. I will tell you why because you must know he will not be the same.

I recently received a new formula for a serum from one of my freelance scientists. It enhances a vampire's powers. So far we have kept it under wraps because it also makes us more violent and lethal, and our thirst more insatiable. He has access to the safe in the clinic with the unreleased

products. After you left, a vision of him screaming sparked
in my mind. I ran to the safe and found the serum gone. Be
alert. I will do my best to find him.—J

"Great," I whisper, then show Alex the message. His eyes scan it quickly.

"I guess we have to be ready for anything. And I want that serum. Sounds like trouble if it gets out."

23

Highgate Cemetery is split into two parts. One is fairly modern and open to the public. You can find Karl Marx buried there beneath his face carved in stone. His statue is of such a magnificent size one can't miss it.

The other side is from the Victorian era. It's overgrown with wild roots bursting through graves, breaking ancient stone. London is a wet place, the perfect climate for moss to cover everything with soft brushstrokes of green. Crops of mushrooms poke from broken graves with all engraving eroded away. The mushrooms are proof of life after death along with the centipedes and earthworms. Beetles and spiders also make their homes in this cradle of death. Life-size angels look down upon the paths. Broken and fallen crosses litter the ground. At all times of the day and night you can hear birds. This area of the cemetery is considered a hazard for visitors because of the sheer number of graves and amount of foliage. And because of its age most of it is protected by the local council. It isn't considered safe enough to allow visitors to wander on their own during certain hours.

We walk up a short flight of stairs, and we are truly inside the cemetery. The stone angels take on demonic shapes as their shadows twist with the moon in and out of the clouds. The large crypts can hide any large creatures or vampires lying in wait. Even the darkness of these crypts sends a chill through my body. The scent of corpses is heavy in the air. The decay sits like an invisible mist caught in the spiderwebs and countless iron gates.

Alex and I stop at the same time—we both smell fresh blood and flesh. Because people are not allowed here at night there is little to no light, and with so little illumination, our other senses are on high alert. We pick up the pace as we walk again toward the line of unmarked crypts housed inside a single long building.

The scent of blood is stronger. I look to Alex, who has a strained look on his face. He is hoping to hear a human heartbeat. There is not one I can detect; however, he is older than I am and may have powers that I do not possess.

Hernán stands beneath a single lit lamp. In one blood-soaked hand he holds a large bone saw. His boots smell like fresh corpses. The scent is heavy from the crypts, which are down a short flight of stairs. Only one gate is open. I step forward, considering he has been hunting me. John was correct. Hernán is not the same. There is definitely something even more unhinged in his eyes. All the death he has caused is reflected back to me.

"Are you ready to die, La Malinche?" he growls.

"Hernán Cortés. You have not even earned the right to touch me let alone have my body. No one will ever have that without my full permission or use me. My destiny and life are mine!"

As these words lash from my tongue, I allow my teeth and

nails to reach their full length. The fresh blood swimming in my body leaks from the tears in my gums and fingertips. My vision sharpens; my breathing grows huskier. All the things I wanted to hide were meant to come out in this moment. The viciousness of my nature has found a place in time to show its beautiful hideousness. I shriek into the night at him. Alex's face has changed to its full vampire form as well. His teeth are longer than before, and the calm softness is gone.

"La Malinche. Look at you in all your beauty. I'm going to enjoy ripping you apart to see what lurks inside. Where are all your little male pets you keep on a sexual leash? You have just the one now? All you bitches are the same."

"Fuck you, Hernán. You will answer for your entire existence," Alexander says in a calm, determined tone.

As slowly as possible I bring my hand to my back pocket and remove the syringe. Half is hidden beneath the cuff of my leather jacket and the other half in my hand. Hernán doesn't acknowledge Alex. His burning eyes that are completely black are fixed on me.

"Malinalli, what makes you all so beautiful is also the very thing I want to see break."

"Well, you will be very disappointed with me. I've been broken more times than I care to recount. There is nothing left for you. I am not the same woman you knew."

"We will see. I can't wait to find out. I admit I underestimated you before, but I won't make that same mistake again."

"Who made you, Hernán? How did you become such a twisted fuck? I know it could not have been Cuauhtémoc."

His face contorts and twitches beneath the lamplight.

"It doesn't matter, but if you must know it was only by a fated moment in battle. A filthy Indian warrior I cornered and killed."

My blood congeals in my brain for a moment as he says this. Enough talking. It is time. Without saying a word, I look to my left. From the rusted and warped stakes around a grave, I rip off the iron chain attaching them with my left hand. My hope is to land enough blows to get close enough to take him to the edge of his life so he can look into my eyes as I do it. Even though I can't consume Hernán's blood for sustenance, I can make sure every drop saturates the ground.

My internal freedom is the most precious part of my journey and now also the love I found with Alex. Hernán can't have either.

I swing the chain side to side while approaching Hernán. The syringe is still in my right hand. In an instant Hernán runs toward me with his mouth open and fangs out. The bone saw is overhead. Alex runs toward him at the same time. I continue to swing the chain, trying to get a hit on Hernán before Alex tackles him. Hernán swerves from me and takes Alex head-on. Alex howls when the bone saw slices into his shoulder.

The two men pummel each other with the sound of rabid jackals fighting to the death. Half of Alex's trench has been ripped off in the process. With Hernán's head exposed for an instant, I kick him straight in the temple with the sharp tip of my boot. He releases Alex for enough time for Alex to scramble for the torn portion of his trench. As I leap toward Hernán, he catches me in the chest with his foot. I fall to the ground, and he is on top of me with his spittle falling on my face. His jaw is clenched.

The bone saw is at my throat. Alex is behind him with the syringe raised overhead. Hernán releases me and swings the saw toward Alex again, catching him across the face. Alex rears back with this blow. I use this opportunity to raise myself up just enough to plunge the syringe into Hernán's shoulder. He screams, "You bloody cunt!" In his rage he jumps to his feet and lifts me into the air before throwing me across the path. I hit a large gravestone in the shape of a Celtic cross. I'm dizzy and losing blood inside of me. Something has ruptured. Still, I get to my feet.

Through blurry vision I can see Hernán and Alex brawling again. I can't tell if Hernán is slowing down or if it's just the impact fucking with my senses. I wobble toward the two with one hand across my waist.

I scream into the air, "Malinalxochitl! One last time. Now!"

With both hands I dig my claws into Hernán's sides just beneath the rib cage. Hernán backhands Alex, sending him across the path into an iron gate and spiked rods linking chains to protect the graves.

With a burst of hot energy, I twist my entire body and throw Hernán in the same direction he threw me. Alex groans. My heart stops when I see him on the ground. He lies wheezing with an iron spear through his neck and a broken stone Virgin Mary lying shattered across his chest. There is bloody foam trailing from his nose and mouth. His eyes are glassy.

Just a short distance away in the trees I see the figure of a woman. I can smell blood and roses on her. A moan escapes her lips as she points in the opposite direction. "Malinalxochitl," I whisper before following the length of her arm with my hazy vision. Hernán is vanishing into the night. I look back at Alex. Seeing him like this pains me.

A rib has punctured my left lung and the side of my heart feels crushed. I'm hemorrhaging internally, or at least what is left from my last feed. My legs are heavier with every step toward Alex.

"There is adrenaline in my pocket. Use it and get yourself about a body full of blood. What I brought isn't enough. This shot won't last long."

With all my strength I shake my head before falling to my knees. The image of Chantico is a dim light in front of me.

I can have rest, at long last, next to the love of my life if I choose, or I can jump into the largest, deepest body of water ever. It is the infinite body we call time that is just a manifestation of the universe. Is it time for me to slumber in the arms of my ancestors?

My heartbeat begins to pound in my left ear. I look down and see Alex has plunged the adrenaline shot into my thigh. Now I face another big choice: I have to be the one to leave him. But I don't want to, not with him in this state.

"I'll be back and I'll call John. He owes us," I whisper to Alex, then feel for my phone. It must have fallen out. I touch Alex's clothing. It's not there.

My eyes shift toward where I thought I saw Chantico. In the spot I can now see Max's dead body. I look back to Alex, who is now unresponsive, though his eyes are still wide open.

I lean in and kiss him on the lips with a lifetime's worth of heartfelt tenderness while pressing the bag of blood back into his mouth so he can heal. I kiss him again. "Come back to me," I whisper. The slight dampness left from his saliva and the blood on my lips is stronger than any ring he could ever place on my finger.

I look to the sky, which is still dark. I have to move fast, but I drag Max next to Alex. "May your soul and your kindness find its way back here. Rest. Find my Chantico and walk with her in gardens. I think you two will get along well."

When I move to run back to the clock shop for blood before

the adrenaline stops working, I see both of our phones are smashed. I have to call John from the landline, and I drink blood until I'm full in order to recover.

Hernán raced through the cemetery, sweating blood. It gushed out his nose. He had watched others experience this rage and power while they experimented to find the perfect dosage. After, the vampires were killed. This potent concoction would not be free, or for just anyone. Until now, it had never been used in an open environment.

His vision appeared red and his throat burned with a fiery thirst. It took all his self-control to run and not kill anything that moved in a frenzied attack in the open. He needed to feed, but there were no humans nearby. John's clinic was not far. He could hide out there and drink what blood was left in the clinic's supply.

That was the downside to this concoction they didn't understand: It raised the user's metabolic rate. So it was excellent in a fight with humans, but for fighting with other vampires, it was best to have blood on hand to replenish. He could feel his body burning through what blood had surged through his system.

Without thought he burst through the front of the Highgate house, breaking the lock. At the basement door leading to the clinic, he rubbed his eyes, trying to see clearly enough to enter the code. The frustration made him scream and kick at the reinforced door.

"Hernán!"

His head jerked to the left. John stood at the top of the stairs.

"It is the one thing we can't get right. The thirst."

John calmly walked down the stairs and entered the code.

When the door opened, Hernán dashed through to rip open the refrigeration unit filled with blood. His teeth and nails tore into each clear pouch before he gulped it with head tilted back. He discarded each one on the floor after he drank.

"Are you done?"

Hernán heaved as he looked back at John.

"Good. Before they killed George, he was able to hack into her computer. I will keep an eye on her movements. We will get her."

Hernán's eyes were less dilated. "I don't care where she is. I want her."

"We stay here until I get more information on her whereabouts. You must also stay here. You can't go running around like a rabid hyena. I will lock this door for your own protection while I get you a fresh body."

"I only want to feed."

"Don't worry. You will."

John turned and left the clinic and locked the door behind him. His phone rang, displaying a number he didn't recognize. He rushed to the top floor of the house to avoid Hernán hearing the conversation.

"He's gone."

It is Malinalli.

John paced in the attic room. "I know. I have him locked in the basement. He will remain high for I don't know how long. He might turn on me, as he has taken two doses of the Hyde. He has fed and is somewhat calm. We never did that in our experiments. This might be a roller coaster. He will have the strength of many. We need backup. This thing we created."

Malinalli paused.

"There is a way. I want you to lure him to Mexico. With Cuauhtémoc's help he won't stand a chance."

"And your lover?" John asked.

"You just focus on your part."

"Fine. Mexico it is. You and I can talk after, maybe come up with an arrangement, especially if your lover does not show."

"Get Hernán to Mexico in the next twenty-four to forty-eight hours. I'll arrange private transport. Wait for further messages."

The line went dead. John didn't like the idea of going to Mexico, but it was the sure way to destroy Hernán. It could also mean the end of him, but without George, what was there left to live for?

I felt pleased John had agreed to everything. Now to lay the final trap. I dial Cuauhtémoc's line. It rings twice, but this time he answers.

"Malinalli, you were in my dream last night. That is why I answered. What is it? Even in my dream I could not see what happened to you beyond this point."

"Are you ready for your revenge? A true reunion of blood and hell?"

"You mean *he* will be here?"

"Yes. Get yourself and your men ready. Cortés might be on some vampire super-serum when he arrives. I got busted up, but I survived."

"You will always survive, mujer. It is in your blood. I will be waiting and arrange for you to stay in Cholula. If he is here, you have all of me at your disposal. Will your friend join?"

I pause with the pain of that question. "I don't know."

"Leave everything to me, Malinalli."

"Thank you, and see you soon."

I have to go back to the Notting Hill flat to retrieve my passport and computer. Then it will be the earliest private flight I can find. Have to get a new phone as well. In fact, I'll buy one for Alex. One day I will gift him with a watch as a reminder of our time at the clock shop and Max.

But first I have to rush to the cemetery with more blood for Alex.

I run to the exact spot where I left the two bodies. The sun will rise within the hour.

I figure I can hide Max's body and help Alex back to the flat. When I arrive both bodies are gone. The dark stain where Alex had bled out still appears wet. I sniff the air, but cannot sense either of them. My eyes squeeze shut to see if I can feel him. Nothing. I feel blocked, shut out. Panic rises in my throat. Maybe the flat. With renewed speed, I head back to Notting Hill, which is a long run. There will be a phone shop along the way I can break into.

The flat is dark, but I do not smell Alex. My heart ignites into the kind of flames that movie vampires die from when exposed to sunlight. We were meant to be in this together and now he has gone rogue. Hernán doesn't have him. Then it hits me that maybe he wanted to leave me and found a way. That Alex has chosen to leave after all. I sit in the dark, pushing thoughts of him away. Like the days when it was about mere survival, I can't cry or mourn. It is death that matters now. My emotions shut down. I open my laptop.

The earliest flights I can find are the following morning and both private. Works for me. Perhaps if I stay here, Alex will come back. However, when the time comes for me to leave, I will choose to walk out that door with or without him.

I have no way to contact him. If I can't reach him, on the flight I can try to see where he might be, feel his energy. I look at my new phone, already synced to the cloud. It is John.

> Hernán is calmer, but still on the warpath in a delirious state. And he is changing. I can't leave him alone like this. What is the plan? We should move fast before he takes another dose. In his distracted state I managed to retrieve some of the serum. —J

I text back:

> Booked you a private flight to Cholula. Tell him you both plan to capture me there. Get him to Cholula then stay out of the way.

It will be another battle. A battle I will not lose no matter the consequences. I call the landline at the clock shop. No answer. I plan to stop on my way to my flight, but maybe Alex has skipped town and skipped out on me. Until the last possible moment before my flight leaves, I wait.

Time has caught up with me in the worst way.

24

My flight has landed at a different airport than John and Hernán's. John continues to send me frantic messages as Hernán is becoming more erratic and out of control. He tried to bust through the cockpit once after consuming the amount of blood of three humans he'd stashed in sterile bottles. Luckily John had called ahead and requested no staff on board except the pilot.

The entire time I could not stop thinking about being abandoned. All that work, and hope. My soul was crushed. When I thought of what Chantico would say, my mind went blank. Maybe all the lonely vampires were alone for good reason. At the very least, I will finally get to see the death of Hernán Cortés. I'll have to settle for vengeance over love after all.

Cuauhtémoc is waiting for me on the tarmac when I arrive. "The mother of the mestizo is back and she has brought her long-dead master Hernán Cortés with her."

"I'm glad you find it amusing."

"No, not at all. The irony and blessing. He can face real justice. Thank you for this ancient gift. It is priceless."

"So where do you have me staying?"

"A villa not far from the church where we will lure him to. Behind me is the car that will take you there. There is plenty of bagged blood, but if you require fresh, then I can arrange whatever type of human you like. And my driver is one of my best fighters. You need not feel unprotected."

This statement makes me think of Alex, how it hurts not to have him here with me. I want to know where he is. Is he okay? I've never missed anyone like I miss him.

"Great, another man who doesn't think I can handle myself."

"I know you can, but we take no chances. This is our opportunity. Don't look so sad, Malinalli. Life is full of surprises. Like you delivering the devil to my doorstep."

The drive to the villa is quiet. It feels good to be home. The sunshine through the open window makes me smile despite the throbbing sorrow in my heart. How I wanted to share this with Alex. To share all this existence with him. All I can attempt to do is harden myself to the pain like I always have before and move on. I didn't survive this long crying about the poison darts in my heart—I pulled them out and ignored the pain. But I wonder if the agony of his absence or the promise of true love will ever heal. My phone pings. It is John.

We landed. We go after dark to avoid human eyes or needless victims. See you at Cholula.

As I walk into the room, I can smell him. My heart leaps.

I didn't expect to see Alex again, had been prepared to take it all on alone, but here he is.

"Malinalli. I'm sorry I left you like that. My fear of loving you and what that means for the rest of my life got the best of me. Like I said, I only do forever."

Alex takes a step closer to me. His energy saturates me with sunlight. I can't stop myself from allowing him to put his arms around me despite feeling furious at his silence. "I will never abandon you or give you anything less than what you deserve. You can trust me."

"Why did you?" I scream. "And how did you know I was here?"

He kisses me with the softness of rabbit fur. Those lips and his body feel like they belong to me. "When you left I could feel my life drifting away. I felt guilty I couldn't protect you and might not have the chance. I felt I would rather die than love you and lose you. Part of me felt I didn't deserve your love.

"Then I saw what Hernán would do if he caught you. His rage sounded like a gong in my brain. There was no way I could let that happen. Max was dead, but his blood still fresh enough . . . I had no choice. I drank what I could of him, then buried him before burying myself beneath the soil to continue to recover and try to sense Hernán.

"Then Cuauhtémoc—damn, he is powerful—spoke to me while I lay there in the cemetery. He told me your plan. I dragged myself out of the dirt to come to you."

Alex hangs his head. "I'm sorry."

I throw my arms around him. "I will bury you myself if you ever do that again."

He kisses my forehead. "Fair enough. What happens next?"

I pull away and grab my phone. "Fuck. John says Hernán is on the run and is heading to where he thinks I am."

"And where is that?"

The blood in my belly sours. "Where I once stood by him during a massacre. Now he will know the pain of true death."

We stare at Iglesia de Nuestra Señora de los Remedios, the church built on the site of the temple of Cholula. "A fitting place for Hernán to die," I say. My desire to kill has not been this strong for a very long time.

"Well, what are you waiting for?" Alex squeezes my hand. Within seconds I am bolting toward the church. I can smell at least twenty vampires surrounding it, but can't see them. No one stops us because we have safe passage. I push the heavy doors open.

Hernán crouches at the altar, snarling, with fresh human blood dripping from his body. If demons existed, they would look like him at that moment, with his eyes intent on torture and pain. The scent of other vampires fills the vestibule.

Hernán sneers at Alex and me. His eyes morph from red to black. The veins in his neck protrude as thick as the ones in his arms. He appears even more deranged than in the cemetery. "The two traitors have each other at long last. What a quaint love story that will now meet its unhappy ending."

"I hope you didn't forget about me, cabrón."

Hernán bites at the air to his right, hearing the voice. Cuauhtémoc stands bare-chested in jeans, his eyes glowing red and nails sharpened to points. His black hair is loose to his shoulders. A large, colorful tattoo of the feathered serpent Quetzalcoatl snakes across his entire chest and onto his back. He has bloodlust in his eyes, not to be mistaken for mere hunger.

"I keep my word, and I vowed to kill you if you ever set foot here again."

"All of your kind . . . filthy. Your stories and your people don't matter. Look at the world. No one cares about your people. In fact, look how they are treated, like common criminals. Spain might not be an empire any longer; however, it is respected in Europe as your country is not."

My hate makes me shake hearing this. It reflects everything I've ever encountered and felt as a Brown woman. His words are cruel but hold truth about how the descendants of this land are treated and viewed.

"I should have hunted you down after I was created and killed you so you would be rotting in the ground now," I scream.

Cuauhtémoc walks closer to Hernán with hands flexing. "I should have as well. However, there was a little matter of staving off the atrocities my people were fighting through."

Without looking at Alex or Cuauhtémoc I run full speed to Hernán, knocking him into the altar below a hanging Jesus Christ. My fangs dig deep into his flesh, but I can't drink his blood despite wanting to. Instead I rip flesh and veins like my life and soul depend on it.

Hernán grabs a gold chalice on the altar and whips it around at me in blind ferocity. He snarls and moves without direction. Truly blind rage. Cuauhtémoc is by my side when he rips Hernán's left arm out of the socket. Blood spews across the altar and splatters the cross. The hand lands on the ground, still clutching the chalice. Hernán thrashes and roars, attempting to catch one of us in his grip. He manages to bite a chunk of flesh from Cuauhtémoc's right forearm. The fallen emperor roars in anger, fueling more of his fight.

Alex stands poised to catch Hernán if he tries to escape again. Blood and viscera continue to fly into the air as our attack doesn't wane. White lace and gold candelabras drip with crimson. These items would not be here in our country if not for this man.

"Die now!" I scream, with bloody tears streaming down my face. I can feel the shadow of Cuauhtémoc's mind lurking in mine. Time to end this nightmare once and for all. We both punch through Hernán's skull and chest with centuries of vengeance and pain. There is no way to recover from those injuries.

He is dead. I look at the man who was once a sort of king.

Cuauhtémoc's eyes drink in the image of a mutilated Hernán Cortés. "I don't take kindly to invaders. And this is my territory."

John walks up the center aisle of the church from the shadows. His face is stained red with eyes fixed on the dead body of Hernán. "Good."

From the confessional a Black man wearing a black suit emerges. "John Hawkins," he says.

John looks back and nods. "Sins are meant to be paid for, I suppose. How fitting that it will happen in a church. Kill me now. I am ready. There is nothing left to live for."

"No, we won't kill you. You will live a little longer to understand and feel the weight of what you created as a human, and of being a vampire running your despicable sort of business."

"Again, I will not fight you."

The Black man stands in front of John and places zip ties on his wrists before shoving a syringe into his neck. "My name is Jacques, and I am here to carry out justice."

John falls unconscious where he stands. Jacques turns to Alexander. "Thank you for your assistance in this matter. My family will be very pleased at his capture."

Alexander bows his head. "Thank you for the business. Anytime. Send my regards to everyone. It cannot erase the past, but perhaps it can bring you some peace."

Jacques turns to Cuauhtémoc. "We should talk about territory. There are more of these cretins walking the world, *our* world. Let us unite."

Cuauhtémoc walks toward Jacques and extends his hand. "Yes, as brothers in blood and vengeance, I am open to this. Speak to your council and we shall meet."

Two Black vampires, both with braids to their waist and wearing suits, approach John's body. One of them hoists him across his shoulder. Jacques nods to Cuauhtémoc and follows the vampires out the back entrance of the church.

Alexander takes my hand. "We should burn the body, then take a long vacation."

Cuauhtémoc kicks one of Hernán's severed limbs out of his way. "I will dispose of this garbage. And if I recall, you have a headdress to get me, Malinalli. Don't stay away too long."

I hate owing people anything. But I had agreed to this condition.

"Don't worry, Cuauhtémoc. I won't keep you waiting."

For now the hunt is over. Instead of keeping the skulls in my home in Tulum, I have them sent to the national museum in Mexico City anonymously. Let them inspire others. Part of me wishes I could fund an entire wing under my known name and identity with items from my entire journey on display to show my pain, evolution, and joy. If I could endure, then anyone could; however, telling my true story is impossible for now, because the world is not ready for vampires.

Alex stands on the balcony of my home in Mexico, overlooking the ocean with his shirt off and his already dark skin a beautiful deep hue. His hair blows in the breeze.

He loves it here in the solitude of my study with books and journals. All that time I spent on my own in the dark and the light was at times soul-crushing in its loneliness, but it also taught me stillness within myself. It prepared me to share my life with another and heal my wounds. Now my inner flame will never be blown out by the slightest drizzle. Being strong first before finding love has been essential. Because now Alexander and I are bound by something greater than ourselves.

Our days here have been a frenzy of lovemaking, in between gathering leads for the next adventure. Cuauhtémoc still wants the Penancho. I'd still like to find Catherine.

But for now, Alex and I celebrate each other in blood and flesh. Maybe one day the world will be ready for the truth of my story and our love story.

Until then, we will walk our immortal path together until our flames are ready to be extinguished.

ACKNOWLEDGMENTS

It was my forty-second birthday, my first postdivorce, when I received the call from my agent that Del Rey had acquired *The Haunting of Alejandra* in a two-book deal. Up until then I had almost given up writing for the millionth time, feeling like my self-belief would simply never be enough to give the world all the stories I held in my heart, the stories exploring my culture and identity. It has always been my mission to carve out space for future generations of women of color.

They say that it takes a village to raise a child; however, I think that the same could be said for writing books! I have to thank Beth Marshea for her constant hustle, taking the time to be present, listening, and being an advocate for even the craziest ideas I pass along to her. She has been a beacon. I also must shout out a woman who has what seem like superpowers—Tricia Narwani. She saw potential in my writing and me. I can't thank her enough for the time she takes with her edits and notes. There is no denying that I have become a better writer because of her meticulous eye and talent. She is the best in the business.

I also want to acknowledge the readers, journalists, podcasters, and reviewers. Thank you for the constant support on this journey.

V. CASTRO is a two-time Bram Stoker Award–nominated Mexican American writer from San Antonio, Texas, now living in the UK. As a full-time mother she dedicates her time to her family and to writing Latinx narratives in horror, erotic horror, and science fiction. Her most recent releases include *Aliens: Vasquez, Mestiza Blood, The Queen of the Cicadas, Goddess of Filth,* and *The Haunting of Alejandra.*

vcastrostories.com
Twitter: @vlatinalondon
Instagram: @vlatinalondon
TikTok: @vcastrobooks
Find V. Castro on Goodreads and Amazon